THE
CURIOUS
WORLD
OF
CALPURNIA
TATE

JACQUELINE KELLY

THE CURIOUS WORLD OF CALPURNIA TATE

SQUARE
FISH

HENRY HOLT AND COMPANY
NEW YORK

The epigraphs at the beginning of each chapter are from
The Voyage of the Beagle by Charles Darwin.

SQUARE
FISH

An imprint of Macmillan Publishing Group, LLC
175 Fifth Avenue
New York, NY 10010
mackids.com

THE CURIOUS WORLD OF CALPURNIA TATE. Copyright © 2015 by Jacqueline Kelly.
All rights reserved. Printed in the United States of America by LSC Communications,
Harrisonburg, Virginia.

Square Fish and the Square Fish logo are trademarks of Macmillan and
are used by Henry Holt and Company under license from Macmillan.

Our books may be purchased in bulk for promotional, educational, or business
use. Please contact your local bookseller or the Macmillan Corporate and
Premium Sales Department at (800) 221-7945 ext. 5442 or by e-mail
at MacmillanSpecialMarkets@macmillan.com.

Library of Congress Cataloging-in-Publication Data
Kelly, Jacqueline.
The curious world of Calpurnia Tate / Jacqueline Kelly.
pages   cm
Sequel to: The evolution of Calpurnia Tate.
Summary: "In rural Texas in 1900, when a storm blows change into town in the form of a
visiting veterinarian, twelve-year-old Callie discovers a life and a vocation she desperately wants.
But with societal expectations as they are, she will need all her wits and courage to realize
her dreams"—Provided by publisher.
ISBN 978-1-250-11502-7 (paperback)   ISBN 978-1-62779-511-1 (ebook)   [1. Family life—
Texas—Fiction. 2. Sex role—Fiction. 3. Veterinarians—Fiction. 4. Texas—
History—20th century—Fiction.] I. Title.
PZ7.K296184Cu 2015   [Fic]—dc23   2015000920

Originally published in the United States by Henry Holt and Company
First Square Fish edition: 2017
Book designed by April Ward
Square Fish logo designed by Filomena Tuosto

1 3 5 7 9 10 8 6 4 2

AR: 5.9 / LEXILE: 860L

To Gwen Erwin—with love and gratitude
for thirty years of encouragement, support,
and laughter. Thanks, Gweni.

CHAPTER 1

ARMAND VERSUS DILLY

> One evening, when we were about ten miles from the Bay
> of San Blas, vast numbers of butterflies, in bands or flocks
> of countless myriads, extended as far as the eye could range.
> Even by the aid of a telescope it was not possible to see a
> space free from butterflies. The seamen cried out "it was
> snowing butterflies," and such in fact was the appearance.
> —Charles Darwin, *The Voyage of the Beagle*

TO MY GREAT ASTONISHMENT, I saw my first snowfall on New
Year's Day of 1900. Now, you might not think much of this, but
it is an exceedingly rare event in central Texas. Why, only the
night before, I'd made the resolution to set eyes on snow just once
before I died, doubting it would ever happen. My improbable wish
had been granted within the space of hours, the snow transform-
ing our ordinary town into a landscape of pristine beauty. I had
run through the hushed woods at dawn clad only in my robe and
slippers, marveling at the delicate mantle of snow, the pewter sky,
and the trees laced with silver, before the cold drove me back to
our house. And what with all the fuss and fizz and pomp of the
great event, I figured I was poised on the brink of a splendid

future in the new century, and that my thirteenth year would be magical.

But now here we were in spring, and somehow the months had slipped away from me, devolving into the usual humdrum round of schoolwork, housework, and piano lessons, the monotony punctuated by my six brothers (!) taking it in turn to drive me, the only girl (!), right around the bend. The New Year had duped me, sure enough.

My real name is Calpurnia Virginia Tate, but back in those days people mostly called me Callie Vee, except for Mother, when she was expressing disapproval, and Granddaddy, who would have no truck with nicknames.

The only solace came from my nature studies with Granddaddy, Captain Walter Tate, a man whom many in our town of Fentress mistook for a crotchety, unsociable old loon. He'd made his money in cotton and cattle, and fought for the Confederate States in the War before deciding to dedicate the last part of his life to the study of Nature and Science. I, his companion in this endeavor, lived for the few precious hours I could eke out in his company, trailing behind him with the butterfly net, a leather satchel, my Scientific Notebook, and a sharp pencil at hand to record our observations.

In inclement weather, we studied our specimens in the laboratory (really just an old shed that had once been part of the slave quarters) or read together in the library, where I slowly picked my way under his tutelage through Mr. Darwin's book *The Origin of Species*. In fine weather, we tramped across the fields to the San Marcos River, pushing our way through the scrub along one of the many deer trails. Our world might not have appeared all that exciting to the untrained eye but there was teeming life everywhere if you only knew where to look. And *how* to look, something Granddaddy taught me. Together we had discovered a brand-new species of hairy vetch now known to the world as *Vicia tateii*. (I confess I'd rather have discovered an unknown species of animal, animals being more interesting and all, but how many people of my age—or any age—had their name permanently attached to a living thing? Beat that if you can.)

I dreamed of following in Granddaddy's footsteps and becoming a Scientist. Mother, however, had other plans for me; namely, learning the domestic arts and coming out as a debutante at age eighteen, when it was hoped I'd be presentable enough to snag the eye of a prosperous young man of good family. (This was dubious for many reasons, including the fact that I loathed cooking and sewing, and could not exactly be described as the eye-snagging type.)

So here we were in spring, a season of celebration and some trepidation in our household on account of my softhearted brother Travis, one year younger than I. You see, spring is the season of burgeoning life, of fledgling birds, raccoon kits, fox cubs, baby squirrels, and many of those babies ended up orphaned or maimed or abandoned. And the more hopeless the case, the bleaker its prospects, the more impossible its future, the more likely was Travis to adopt the creature and lug it home to live with us. I found the parade of unlikely pets quite entertaining but our parents did not. There were stern talks from Mother, there were threatened punishments from Father, but everything went out the window when Travis stumbled across an animal in need. Some thrived and some failed miserably, but all found space in his susceptible heart.

On this particular morning in March, I got up very early and unexpectedly ran into Travis in the hall.

"Are you going to the river?" he said. "Can I come too?"

I generally preferred to go alone because it's so much easier to spy on unsuspecting wildlife that way. But of all my brothers, Travis came closest to sharing my interest in Nature. I let him come along, saying, "Only if you're quiet. I'm going to make my observations."

I led us along one of the deer trails to the river as dawn slowly warmed the eastern sky. Travis, ignoring my instructions, chattered the whole way. "Say, Callie, did you hear that Mrs. Holloway's rat terrier Maisie just had puppies? Do you think Mother and Father would let me have one?"

"I doubt it. Mother's always complaining about the fact that we have four dogs already. She thinks that's three too many."

"But there's nothing better in the world than a puppy! The first thing I'd do is teach it to fetch sticks. That's part of the trouble with Bunny. I love him, but he won't play fetch." Bunny was Travis's huge, fluffy, white prizewinning rabbit. My brother doted on him, feeding and brushing and playing with him every day. But training was a new development.

"Wait," I said, "you're . . . you're trying to teach Bunny to retrieve?"

"Yep. I try and try, but he just won't do it. I even tried him with a carrot stick, but he just ate it."

"Uh . . . Travis?"

"Hmm?"

"No rabbit in the history of the world has ever fetched a stick. So don't bother."

"Well, Bunny's awful smart."

"He may be smart for a rabbit, but that's not saying much."

"I think he just needs more practice."

"Sure, and then you can start piano lessons for the pig."

"Maybe Bunny would catch on faster if you helped us."

"Not so, Travis. It's a hopeless dream."

We continued our debate until we had nearly reached the river, when we suddenly spied some creature snuffling in the leaf mold at the base of a hollowed-out tree. It turned out to be a young *Dasypus novemcinctus*, a nine-banded armadillo, about the size of a small loaf of bread. Although they were becoming more common in Texas, I'd never seen one up close before. Anatomically speaking, it resembled the unhappy melding of an anteater (the face), a mule (the ears), and a tortoise (the carapace). I thought it overall an unlucky creature in the looks department, but Granddaddy once said that to apply a human definition of beauty to an animal that had managed to thrive for millions of years was both unscientific and foolish.

Travis crouched down and whispered, "What's it doing?"

"I think it's looking for breakfast," I said. "According to Granddaddy, they eat worms and grubs and such."

Travis said, "He's awfully cute, don't you think?"

"No, I don't."

But there was no use telling him that. The heedless armadillo then did the one surefire thing guaranteed to earn itself a new home with us: It wandered over to my brother and sniffed at his socks.

Uh-oh. We'd have to get out of there before Travis could say—

"Let's take it home."

Too late! "It's a wild animal, Travis. I don't think we should."

Ignoring me, he said, "I think I'll call him Armand, Armand the Armadillo. Or if it's a girl, I could call her Dilly. How d'you like the name? Dilly the Armadillo."

Drat, now it really was too late. Granddaddy always warned me not to name the objects of scientific study because then one could never be objective, or bring oneself to dissect them, or to stuff them and mount them, or dispatch them to the slaughterhouse, or set them free—whatever the particulars of the case called for.

Travis went on, "Is it a boy or a girl, do you reckon?"

"I don't know." I pulled my Scientific Notebook from my pinafore pocket and wrote, *Question: How do you tell an Armand from a Dilly?*

Travis scooped up the armadillo and hugged it to his chest.

Armand (I had decided to refer to it as Armand for now) showed no sign of fear and proceeded to inspect Travis's collar with an avidly twitching snout. Travis smiled in delight. I sighed in aggravation. He crooned to his new friend while I rooted around with a stick to find it some food. I dug up an immense night crawler and gingerly presented it to Armand, who snatched it from me with his impressive claws and gobbled it down in two seconds flat, spraying messy bits of worm about. Not a pretty sight. No, not at all. Who knew armadillos had the world's worst table manners? But here I was doing it again, applying human sensibilities where they didn't belong.

Even Travis looked taken aback. "Eww," he said. I almost said the same thing, but unlike my brother, I had been annealed in the furnace of Scientific Thought. Scientists do not say such things aloud (although we may *think* them from time to time).

Armand licked shreds of worm off Travis's shirt. My brother said, "He's hungry, that's all. Boy, he doesn't smell so good."

It was true. As if his atrocious manners weren't enough, up close Armand emitted an unpleasant musky smell.

I said, "I think this is a bad idea. What's Mother going to say?"

"She doesn't have to know."

"She *always* knows." Exactly how she always knew was a matter of considerable interest to all seven of her children, who'd never been able to figure it out.

"I could keep him in the barn," Travis said. "She hardly ever goes out there."

I could see this was both a losing battle and not really mine to fight. We put Armand into my satchel, where he proceeded to scratch at the bag's interior all the way home. To my annoyance, I found several deep gouges in the leather when we finally unloaded him in an old rabbit hutch next to Bunny in the farthest corner of the barn. But first we weighed him on the scale used for rabbits and poultry (five pounds) and measured him from stem to stern (eleven inches, not including the tail). We debated for a minute whether to include the tail but decided that leaving it out was a better representation of his true dimensions.

Armand didn't seem to dislike this attention; on the other hand, he didn't seem to like it much either. He investigated the confines of his new home and then started scrabbling at the bottom of the hutch, ignoring us completely.

We didn't know it then, but this was going to be the extent of our relationship: scrabbling and ignoring, followed by more scrabbling and more ignoring. We watched him scrabbling and ignoring us until our maid, SanJuanna, rang the bell on the back porch to signal breakfast. We bolted into the kitchen and were met with the delightful fragrance of frying bacon and fresh cinnamon rolls.

"Warsh," commanded our cook, Viola, from the stove.

Travis and I took turns operating the pump and scrubbing our hands at the sink. A few slimy strings of Armand's breakfast still clung to my brother's shirt. I signaled to him and handed him a damp dish towel but he only smeared the stuff around and made things worse.

Viola looked up and said, "What's that smell?"

I said hastily, "Those rolls sure look good."

Travis said, "What smell?"

"That smell I smell on you, mister."

"It's just, uh, one of my rabbits. You know Bunny? The big white one? He needs a bath, that's all."

This surprised me. Travis was a notoriously bad liar on his feet, but here he was, making a pretty good job of it. In addition to my nature studies, I was making a project of building my vocabulary, and the word *facile* popped into my mind. I'd had no opportunity to use it before, but it certainly applied here: Travis, the *facile* fibber.

"Huh," said Viola. "Never heard of no rabbit needing a bath before."

"Oh, he's filthy," I chimed in. "You should see him."

"Huh," she said again. "I'll just bet."

She loaded a platter high with crispy bacon and then carried it through the swinging door into the dining room. We followed behind and took our assigned places at the table with my other brothers: Harry (the oldest, my favorite), Sam Houston (the quietest), Lamar (a real pill), Sul Ross (the second quietest), and Jim Bowie (at age five, the youngest and the loudest).

I should say here that Harry was quickly sinking in his rating as Favorite Brother due to his stepping out with Fern Spitty. Even though he was eighteen and I'd finally resigned myself to his marrying one day, his courtship meant that he spent more and more time away from the house. Fern was pretty and sweet-tempered and fairly sensible in that she didn't recoil all that much when I walked through the house with some blobby specimen sloshing around in a jar. And even though I generally approved of her, the sad truth was that she would likely break up our family one day.

Father and Granddaddy came in and sat down, nodding to us all and solemnly proclaiming, "Good morning."

Granddaddy gave me a good morning of my own, and I smiled at him, warmed by the knowledge that I was *his* favorite.

Father said, "Your mother is having one of her sick headaches. She won't be joining us this morning."

This was something of a relief, as Mother could have spotted a wormy shirt at thirty paces. And if she rather than Viola had interrogated Travis, there was a good chance he'd have buckled and confessed all. I, on the other hand, had adopted the tactic of stout denial, no matter what. I had become so good, so *facile* at denial—even in the face of incontrovertible evidence—that Mother often didn't bother interrogating me at all. (So you see, being considered unreliable does have some use, although I don't encourage it in others.)

We bowed our heads while Father said the blessing, then SanJuanna passed the platters of food. Without Mother present, we were relieved of the burden of making the light and pleasant conversation that she required at mealtimes, and we pitched into our breakfast with a right good will. For several minutes there was only the scraping of forks and knives, muffled sounds of appreciation, and the occasional request to please pass the syrup.

AFTER SCHOOL, Travis and I ran to check on Armand and found him hunched in a corner of his cage, every now and then scrabbling halfheartedly at the wire. He looked sort of, well, depressed, but with an armadillo, how could you tell for sure?

"What's wrong with him?" said Travis. "He doesn't look too happy."

"It's because he's a wild animal and he's not supposed to be here. Maybe we should let him go."

But Travis was not ready to give up on his novel pet. "I'll bet he's hungry. D'you have any worms on you?"

"I'm fresh out." This wasn't exactly true. I had one giant worm left in my room, the biggest one I'd ever seen, but I was saving it for my first dissection. Granddaddy had suggested we start with an annelid and work our way up through the various phyla. I figured, the bigger the worm, the better to see its organs and the easier the dissection.

Nevertheless, I applied myself to the problem of Armand. He was a ground dweller and an omnivore, which meant he would eat all different kinds of animal and vegetable matter. I wasn't in the mood for digging grubs, and it would take forever to trap enough ants to make him a decent meal, so I said, "Let's go see what's in the pantry."

We ran to the back porch and into the kitchen, where Viola sat resting between meals, drinking a cup of coffee, Idabelle the Inside Cat keeping her company in her basket by the stove. Viola paged through one of Mother's ladies' magazines. She couldn't read or write but enjoyed looking at the latest fashionable hats. One of them had what appeared to be a stuffed bird of paradise perched in a nest of tulle, one wing swooping artfully over the wearer's brow. I thought the hat thoroughly ridiculous, along with being a terrible waste of a rare and wonderful specimen.

"What do you want?" Viola said, not looking up.

"Oh, we're just a little hungry," I said. "We thought we'd see what's in the pantry."

"All right, but don't you touch those pies. They're for supper, you hear?"

"We hear."

We grabbed the first thing at hand, a hard-boiled egg, and ran back to the barn.

Armand sniffed at the egg, rolled it around with his claws, and then cracked it open. He ate with messy enthusiasm, grunting all the while. When he'd finished, he retired to the far corner of his cage and resumed his hunched, miserable posture. I stared at him and thought about his environment. He lived in the ground. He was nocturnal. Which meant he liked to sleep in a burrow all day. But here he was in broad daylight without a burrow for protection. No wonder he looked unhappy.

I said, "I think he needs a hole in the ground, a burrow to sleep in."

"We don't have one."

"If you let him go," I said hopefully, "he could make himself one."

"I can't let him go. He's my Armand. We just have to make one for him."

I sighed. We cast about for materials and found a pile of old newspapers and a scrap of blanket used to wipe down the horses after their day's work. We put these items in the cage where Armand did his usual sniffing routine and then started industriously shredding the paper. He hauled it, along with his blanket, to the back corner of the hutch and, within minutes, had built himself a nest of sorts. He pulled the blanket over himself and thrashed this way and that. Then he grew still. Faint snores emanated from the mound.

"There," Travis whispered, "see how happy he is? You're so smart, Callie Vee. You know everything."

Well, of course this puffed me up quite a bit. Maybe it wasn't such a bad idea after all to keep Armand. (Or Dilly.)

THAT NIGHT we lined up to receive our weekly allowance from Father. We stood outside his door in order of age, and he called us in one at a time, doling out a dime apiece to the older boys; the younger boys and I each got a nickel. I understood the reasoning behind this—sort of—but looked forward to the day when I reached dime age. The small ceremony concluded with him admonishing us not to spend it all in one place, which most of us did right away at the Fentress General Store on jujubes, taffy, and chocolate. Father's point was to teach us the value of saving money, but what we learned instead was how to calculate complex ratios of the maximum pleasure that could be extracted from each item for the longest time, as in, for example, the value of getting five cinnamon red hots for a penny versus three caramels for two pennies, and which brother would trade licorice for gumdrops, and at what exchange rate. Intricate calculations indeed.

Despite this, I had managed to save the sum of twenty-two cents, which I kept in a cigar box under my bed. A mouse, apparently finding the box attractive, had nibbled on the corners. Time for a new box from Granddaddy. I knocked on the door of his library, and he called out, "Enter if you must." I found him squinting at something through a magnifying glass, his long silver beard a pale lemon color in the faint wash of the lamplight.

"Calpurnia, fetch another lamp, won't you? This appears to be *Erythrodiplax berenice*, or the seaside dragonlet. It is the only true saltwater dragonfly we know of. But what is it doing here?"

"I don't know, Granddaddy."

"Ah, of course not. That is what we call a rhetorical question; no answer is actually expected."

I almost said, "Then why ask it?" But that would have been impertinent, and I would never be impertinent with my grandfather.

"Strange," he said. "You don't normally see them this far from the salt marsh."

I brought him another lamp and leaned over his shoulder. I loved spending time with him in this room, piled high as it was with all sorts of intriguing things: the microscope and telescope, dried insects, bottled beasts, desiccated lizards, the old globe, an ostrich egg, a camel saddle the size of a hassock, a black bear-skin rug with a gaping maw the perfect size for catching the foot of a visiting granddaughter. And let's not forget the books, great stacks of them, dense scholarly texts bound in worn morocco with gilt lettering. And in pride of place on a special shelf, a thick jar containing the *Sepia officinalis*, a cuttlefish that had been sent to my grandfather years ago by the great man himself, Mr. Charles Darwin, whom Granddaddy revered. The ink on the cardboard tag was faded but still legible. My grandfather prized it above all things.

He raised his head, sniffed the air, and said, "Why do you smell like an armadillo?"

There was no putting anything past him, at least not anything having to do with Nature.

"Uh," I said, "it's probably better that you don't know."

This amused him. He said, "The name in Spanish means 'little armored one.' The early German settlers referred to it as the *Panzerschwein*, or 'armored pig.' The flesh is pale and resembles pork in taste and texture when properly prepared. My troops and I occasionally made a grateful meal of one when we could find it. During the War, they were not so common, having only recently migrated to our part of the world from South America. Darwin was quite taken with them and called them 'nice little animals,' but then he never tried to raise one. Although they rarely bite, they make terrible pets. They live alone as adults with no social tendencies, which might explain why they do not value human company in the slightest."

Granddaddy would occasionally mention the War Between the States, but not often. Probably best, as several Confederate veterans lived on in our town, and the War—or at least its outcome—still rankled with many of them. I also thought it best not to mention to Travis that his own grandfather had dined on Armand's ancestors and found them good eating.

"Granddaddy," I said, "I would like a new cigar box, please, if you can spare one, and I need to borrow a book. So I can read about the armadillo we don't have."

He smiled and produced a box for me, and then pointed to *Godwin's Guide to Texas Mammals*. He said, "There are certain animals that apparently cannot be domesticated, for reasons that are not well understood. It isn't only the armadillo. Consider the beaver, the zebra, and the hippopotamus, to name a few others. Many people have tried to domesticate them and all have failed miserably, often in a spectacular and sometimes deadly fashion."

I could just imagine Mother's reaction to Travis coming home with a baby hippopotamus on the end of a string, and I thanked my lucky stars we lived in a hippo-free county. I opened my reference text, and Granddaddy and I worked together in contented silence.

Right before bed, Travis and I checked on Armand. (We had agreed to call him Armand, even though we still couldn't rule out Dilly.) He rooted and scrabbled and ignored us, so we left him to it.

The next morning, Travis gave him another boiled egg. He ate it, ignored us, and retired to his burrow.

Travis said, "I wish he'd be my friend. I bet if I keep feeding him, he'll be my friend."

"That's only 'larder love.' Do you really want a pet that's only glad to see you because you bring it food?"

I told him what I'd learned about the species from Granddaddy, but he shrugged it off. I figured he'd have to find out for himself. Some lessons can only be learned the hard way.

CHAPTER 2

THE ARMADILLO CRISIS

In the Pampæan deposit at the Bajada I found the osse-
ous armour of a gigantic armadillo-like animal, the inside
of which, when the earth was removed, was like a great
cauldron.

A COUPLE OF DAYS LATER, Travis appeared at breakfast with dark
circles ringing his eyes. And he smelled something fierce.

Mother, alarmed, said, "Do you feel all right? What's that
terrible odor?"

"I'm all right," he mumbled. "It's the rabbits. I fed them
early."

"Hmm," said Mother. "Perhaps you need a teaspoon of
cod-liv—"

"No, I'm fine!" he shouted. "Time for school!" And he
bolted from the room.

He'd come perilously close to being dosed with the dreaded
cod-liver oil, Mother's all-purpose remedy for whatever ailed you,
and the foulest substance known to man. If you weren't sick before
taking a dose, you certainly were afterward; the mere threat of
one small spoonful was enough to cause the sickest child to

levitate from his deathbed and gallop off to school or church or whatever onerous chore awaited him in a state of glossy good health.

On our way to school, I asked Travis what was wrong.

He said, "I brought Armand in last night."

"What do you mean?"

"He slept in my bedroom."

I stared at him. "You're kidding me. You brought his cage inside?"

"No, just him."

I stared at him some more. "You mean . . . he was loose in your room?"

"Yes, and you should have heard the noise he made."

The mind reeled. He went on, "He wouldn't go to sleep, so I sneaked down to the pantry and got him an egg, but he still wouldn't settle down. He kept digging in the corners and rubbing his armor against the legs of my bed. A horrible scraping noise, all night long."

"I don't believe it," I said. "What about the others?" Travis shared a room with the little boys, Sul Ross and Jim Bowie.

"They both slept right through it," he said bitterly. "They didn't even notice."

"You know keeping Armand isn't a good idea," I said, and was about to deliver a sisterly lecture on the many reasons why not, when we were joined by my friend and classmate Lula Gates, who sometimes walked to school with us. A whole bunch of my brothers—including Travis—were sweet on her. Lula wore a new ribbon in her long silvery-blond hair that made her eyes look especially green. Mermaid eyes, Travis called them. When he saw her, all his fatigue dropped away. (I should mention here that Travis had a special gift for happiness. He was one of those rare individuals whose face lit up like the sun when he smiled, his entire being suffused with contagious happiness. The world could not help but smile back.)

"Hey, Lula," he said, "guess what I've got? A pet armadillo!"

"Really?"

"You should come and see him. He'll eat right out of your hand. I'll let you feed him if you like. Would you like to?"

"Gosh, you always have the most interesting pets. I'd love to see it."

And that's how—probably for the first time in history—the nine-banded armadillo became a tool of courtship and an implement of wooing.

Lula came the next day, to Travis's delight. I could tell he was pulling ahead of my other brothers in the Lula stakes. He took Armand from his cage and fed him an egg, which Armand tore into with his usual relish. Lula watched in fascination but, being a bit of a delicate flower, declined to hold the beast when offered the chance. (Although we could not have known it at the time, this turned out to be a fortunate choice on her part.)

On the weekend, Travis spent hours in the barn with Armand, fruitlessly trying to turn him into a pet. He cuddled him and fed him by hand and buffed his armor with a soft cloth, but Armand simply did not care.

One night at dinner, Travis surprised me by speaking directly to Granddaddy, something he seldom, if ever, did. He started out with, "Sir?"

No response.

"Sir? Grandfather?"

Granddaddy snapped out of his reverie and looked around the table, trying to locate the speaker. His gaze finally settled on Travis.

"Yes, uh . . . young man?"

Travis quailed under the direct and curious gaze. He stammered, "I-I was wondering, sir. Do you know how long armadillos live? Sir?"

Granddaddy stroked his beard and said, "Generally, in the wild, I would say about five years. However, in captivity, they have been known to survive as long as fifteen."

Travis and I glanced at each other in dismay. Granddaddy noticed this and looked amused but said nothing more.

WE FED ARMAND twice daily, and he put on weight nicely, no doubt due to the fact that he no longer had to wander afield for his dinner. He tolerated Travis briefly cradling him but that was all. He never seemed to welcome us, despite the fact that we brought him his daily hard-boiled eggs. He never stopped digging at the corner of his cage, to the point that we had to reinforce it with bits of scrap lumber. But Travis, inexplicably, loved Armand as he loved all animals and would not give him up.

One morning I visited the pantry and found no hard-boiled eggs. Viola sat at the kitchen table peeling a giant mound of potatoes. My brothers, growing boys all, managed to plow their way through a hillock of spuds every day. I said, "Why don't we have any eggs?"

"So it's you," she said. "I wondered how those eggs was walking off. What are you doing with 'em?"

"Nothing," I said stoutly.

"You eating them all yourself?"

"Yup."

"I doubt that, missy. You feeding some hobo at the river? Your momma ain't gonna like that."

"Then perhaps you shouldn't *tell* her," I said, a shade more pertly than I'd intended.

"Don't take that tone with me, little miss."

"Sorry." I sat down and peeled with her, marveling at the speed at which her nimble fingers worked, finishing two clean spuds to my single eye-pocked one. We worked together in silence for a while and then I said, "It isn't a hobo; it's something else. I'll tell you if you promise not to tell anyone."

"Anyone" meaning, of course, Mother.

"Don't be doing that to me. You know better."

I sighed. "You're right. I'm sorry."

"You certainly are."

"Ha-ha, very funny. If you must know, it's for a sort of experiment."

"Don't tell me. I don't want to know."

"It seems like people often say that to me."

"Huh."

I noticed that Idabelle the Inside Cat was not in her basket by the stove. No doubt this was part of Viola's tetchy mood. She tended to fret when her constant feline companion and helper was off patrolling for mice or lolling in a patch of sunlight upstairs. Idabelle's job was to keep the vermin down in the pantry, and she did a fine job of it. In winter, she made an excellent bed warmer. We also had the Outside Cats that looked after the back porch and the outbuildings. They occasionally wandered into the barn to stare at Armand who, naturally enough, ignored them.

We finished the spuds. As I went out, I kissed Viola's cheek, and she swatted me away.

At dusk, Granddaddy called me into the library and gestured for me to sit down in my usual place on the camel's saddle. Holding up a magazine, he said, "Calpurnia, I have here the latest edition of *The Journal of Southwestern Biology*. It contains a report of a naturalist in Louisiana who appears to have contracted Hansen's disease from handling an armadillo that served as a vector."

"Oh, really?"

"Therefore, I suggest that if you by any chance have an armadillo in your possession—and I'm not saying you do, mind—that you release it into the wild as soon as practicable."

"Uh . . . all right. What's Hansen's disease?"

"A strange and terrible malady for which there is no cure. It is commonly known as leprosy."

I rocketed from my chair like a pheasant flushed from the scrub. I bolted from the room, my mind racing, my heart pounding—no, no, not Travis! Not the hideous fleshy tumors that deformed the face and hands, leaving the victims shunned and helpless, living out their lives quarantined in leper colonies behind barbed wire. It was unthinkable that softhearted Travis would be banished to the land of the damned!

I careened into the barn, causing the stabled horses to shy and the Outside Cats to streak away in alarm.

There stood Travis, cradling Armand. I charged, screaming, "Put it down! Put it down!"

Travis flinched and looked stunned. "What?"

"Put it down—it's dangerous!"

Travis stared at me stupidly.

I reached for the armadillo and then pulled back, unable to bring myself to touch it.

"Put it down," I panted. "They can spread diseases, Granddaddy said so." I took the skirt of my pinafore and, using it as a protective wrapping, grabbed the creature and dumped it to the ground.

"Hey," Travis protested. "You'll hurt him. What diseases, anyway? Look at him, Callie. He's perfectly healthy."

He stooped to pick Armand up.

"Leprosy," I gasped.

He froze. *"What?"*

"Granddaddy says they can spread leprosy. If you catch it, you have to live in a leper colony and never see your family again."

He blanched and stepped back.

Armand sniffed casually at a loose wisp of hay while we stared at him as if he were an unexploded bomb. I caught my breath and patted Travis on the arm. "It's probably okay," I said. "He's probably one of the healthy ones."

Travis shivered. Armand snuffled and wandered around the barn for a minute.

"Maybe you should go and wash your hands."

Saucer-eyed, he stared at me and croaked, "Will that help?"

I had absolutely no idea but lied through my teeth: "Of course it will."

We hightailed it to the horse trough, where I worked the pump handle for all I was worth, while Travis frantically scrubbed his hands, teeth chattering.

We turned in time to see Armand mosey toward the scrub at the edge of the property. I wondered how a creature so seemingly oblivious of everything around it could possibly survive in the wild. I compared Armand with Ajax, Father's prize bird dog, driven by curiosity, constantly policing his territory, alert to every small change, aware of every subtle scent. His intense vigilance served as a highly tuned survival mechanism. That was apparently missing from Armand.

Question for the Notebook: Is it Armand's protective armor that fosters his nonchalant attitude? Maybe if you toted a shell around on your back and could curl into it at a moment's notice, you didn't have to pay much attention to your environment. Was that why he appeared deaf and dumb to his surroundings? Or was he in fact acutely attuned to his world, but we, as humans, simply played no part in it?

We watched him scrabble away in the gathering darkness.

Travis waved sadly. "Bye, Armand. Or Dilly. You were my favorite armadillo. I hope you don't get sick."

Armand or Dilly stayed true to form and ignored him.

Travis spent the next week scrubbing his hands raw. Mother noticed this and complimented him on his hygiene, saying, "I am glad to see that at least one of my boys finally understands the importance of clean hands. What brought this on?"

"Well, I found this ar—"

"No, no," I gurgled. "Miss Harbottle gave a talk about it at school. Yes, ha-ha. Now we all wash our hands a lot. Heh-heh."

Mother narrowed her eyes but said nothing.

Oh, Travis, Travis, my downy little chick of a brother. How you survived each day without being squashed under life's passing wheels was beyond me. Later I told him, "Look, if Mother ever finds out about Armand, you'll never be allowed to adopt any other animal. Of any kind. Ever again. D'you want that?"

"I guess not."

"I didn't think so."

He said, "I feel kind of itchy. And sick to my stomach. And dizzy all over. Oh, and my hair hurts. Do you think it's leprosy?"

I didn't know, so I looked up the symptoms in Granddaddy's *Contagious and Tropical Diseases of Man*, a book full of dreadful pictures that were best not gazed at directly (or at all if one could help it), what with the creeping larval eruptions and rotting body parts.

It turned out that the early symptoms of leprosy included loss of the eyebrows, along with loss of sensation in the cooler areas of the skin, such as the knees. Travis inspected his eyebrows in the mirror a hundred times a day, and at least once daily asked me to pinch him hard on the knees. Each time he said "ow" and sighed in relief. (He was still in short pants at that point, and walked around with bruised knees on display. If Mother noticed, she made no comment.)

CHAPTER 3

THE BAROMETER SPEAKS

At the place where we slept water necessarily boiled, from the diminished pressure of the atmosphere, at a lower temperature than it does in a less lofty country....

SPRING TURNED SLOWLY into summer with its inevitable crushing heat and our inevitable grousing about it. Viola said it was so hot, the hens were laying hard-boiled eggs. I complained about the heat less than the others because I often slipped away to the river at midday while they took to their shuttered rooms for a sweaty, fretful nap. Since I owned no bathing costume, I stripped down to my chemise, then floated on my back in the gentle eddies, examining the clouds overhead for fanciful shapes and scenes: There stood an Indian teepee; there, a waltzing gopher; there, a puffing dragon.

The scenes overhead formed and broke apart and re-formed endlessly. I noted that the thick, puffy cumulus clouds were excellent fodder for the imagination while the thin, sparse cirrus ones were useless. Question for the Notebook: What shapes the clouds? It must have something to do with moisture in the air. And what about a mackerel sky? Discuss further with Granddaddy.

I could hear the shouting, splashing, uncouth town boys at the bridge downstream, and though I envied them their rope swing, nothing could have induced me to join them, swimming as I was in my underclothes. After my refreshing dip, I made order of my hair and clothes as best I could with a comb and towel I kept secreted in a brown paper bag at the base of a hollow tree, then sneaked back to my room.

Later that day, I asked Granddaddy about the weather. He said that scientists had actually ridden in a huge balloon two miles above the earth and discovered that the puffy lower clouds were composed of tiny droplets of water like fog, while the higher wispy clouds were made of tiny ice crystals. And mackerel skies were formed by a rare type of cloud in between them. I marveled at the courage it must have taken to be the first person to make that flight.

We started my study of the weather with wind direction. This was easy, as there was a weather vane mounted at the very top of the house next to the lightning rod. The vane was cut from a sheet of tin in the shape of a longhorn steer; it swiveled automatically to point into the direction of the wind. Any nitwit could figure it out. After several days' observation, I noted that when the wind blew from the west, it generally signaled good weather to come. I wrote my findings in my Notebook.

To measure wind speed, I built an "anemometer" out of four cardboard cones glued together in the manner of a whirligig, but my materials weren't up to the job, and the first good gust tore my instrument apart, scattering bits of debris across the front lawn.

"Was that another one of your 'science experiments'?" said Lamar, standing on the porch with Sul Ross.

What a pill. I said, "Lamar, you'd probably flunk out of a school of fish."

Sul Ross hooted with laughter at this, and Lamar rabbit punched him but could not come up with a decent retort. In a battle of wits, Lamar was unarmed.

I went to Granddaddy and said, "My anemometer blew apart."

"That's a shame," he said. "The homemade ones often do, but at least you are now familiar with the principles involved."

Our next lesson involved something called "air pressure" that you measured with a barometer. I'd had to build the anemometer because we didn't own one, but we—or rather Grandaddy—owned a barometer, so I figured we'd use that one for my lessons. I figured wrong.

He said, "We will need a jar, a balloon, a rubber band, a straw, a sewing needle, a metric ruler, and a pot of glue."

Now, that was certainly an intriguing list, but I could make no sense of it.

"Why do we need those things?"

"You're going to build your own barometer."

I gestured at the handsome brass instrument mounted on the library wall, saying, "What's wrong with that one?"

"Not a thing, as far as I know."

"Oh, I see. This is going to be one of those lessons about learning something from the ground up, right?"

"That's correct," he said, licking a forefinger and turning a page. "I'll wait here for you."

I considered the list of things we needed. I had no balloon, and was pretty sure none of my brothers did, either, so I ran to the general store and bought one for a nickel. (Normally I would have kicked at the exorbitant price, but it was all worth it for Science.) I also filched a paper straw from the soda fountain.

Then I ran to the laboratory and found a ruler and an empty jar and pot of glue among the jumble of tubing and beakers and the hundreds of small bottles filled with a nasty-looking brown liquid. Granddaddy had been trying to distill whiskey from pecans for years, and the shelves were crammed with his many failures.

I returned with all the necessary equipment and placed it on his desk.

"Now," he said, "before we begin, you need to understand what we will be measuring. The concept of air pressure was not fully understood until 1643, when the Italian scientist Torricelli, who built the first barometer, said famously, 'We live submerged at the bottom of an ocean of air.'"

Granddaddy went on to explain the astounding fact that although air is invisible, it actually weighs something, and that the many miles of air in the atmosphere above us actually weigh a *lot*. He reminded me of how my ears popped when I dove deep in the river, down to where the catfish live, due to the growing weight of water above me and its pressure on my eardrums. And in that same way, the air pressed down on us with a mighty force of 14.7 pounds per square inch. Fortunately we were able to stand the pressure, and in fact didn't even notice it, because it compressed us from all directions at once, and because our bodies were rigid enough to push back.

I found this information rather disconcerting, but being a Fact of the Universe, there was no getting around it.

He went on, "The barometer we will make is different from Torricelli's barometer because they didn't have rubber balloons in his day. But the idea of measuring air pressure was his real contribution. He got the idea in part from his friend and colleague Galileo, now revered as the 'Father of Modern Science,' who was imprisoned during his lifetime for heresy. And Torricelli actually had to hide his first barometer from his neighbors to avoid accusations of witchcraft. Ah, me. Such is the lot of the scientist bold enough to advance the boundaries of knowledge. But enough history, let us begin. You will find the device is simplicity itself."

Under his instruction, I cut the neck off the balloon and stretched it tight over the open top of the jar, securing it in place with the rubber band. Then I dabbed glue onto one end of the straw and placed it horizontally on top of the balloon so that the end of the straw was stuck to the center of the balloon. Finally, I glued the needle to the far end of the straw.

I stepped back and studied my creation. How could such an unimpressive instrument possibly work?

As if reading my mind, Granddaddy said, "I admit it's rather a crude model, but eminently workable. Now measure the height of the needle and write it down."

I stood the ruler up and made a note of where the needle pointed.

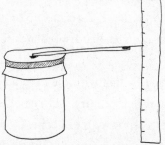

"As the air pressure increases, it presses down on the balloon, compressing the air inside the jar. This causes the glued end of the straw to go down, which causes the needle end to rise. Conversely, as the air pressure falls, the needle will fall. Measure the height of the needle several times per day, and you will see that rising pressure and a rising needle generally indicate good weather is on the way. Falling pressure and a falling needle presage rain and stormy weather. You could also try using the jar of bear grease I have somewhere, but I remain skeptical about its efficacy."

"The jar of what?" I didn't think I'd heard him right.

"I was given a jar of bear fat some years ago by Gordon Poteet, who had been snatched by the Comanche outside Fredericksburg when he was nine years old. I was a member of the Rangers' posse that pursued his captors across Texas to bring him back, a long tale of woe I prefer not to delve into at the moment. But we did eventually return him to his parents a few years later, by which time he had turned mostly Indian. He changed his name to Gordon Whitefeather and now lives halfway between the two societies, happy neither here nor there. He gave me a jar of grease and claimed that the medicine man had taught him to predict the weather from observing certain changes in the fat, changes that I speculate are caused by varying air pressure."

"Huh. I think I'll stick with the barometer." We had just stepped into a brand-new century, and a jar of bear grease struck me as too much of a retreat to the old one. I took my instrument to the farthest corner of the front porch and parked it out of harm's way behind a couple of Mother's potted plants.

The next morning was mostly overcast and gloomy with low, patchy clouds. I sat on the front steps and made my usual observations of flora and fauna. I added the following: *Needle is rising, which is supposed to mean higher pressure, which is supposed to mean fine weather. Seems doubtful. Maybe go with bear grease next time?*

But by recess, the clouds had dissipated and the sun smiled down from a blue enamel sky. The barometer had spoken.

OUR ANNUAL SCHOOL PICNIC—a special treat that we all looked forward to with great anticipation—was scheduled for the following Friday afternoon. When I checked the barometer at 6:15 that morning, my heart sank. The needle was falling, a harbinger of bad weather. Ugh. When I arrived at school, the sky was aquamarine with not one single cloud. Nevertheless, I went up to Miss Harbottle and told her that we might be in for some rain on our picnic.

She waved a dismissive hand at the heavens and sighed. "Calpurnia Tate, wherever do you get these ideas?"

"From the barometer, Miss Harbottle."

"Well, I suggest you use the eyes God gave you instead. There's nothing *wrong* with them, is there?"

"Not that I know of, Miss Harbottle."

"Thank goodness for that. Now, please go in. You're holding up the line."

A couple of my classmates tittered and elbowed each other, one of them being Dovie Medlin, my least favorite of all, a self-important nincompoop with delusions of grandeur over the fact that her older sister was the town's Telephone Operator. The odious Dovie enjoyed lording this over everyone and would not concede that having one's name attached to a new species of plant could possibly rise to such a level of magnificence. Gah.

But when the first ominous roll of thunder sounded at noon, Dovie's mouth fell open in a perfect O of disbelief, and Miss Harbottle glared at me as if I were somehow responsible for ruining our outing. How ridiculous! How satisfying! I bit back a giggle and fought to keep a suitably bland expression on my face.

UNBELIEVABLY, TRAVIS CONTINUED to mope over the loss of his armadillo. He spent his free time brushing and hugging Bunny (who still did not fetch), and playing with the barn cats, whom he had named after famous outlaws (Jesse James, Belle Starr, etc.), but this was apparently not enough. To cheer him up, I suggested we go and see the Holloways' new pups. We walked half a mile up the Lockhart Road to the Holloways' sagging farm-house. Mrs. Holloway answered the peeling door wearing a dirty apron. Maisie, a medium-sized brown-and-white rat terrier, whined in distress at her feet.

"Good afternoon, Mrs. Holloway," I said.

"Hi, Maisie," Travis said. "What's wrong with her? Why is she crying like that?"

"She had some puppies," Mrs. Holloway said, "and now they're gone."

"Where are they?" Travis said.

Mrs. Holloway looked uncomfortable. "Well, you got to understand about those pups. Best we can tell, a coyote jumped the fence when Maisie was in heat, and we got seven of these real ugly pups. Seven! Can you imagine? You never saw the likes. We couldn't even give 'em away. Mercy me."

"I'll take one," Travis said quickly.

I glanced at him in consternation. We hadn't discussed this with our parents.

"I'll take two," he said.

I frowned at him.

"I'll take three," he said.

I glared at him and nudged him with my foot.

"Why, honey," Mrs. Holloway said, looking uncomfortable again, "you're too late. Mr. Holloway finally got fed up with their yapping and took 'em to the river in a sack ten minutes ago."

"Oh no!"

"If you run, you might catch him, but maybe it's best that you don't. Ugly, I tell you. Mercy me."

Travis wheeled and took off like a madman. I managed to stutter a good-bye to Mrs. Holloway and ran after him at top speed.

"Travis, stop! Don't look!"

He ran even faster. I kept up with him halfway until I got a sudden agonizing stitch in my side, slowing me to a trot a hundred yards back. Off in the distance, I could see a figure on horseback heading our way. Mr. Holloway. Returning from the bridge. Travis shouted something I couldn't hear. Mr. Holloway shook his head and jabbed his thumb over his shoulder at the bridge. Travis ran on.

As I passed Mr. Holloway, he said, "You don't want no coyote cross."

I hurried on. Travis stood on the bridge feverishly scanning the slow-moving river for signs of life. But there was nothing to see. No sack, no puppies, not even bubbles. For Travis's sake, I was grateful.

"They're gone," I said.

We stood there a few minutes longer. He said not a word. I put my arm around him, and we turned for home. It would be months before we spoke of it again.

CHAPTER 4

DEVIL BIRDS

[The tameness of the birds] is common to all the terrestrial species. . . . One day, whilst lying down, a mocking-thrush alighted on the edge of a pitcher, made of the shell of a tortoise, which I held in my hand, and began very quietly to sip the water.

A FEW WEEKS LATER, I was in the kitchen with Viola, petting Idabelle and generally getting in the way, when Travis came through the back door, beaming and carrying an old straw hat covered with a red bandanna, from whence issued rustling sounds.

"Hey, everybody, you'll never guess what I found!"

Viola looked up sharply. "Whatever it is, I don't want it in my kitchen."

"What is it?" I said, with both interest and trepidation.

He whipped back the cloth like a conjurer to reveal two baby blue jays, scrawny, stringy, partially feathered, pink mouths agape, and ugly enough to turn sweet milk into clabber. They strained upward, quivering for food, emitting grating high-pitched cries.

Now, it wasn't all that unusual to occasionally run across a stranded young bird that had fallen or been dumped from the nest. But two? I found that . . . suspicious.

"You *found* them? Really? Where?"

Travis wouldn't meet my eye. "Down near the gin."

Viola said, "I don't care where you found 'em, you get them nasty things out of here right now. Those are devil birds."

As if to confirm her opinion, both birds threw back their heads, much too big for their wobbly necks, and screamed like, well, the devil. You wouldn't think such frail-looking organisms would be capable of such a racket, but this was how they begged for food from their parents.

Viola yelled over the noise, "Get 'em out of here."

Travis chattered on our way to the barn. "I've heard they make good pets. Have you heard that? They say they're really smart, and you can teach them tricks. I've been thinking about their names. How about Blue for one and Jay for the other? Blue is this one here. Look, he's a little bit smaller. And Jay, well, he's a little bit bigger, but one of his wings looks kind of funny. I hope it's okay. But that's how you tell them apart. I wonder when they ate last? Do you think they'll eat chicken feed? Or will we have to dig for worms?"

"Travis, you know how Mother and Father feel about wild animals."

"But these aren't even animals, Callie. They're birds. So it's different."

"Not really. Birds are a class of vertebrate within the kingdom Animalia."

"I don't know what that means, but boy, they sure are noisy."

And boy, they sure *were* noisy. Their cries were an annoying sound halfway between a squeak and a screech, and about six octaves higher than I could sing. I followed him to the barn, where he looked for some kind of home for them. But the raucous cries of Blue and Jay quickly drew an attentive circle of the Outside Cats, eyes agleam and tails atwitch.

"They'll have to go into the chicken pen," I said. "It's the only place they'll be safe." The chicken pen had a stout roof to discourage cats, coons, and hawks. We filled a wooden box with combings from Snow White, Mother's favorite ewe, and put the birds in their new home. They aggressively demanded food without ceasing, being basically two oversized mouths attached to two undersized bodies. They stopped their terrible noise only long enough to choke down beakfuls of a soft mash of chicken feed, fluttering their wings in excitement.

"Do you think we should give them water too?" asked Travis.

"I reckon it can't hurt."

Travis dipped his finger in the hen's basin, and then, wiggling his wet finger, let fall a couple of drops of water into each beak. The birds liked it. As far as I could tell.

The offended hens huddled on the far side of the enclosure and clucked in consternation. Finally, to shut the hatchlings up, Travis draped the bandanna over them and they fell quiet in the artificial dark.

But calamity struck the next morning when we found Blue, the smaller of the birds, dead. Its sibling ignored the corpse and screamed at the top of its lungs for breakfast. From Travis's reaction, you would have thought there was no greater tragedy in our family.

"I killed him," Travis said, fighting back tears. "I should have sat up with him. Poor old Blue. I failed him."

"No, you didn't," I said in a vain attempt to console him. "It always goes that way with the runts. It can't be helped; it's the survival of the fittest. That's the way Mother Nature works."

Well, there was nothing for it but we had to have a funeral, interring "poor old Blue" in the patch of land behind the smokehouse that Travis had staked out as a sad little cemetery over the years for his unsuccessful projects. (I myself would have left Blue to the ants and beetles to strip down to the bone so that I could have a nice clean skeleton to study, but Travis looked too distraught for me to suggest it.)

We placed the carcass in a nest of shredded newspapers in one of my cigar boxes, a brightly colored one with a dancing lady in a red dress and mantilla. I almost apologized to Travis for not having something more somber, so contagious was his grief. He dug a hole and gently deposited the colorful casket in the dark soil.

"Callie, would you like to say some words?"

Startled, I said, "Uh, you go ahead. You knew him better than I did."

"Okay, then. Blue was a good bird," said Travis, choking up a little. "He liked his mash. He did his best. And he never learned how to fly. We'll miss you, Blue. Amen."

"Amen," I said, for want of something to say, wondering if you were allowed to pray over a dead bird.

He filled in the hole and tamped it down with the back of the shovel. Thinking we were done, I turned to go.

He said, "Wait, we need some kind of marker."

We found a smooth river rock, and then he fretted over how to scratch the bird's name on it. The bell rang for breakfast, and I said, "You'll have to come back later." I handed him my handkerchief and put my arm around him as we trudged back to the house.

At the table Mother took one look at Travis's swollen red eyes and said gently, "Darling? Is something the matter?"

"One of my blue jays died in the night," he mumbled, eyes downcast on his plate.

"One of your what?" said Mother, cocking her head and fixing him with a bright beady gaze; she so resembled a bird that I almost giggled.

"I found two baby jays. One of them died in the night."

"That," said Mother, "is what I thought you said. But I can't believe my ears. How many times have we talked about this?"

"Ah," said Granddaddy, choosing that moment to snap out of his usual mealtime musing. "The North American blue jay, *Cyanocitta cristata*, a member of the corvid family, which also includes crows and ravens, although the jay is strictly a New World bird. They are known to be intelligent and inquisitive and are excellent mimics who can often be taught to speak. Some experts consider them as intelligent as the parrot family. Many of the Indian clans view the jay as a trickster, mischievous and greedy but also clever and resourceful. You say you have one of these, my boy?"

Encouraged, Travis said, "Yessir, although it's just a baby."

"In that case, it will bond with you, so you'd best be prepared to support it through its adult life, which could easily last a decade or more. Yes, indeed, they are quite long-lived birds." He resubmerged himself in his scrambled eggs and deep thoughts.

Mother, clearly wishing to shoot daggers at Granddaddy, instead turned them on Travis.

"We agreed there would be no more wild animals, did we not?"

"Yes, ma'am."

"And?"

"And . . . uh."

I interjected on his behalf: "They're only babies, Mother. They both would have died if he hadn't picked them up. At least he saved one of them."

"Calpurnia, keep out of this," she said. "Travis can speak for himself."

"Yeah, Calpurnia"—Lamar snickered under his breath— "let the little birdbrain speak for himself. That's if he doesn't start bawling."

"And *you*." She wheeled on Lamar. "Do you have something useful to add to this conversation? No? I didn't think so."

Oh, Lamar, how had you become such a pill? And why? And more important, could anything be done about it?

Travis rallied his arguments. "I've got him in the chicken pen, Mama. He won't be any trouble in there, I promise."

Did anyone else besides me notice the change in his form of address? He hadn't called her Mama since his eighth birthday. She visibly softened and said, "But, darling, they're *always* trouble."

"Not this time, I promise."

"You *always* promise." Mother massaged her temples, and I could read in that gesture that Travis, the beamish boy, had won again.

Sure enough, Jay quickly grew attached to his master. He became more attractive as his feathers filled in and turned bluer, but his gimpy right wing was a problem. Every time Travis and I tried to splint it, Jay turned into an exploding ball of blue feathers in our hands, furious, flapping like mad, and screaming blue murder (ha!). It turned out that all the flapping we provoked was probably the best thing for the wing, and it slowly grew stronger. Even so, when he was finally ready to fly, I noticed that he always flew in a circle, the stronger left wing propelling him clockwise.

Jay lived mostly in the pen, but sometimes Travis would take him for a "walk," and Jay would either ride on his shoulder or flap from tree to tree alongside. Jay became a good mimic. He learned to cackle like the hens and crow like our rooster, General Lee, driving the normally prideful bird to distraction so that he fretfully paced the yard, seeking his invisible rival in vain.

Jay's plumage grew beautiful; his voice did not. When he was separated from his boy-god, he screamed down the heavens in rage; sometimes we could even hear his strident calls as we sat at the dining table, a good fifty yards or so from the pen. We all pretended not to notice.

Travis started giving Jay a weekly bath in a shallow pan of warm water, and the bird thrashed about in great delight. They spent more and more time together out of the pen. We grew used to seeing Travis with streaks of white on his shoulders, to our maid SanJuanna's vexation. He even took Jay to show-and-tell at school, where he proved to be a big hit, although Miss Harbottle flinched every time he screamed or flapped, fearing for her black dress and lofty coiffure, with good reason.

Jay took special delight in taunting the cats, but for some reason, he particularly singled out Idabelle, swooping down and screeching at her whenever she went outside to take some sun. Viola told Travis more than once, "You keep that devil bird away from my cat."

Then, of course, the calamitous, the gruesome—and the entirely predictable—happened. Idabelle ran through the back door bearing a limp bundle of blue feathers in her mouth.

Now, you can't exactly fault a cat for eating a bird, can you? That doesn't seem fair; it's just the way Nature goes. There wasn't much to bury, only a wing and a handful of tail feathers.

I'd never attended an actual funeral (and by that I mean for a real person) and had always wanted to see one, but after our ceremony for Jay, I changed my mind. Travis's grief was terrible to behold. And although I felt disloyal for thinking so and would never have said it aloud, I suspect that all the rest of us were relieved to see the end of Jay.

CHAPTER 5

RARA AVIS

The jaguar is a noisy animal, roaring much by night, and especially before bad weather.

I WOKE UP with a small thrill of anticipation coursing through my veins. It took me a moment to remember why, but then it came to me: I was due to crack open a new Scientific Notebook. I'd jammed my first one chock-full of many Questions, a few Answers, and various observations and sketches. It had been my faithful companion for the past year, and it included my notes about the brand-new species of hairy vetch that Granddaddy and I had discovered, the *Vicia tateii*. Maybe one day the book would be an object of scientific and historic interest. Who could say?

But now it was time to bid adieu to the old one and start the cheerful new red one Granddaddy had given me. I opened it and inhaled the smell of fresh leather and paper. Could anything top the promise and potential of a blank page? What could be more satisfying? Never mind that it would soon be crammed with awkward penmanship, that my handwriting inevitably sloped downhill to the right-hand corner, that I blotted my ink, that my drawings *never* came out the way I saw them in my head. Never mind all that. What counted was possibility. You could live on possibility, at least for a while.

I crept downstairs, avoiding the treacherous spot in the middle of tread number seven that cracked like a pistol shot. The house was just beginning to stir. If I hurried, I could have some time alone to myself. I eased the front door open and stepped outside into the freshness of the morning to make my notes.

And there, to my surprise, stood a strange gray-and-white bird on the front lawn. It was about the size of a chicken but of an entirely different shape. The plumage was sleek; its beak was curved and wicked and reddish in color; its legs were yellow and ended in, of all things, webbed feet. So it was a bird that could swim as well as fly. And that beak, it didn't look as if it was meant for picking fruit or catching bugs, but rather for tearing flesh. So, a carnivorous bird? A flesh-eating duck? I sat down on the porch, moving slowly and quietly so as not to alarm it. I opened my new book and wrote, *Saturday, September 8, 1900. Vy cloudy, SW winds. Strange bird on lawn, looks like this:*

I worked hurriedly to finish my sketch before my subject flew away. I was shading in the finishing touches when the front door opened and Harry came out. "Pet," he called, "it's breakfast."

The startled bird took off and flew toward the live oaks bordering our lawn, where it landed on the ground. This surprised me. Then I thought about it. Of course, it wouldn't be a passerine, or perching bird, not with webbed feet like that.

"Harry, did you see that? What is it, do you think?"

But Harry had gone inside.

I made a quick check of my barometer before following him and noted that the pressure was down significantly. Was there something wrong with it? I flicked it with my fingernail but it held steady. Huh. Maybe you had to change the balloon from time to time to keep it fresh.

I went inside, and right at that moment, the wind picked up and slammed the door behind me with a loud crash. It meant nothing to me at the time.

Since it was a Saturday, I got my obligatory half hour of piano practice over with right after breakfast and then tracked down Granddaddy in the library. I tapped on the door, and he called out, "Enter if you must." He sat at his desk reading *Thallophyta of North America*. I confess, fungi were not exactly my favorite subject, but as he always reminded me, all of life was intertwined and we could neglect no aspect of it. To do so indicated shallowness of intellect and shabby scholarship.

"Granddaddy," I said, "can I use the bird atlas?"

"I believe the question is '*may* I use the bird atlas?' And the answer is, of course, you may. My books are your books."

I left him to his work and pulled the weighty *Thompson's Field Guide to the Birds* from the shelf. I thumbed through it, briefly diverted by the stunning display of the peacock and the awkward form of the flamingo before coming to a section I'd never browsed before: Sea Birds of the Gulf of Mexico. For a girl who had never been to the seashore, this was interesting stuff.

"Gosh," I said, poring over the pages.

"Calpurnia, I know you are capable of expressing yourself without resorting to popular exclamations. The use of slang betrays a weak imagination and a lazy mind."

"Yessir," I murmured. But my mind was not attending to him. I stared at an illustration of the bird I'd seen on the lawn. "Golly."

"Calpurnia."

"Hmm? Oh, sorry. Granddaddy, look at this bird. I saw one just like it this morning."

He got up and looked over my shoulder. "Are you sure?" He frowned.

I opened my Notebook and showed him my sketch, saying, "It's the same one, isn't it?"

He compared the two drawings, his gnarled forefinger moving back and forth between them. He muttered, "The silhouette is correct, as is the gorget, and the primary and secondaries. And you're sure about this dark area here? Between the upper wing and the distal wingtip?"

"Yessir."

"And there was no white window here on the wing?"

"No, sir, not that I could see."

"Then it is a laughing gull, or *Leucophaeus atricilla*. Strange. A gull with a typical inland range of twenty-five miles, and yet here it is, two hundred miles from the coast." He leaned back in his chair, steepled his fingers, and frowned at the ceiling, lost in thought. There was silence, except for the ticking of the mantel clock. I dared not interrupt his pondering. After a few minutes, he got up and peered at his own barometer on the wall. His expression was remote, and grave.

I said, "Is there something wrong with your barometer? There's something wrong with mine too."

"No. There's nothing wrong with the barometers. But we must warn them. I hope it's not too late."

A thrill of fear shot through me. "Warn who? Too late for what?"

He was deep in thought and did not answer. He put on his coat and hat, grabbed his walking stick, and headed for the door. What was going on? I trailed behind him, sick with anxiety. He walked briskly, casting uneasy glances at the sky and murmuring, "Don't let us be too late."

"Too late for what?"

"A terrible storm might be coming," he said. "I fear the worst. We must warn them on the coast. Your mother has family in Galveston, does she not?"

"There's Uncle Gus and Aunt Sophronia and their daughter, Aggie. That makes her my cousin, but I've never met her."

"Your mother should telephone them right away."

"Telephone? Galveston?" I marveled at the idea. We'd never done such a preposterous thing; the expense and inconvenience were unimaginable. I examined the plump cumulus clouds on the horizon, and although there were a lot of them, I saw no portent of doom. They looked like ordinary clouds to me.

We passed the cotton gin once owned by Granddaddy and now by Father. A row of old Confederate soldiers and Indian fighters rocked back and forth out front, arguing over past glories and defeats, pausing from time to time on the forward swing to spit tobacco. The ground around them was dotted with foul, shiny gobs that looked like dead brown slugs. Willy Medlin had the sharpest aim, despite being the oldest and most decrepit, maybe because he'd practiced the longest. He could hit a cockroach, *Periplaneta americana*, dead-on from ten feet, an accomplishment much admired by my brothers. The old coots hailed Granddaddy, who had fought by their side during the War, but if he heard them, he gave no sign.

We hurried to the Western Union office housed next to the newspaper and the telephone switchboard. The bell over the door signaled our arrival, and the telegrapher, Mr. Fleming, came out to greet us.

On spying Granddaddy, he drew himself to attention and saluted smartly, saying, "Cap'n Tate."

"Good afternoon, Mr. Fleming. No need to salute. We are both old men. The War is long over."

Mr. Fleming stood at ease and said, "The War of Northern

Aggression will never be over, Captain. The Cause is not lost! The South shall rise again!"

"Mr. Fleming, let us not live mired in the past. Let us be forward-thinking men."

I had heard similar exchanges before. Mr. Fleming was easily riled up and could spew pure vitriol on the subject of Yankees. Under normal circumstances, it could be quite entertaining, but today was not a normal day.

Granddaddy continued, "We must hurry. I need to send three telegrams immediately."

"Certainly, sir. If you'll pencil your message in this blank here, I'll get them out as soon as I can. Who are they going to?"

"The mayors of Galveston, Houston, and Corpus Christi. But I'm afraid I don't know their names."

"That's not a problem. We'll address them to His Honor the Mayor, and that should do it. I know all the head telegraphers. We'll make sure they get delivered."

Granddaddy wrote his message and handed it to Mr. Fleming, who peered at it through his half-moon spectacles and read aloud: "'Seagull sighted two hundred miles from coast, stop. Evidence of major storm coming, stop. Evacuation may be necessary, stop.'" He lifted his glasses to his forehead and frowned. "That it, Cap'n?"

"That's correct, thank you. Galveston Island lacks a seawall and is the most vulnerable, so please send that one first."

"This is mighty serious business. You really think they should get out because of a bird?"

"Mr. Fleming, have you ever seen a laughing gull in Caldwell County?"

"Well, no, I guess not. But it still strikes me as a pretty drastic measure. I'll bet they're used to big winds down there."

"Not like this, Mr. Fleming. I fear a calamity of the worst magnitude."

"You really saw a seagull?"

"My granddaughter saw one earlier this morning."

Mr. Fleming cut his eyes sideways at me, and I flinched. I could read his thoughts, something along the lines of, *Evacuate Texas's largest cities on the word of a child? What madness is this?*

Granddaddy continued, "There is evidence that the animals have some senses that we do not, which may warn them of natural disasters. There are many anecdotal accounts of such things. The elephants of Batavia are said to foretell tidal waves; the bats of Mandalay are said to predict earthquakes."

Mr. Fleming spoke slowly. "Well . . . the lines are all jammed up right now. The price of cotton is swinging pretty good today, so there's lots of commercial traffic. I've got a bunch of buy and sell orders stacked up ahead of you. I'd say there's a couple of hours' wait."

I had never heard Granddaddy raise his voice, and he did not do so now, but ice entered his gaze, and steel, his tone. He leaned over the counter and fixed Mr. Fleming with a piercing blue stare from beneath his bushy dragon eyebrows. "This, Mr. Fleming, is a matter of grave importance, possibly of life and death. Mere commercial transactions will have to wait."

Mr. Fleming squirmed and said, "Well, Cap'n, since it's you, I'll move you up to the head of the line. Be another ten minutes, though."

"Good man, Mr. Fleming. Your service in this time of need shall not be forgotten."

Granddaddy took a chair and stared into space. I felt too jittery to sit still on a bet. Since nothing was going to happen for a spell, I ran across the street to the gin, where Father was conducting business in his glassed-in office. He waved at me briefly through the glass. The place was a hive of activity as usual, engaged in the never-ending business of separating the cotton from its seeds and packing the fiber into huge bales for shipment downstream. The thrumming of the great leather machinery belts, the deafening noise from the floor, the shouting of orders back and forth, all of it served only to increase my tension. I wandered into the relative quiet of the assistant manager's office to study the resident bird, Polly the Parrot, from a safe distance.

Polly (it seemed that all parrots were named Polly, regardless of gender) was a three-foot-tall Amazon parrot that Granddaddy had bought for my twelfth birthday, the most gorgeous bird anyone had ever seen, with a golden chest, azure wings, and crimson tail. He was also touchy and irritable, unfortunate personality traits in a bird possessed of such an alarming beak and tremendous claws. He had proved so disturbing a presence in our house that, to everyone's relief (including mine), he'd been donated to the gin's assistant manager, Mr. O'Flanagan, an old salt who dearly loved a parrot. They were known to sing rude sea chanteys together behind closed doors.

I compared the gull with the parrot, both so far from home, one displaced by Nature, one displaced by Man. Did Polly dream of tropical climes? Did he dream of lush jungles filled with sticky ripe fruits and tasty white grubs? Yet here he lived chained to a perch in a cotton gin in Fentress, Texas, and I was technically part of the reason. For the first time, I felt sorry for him.

I took a cracker from a bowl on the desk and gingerly approached him. He fixed me with his fierce yellow eye and yelled, "Braawwkk!" I gulped and slowly extended my peace offering to him, pincered between the very tips of my fingers. Fingertips that might not be mine for long. I whispered, "Polly want a cracker?"

He extended a terrifying claw, and I suddenly questioned my own sanity. Was I completely *mad*? Retreat now with all digits intact! But he plucked the cracker from my trembling hand with surprising gentleness, then said in his nasal otherworldly voice, "'Ank you."

I blinked at him. He blinked at me. Then he delicately nibbled his treat, as precise and genteel as any fancy lady at a society luncheon. So. We had a truce of sorts.

Mr. O'Flanagan came in and greeted us. "I see you're talking to Polly. Polly's a good bird, aren't you, my lad?" He ruffled the feathers on the back of the bird's neck, a move I thought would surely irritate him, but he only leaned into Mr. O'Flanagan's hand, muttering liquid sounds of pleasure. I marveled at this side of

Polly and figured that maybe we could be friends too. But far more pressing matters awaited, and it occurred to me that Mr. O'Flanagan could help.

"Sir? Mr. O'Flanagan? You've sailed around the world, haven't you?"

"I have that, my girl. I've seen the sun rise over Bora-Bora; I've seen the beacon fires at Tierra del Fuego."

"Is it true . . ." I hesitated, torn about questioning Granddaddy's judgment. But so much was at stake, including my own peace of mind.

"Yes, darlin'?"

I plunged ahead. "Is it true that the animals can predict a coming disaster?"

"I believe they can, my dear. Why, once when I was in New Guinea, I saw the snakes fleeing their homes in great numbers only an hour before an earthquake struck."

Relief washed over me. I dashed from the room, crying "Thank you!" over my shoulder, and was gone.

I got back to the telegraph office in time to catch Mr. Fleming enter his call sign on the "bug" and begin rattling off the first message. I craned over the counter to watch, fascinated by this miraculous ability to instantaneously "talk" to someone hundreds of miles away. His fingers bounced on the bug, clicking out the shorter dots and longer dashes, sending actual language sparking along an electrical wire at the amazing speed of forty words per minute. It was a wonderful tool, and I coveted one of my own. Perhaps one day in the future we would each have our own personal telegraphs and shoot messages back and forth to our friends along an electrical wire. Far-fetched, but still a girl could dream.

Three minutes later, Mr. Fleming said, "Well, that's done. Here's your receipt, Cap'n."

"Mr. Fleming, I thank you for your commendable service."

Mr. Fleming leaped to attention and saluted again. "Thankee, Cap'n."

We walked to the gin, Granddaddy again lost in silence. He conferred with Father behind the glass; Father at first looked puzzled, then concerned. Granddaddy emerged a few minutes later, and we headed back to the house.

With trepidation, I asked, "Will we be safe here? Should we evacuate too?"

"What was that? Oh no. We may have some high winds and heavy rain, but I don't expect any loss of life. Not this far inland."

"Are you sure? How can you tell?"

"The gull could have flown farther inland into the Hill Country, and yet it stopped here. Did it appear to be hurt in any way?"

"No, sir."

"Then it stopped here not because of injury but because it deemed Fentress a safe place. Hurricanes quickly lose their force as they begin to travel overland. I trust the gull. Don't you?"

Despite Mr. O'Flanagan's confirmation, I could not answer, due to my worry about what I had set in motion. Three great cities might be thrown into panic, all based on Calpurnia Virginia

Tate's brief sighting of an unknown bird. Me. A Nobody from Nowhere. What had I done? Nervous hives erupted on my neck.

"Granddaddy," I said, my voice quavering, "what if . . . what if it was some other kind of bird? What if I'm wrong?" The hives spread to my chest.

"Calpurnia, do you or do you not believe in your own powers of observation?"

"Well . . . yes. But."

"But what?"

"I guess I need to know . . . do *you* believe in them?"

"Have I taught you nothing?"

"No, sir, you've taught me plenty. It's just . . ."

"Just what?"

I struggled to hold back my tears. The burden thrust upon me was too great. Then, just as despair was about to overwhelm me, we turned the bend in the road—and there stood the gull, in our own drive. We stopped in our tracks. The gull opened its beak and laughed at us, *Ha-Ha-Haaaah*, a jeering, abrasive, unearthly cry, even worse than Jay's. Then it ponderously flapped away. I looked up at Granddaddy with a palpitating heart.

He said, "Do you see why they call it the laughing gull? Once heard, never forgotten."

Relief flooded through me, and my welts subsided. I slipped my hand into his and took comfort in the huge rough palm. "I see," I said shakily. "I do see."

The wind picked up and shifted to the east. Despite the freshening breeze, the air felt strangely thicker, if that were possible.

We went into the library, where he peered at the barometer again. "The mercury is still falling. It's time to batten down the hatches."

"We have hatches?"

"It is a nautical expression, and I am speaking metaphorically. Sailors secure the hatches on the ship's deck in preparation for a storm."

"Oh."

"We should have further discussions about weather in general, but now is not the proper time." He crossed the hall into the parlor, where Mother sat working out of her mending basket.

I crept to the parlor door. It wasn't *exactly* eavesdropping, was it? I mean, if they'd wanted a private conversation, they'd have closed the door, wouldn't they?

Mother's voice rose: "Because of a *bird*? You would spread fear through half the state because of a *bird*?"

My hives resurged. I clawed savagely at my neck.

Granddaddy's voice remained calm. "Margaret, the seagull and the falling barometer are cause for serious concern. We disregard these signs at our peril."

At that moment Sul Ross and Jim Bowie burst through the front door, and I jumped like a scalded cat. I ran upstairs to my room before they could reveal my presence with their pestering questions about why I looked so guilty and what I had heard.

MOTHER WAS QUIET at lunch, casting apprehensive glances from Granddaddy to the window, back and forth, back and forth. She then went to the telephone office at his insistence and placed a long-distance call to Galveston, an unprecedented extravagance that cost three whole dollars (!) and required the relaying services of four separate operators, all of whom no doubt listened in. The connection was bad, but in a minor miracle, Mother had actually talked to her sister Sophronia Finch, who shouted down the line that, yes, they were already experiencing high winds, but not to worry, they were used to such things, and Gus was at that very moment outside in his rubber boots securing the shutters on the house. Plus, the Weather Bureau, the government's own experts, did not seem overly alarmed.

After dinner, we sat on the porch and looked in vain for fireflies. Their season was coming to an end, or perhaps they were cowering in the long grass, battening down their own tiny hatches. The air was still and oppressive, but my younger brothers raced one another across the lawn and turned cartwheels and fell into wrestling piles that formed and broke apart and reformed again in fleeting combinations of foes and allies.

I sat at Granddaddy's feet as he slowly rocked back and forth in his old wicker rocker and smoked his cigar, the tip glowing in the dark like the biggest, reddest firefly of all. He said, "The barometer is still dropping. I can feel it in my bones."

"How can that be?"

But before he could answer, Mother called, "Bedtime."

I whispered, "Good night, Granddaddy," and gave him a kiss. He didn't seem to notice. I left him slowly rocking, staring off to the east, his face now in shadow.

That night Idabelle prowled up and down the stairs, meowing all the while in a most irritating manner. I scooped her up and took her to bed with me, where I quieted her with soothing pats and honeyed words until she finally settled down. Was her uneasiness also a warning? Question for the Notebook: Wouldn't you expect cats to be especially sensitive to such things, with their fur and whiskers picking up strange vibrations and such? I imagined that if I were so equipped, I'd be able to pick up lots of distant signals of strange events. I fell asleep and dreamed I was a cat.

I woke up once in the middle of the night. The temperature had fallen, and there was no sign of Idabelle. Rain lashed my window. The glass shivered in its frame; its nervous rattling rhythm set my teeth on edge. I hauled up my quilt and eventually fell into an uneasy sleep, this time filled with strange birds and whistling winds.

The next day, Father reported that all the lines to Galveston Island were down. There was no news going in. And no news coming out.

CHAPTER 6

A CITY DROWNED

[D]uring the previous night hail as large as small apples, and extremely hard, had fallen with such violence as to kill the greater number of the wild animals.

ALL NEXT DAY, the gusting winds spat intermittent rain. The newspaper reported that the city of Galveston lay silent, but that a mighty storm had lashed the coast, and the few survivors who had reached the mainland reported catastrophic destruction.

We walked to the Methodist church under a clutch of dripping black umbrellas. Reverend Barker offered up a special prayer for the people of Galveston, and the choir sang "Nearer My God to Thee." Everyone either had friends or family there or knew someone who did. Several of the adults sobbed openly; the others looked drawn and spoke in hushed tones. Tears rolled down Mother's face; Father put his arm around her shoulder and held her tight.

When we got home, Mother retired to her room after dosing herself with a headache powder and Lydia Pinkham's tonic. She'd forgotten to make me do my piano practice, and I, the soul of consideration, did not bother to remind her, reckoning that she had more than enough to worry about.

Next day there were whispers of water six feet deep in the streets, of whole families drowned, of the city washed away. Somber clothes marked the somber mood in our town. Some of the men wore black armbands; some of the women wore black veils. The whole town—no, the whole State—seemed to hold its breath while we waited for the downed telegraph and telephone wires to be restored. Ships all the way from Brownsville to New Orleans were steaming to the ruined city at that very moment, loaded with food and water and tents and tools. And coffins.

I went looking for Harry and finally tracked him down in the storehouse off the barn, where he was taking an inventory.

"Harry, what's going on?"

"Shh. Seven, eight, nine barrels of flour." He made a checkmark on a list.

"Harry."

"Go away. Beans, coffee, sugar. Let's see, bacon, lard, powdered milk."

"Harry, tell me."

"Sardines. Go away."

"Harry."

"Look, we're going to Galveston. But Father said not a word to the others."

"Who's going? Why can't you talk about it? And I am not 'the others'—I'm your pet, remember?"

"Stop it and go away."

I stopped it and went away.

I wandered around morosely for a while before I got the bright idea of checking in the *Fentress Indicator*, our daily newspaper. Harry was normally the only one of the children allowed to read the paper (the rest of us were still deemed too young, something to do with our "tender sensibilities"). I found a stack of discarded papers in the pantry where Viola stored them. She saved them for mulch in the kitchen garden. I grabbed the latest paper and ran outside to the back porch. The headlines read: Galveston Tragedy. Devastating Flood. Pride of Texas Washed to Sea by Hurricane. Most Deadly Natural Disaster in American History. Thousands Feared Lost.

Thousands. *Thousands.* The terrible word pounded in my brain. My marrow froze, and my knees turned to jelly. A part of me could not believe it, but the rest of me knew it was true. And my relatives, the Finches, were they included in those thousands? They were our kinfolk, bound to us by ties of blood. And Galveston itself, the finest city in Texas, our capital of culture, with its glittering opera house and magnificent mansions, all gone.

I dropped the paper, ran to my room, and threw myself on my tall brass bed, stricken. I wept without ceasing until Mother came upstairs and dosed me with Lydia Pinkham's, which only made me dizzy; then she dosed me with cod-liver oil, which only made me sick. Finally I crawled from my bed and sought out Granddaddy in the laboratory. He perched me on the tall stool at the counter where I normally worked as his assistant, patted my hair, and said, "There, there, now. These things happen in Nature. You are not responsible for this. There, now. You're a good girl, and brave."

Ah, brave. Normally that word from him would have filled me with elation, but not now.

"Why wouldn't they listen?" I hiccuped.

"People often don't. You can lay the evidence before them but you cannot make them believe what they choose not to."

He uncorked a small bottle filled with murky brown liquid and raised it in a toast, saying, "To the Galveston that once was; to the Galveston that yet will be." He sipped and grimaced. "Damn, that's awful. Would you like a drink? Oh, I forgot, you don't drink. Just as well. This stuff is still terrible. I'm thinking of giving up on this particular branch of research."

I was so startled I stopped crying.

"Give up?" I'd never known him to give up on anything, not even me. Not even the time I'd heartily deserved to be given up on when I'd temporarily lost the precious *Vicia tateii*, the new species of hairy vetch we had found.

"But, Granddaddy, after all the work you've done." I looked at the scores of bottles jamming the shelves and counter, each labeled with its run date and method of distillation. Such a lot of work to abandon.

"I'm not giving it up entirely, mind, merely changing direction. I now realize that the pecan is much more suited to a sweet drink, such as an after-dinner liqueur. Besides, none of the work has been for naught. Remember, Calpurnia, you learn more from one failure than ten successes. And the more spectacular the failure, the greater the lesson learned."

"Are you saying I should be aiming for spectacular failures? Mother really won't like that. She has a hard enough time with my ordinary ones."

"I'm not saying you should aim for them, merely learn from them."

"Oh."

"Strive to make each subsequent failure a better one. And as for regrets . . ."

"Yes?"

"They are only useful as instructional tools. Once you have learned all you can from them, they are best discarded."

"I see. I think."

"Good. Now, if you don't mind, I'd appreciate your taking notes while I check the last of these runs."

I plucked a pencil from the cracked shaving mug on the counter and sharpened it. If we were not exactly back in business as usual, we were at least heading in that direction.

ON WEDNESDAY, Father, Harry, and our hired man, Alberto, heaped the long-bed wagon with blankets and tools and barrels of food. Mother tearfully embraced Father, who whispered some private words of comfort to her. Then he shook Granddaddy's hand and shook all our hands, and kissed each of us on the cheek.

"Mind your mother, now," he said, and if his gaze lingered on me a tad longer than the others, well, I deemed that unfair.

Alberto shyly kissed his wife, SanJuanna, good-bye. Her lips moved in a silent prayer, and she made the sign of the cross.

Father and Alberto climbed upon the wagon, Father taking the reins. Harry mounted King Arthur, one of our big work-horses. Not the most comfortable ride over the long distance, with his deep chest and broad back, but his massive power would be useful for clearing roads and hauling lumber. Their plan was to drive to Luling, where they would load the wagon on either a steamboat or a train for the coast, depending on the amount of relief traffic. Men and supplies were said to be racing to Galveston from all over the state, and my family was determined to do its part. And to find Uncle Gus and Aunt Sophronia and Cousin Aggie.

Father clapped the reins and called, "Get up, now." The horses dug in and strained against the harness. Slowly, slowly, the wagon creaked away. Travis held Ajax's collar. The dog, unaccustomed to being separated from Father, squirmed and fought and barked. Mother turned and fled inside. My brothers and I accompanied the wagon to the end of the street, waving and calling our good-byes. A few minutes later, we watched it disappear around the bend in the road.

We didn't know that they'd be gone for over a month. Nor did we know how changed they'd be on their return.

CHAPTER 7

AMPHIBIA AND REPTILIA IN RESIDENCE

The expression of this snake's face was hideous and fierce; the pupil consisted of a vertical slit in a mottled and coppery iris; the jaws were broad at the base, and the nose terminated in a triangular projection. I do not think I ever saw anything more ugly, excepting, perhaps, some of the vampire bats.

FATHER'S AND HARRY'S CHAIRS stood empty. The gap at the head of the table so depressed Mother that she asked Granddaddy to sit in Father's place. He did so to oblige her but was not much of a mealtime conversationalist and spent most of his time staring into space. When addressed, he would blink and murmur, "Hmm? What was that?" The others probably thought him rude, possibly senile, but I knew that his placid exterior concealed a furiously active mind, contemplating what he called the Mysteries of the Universe. I loved him for it.

Most days, Mother received a letter from Father. I noticed that she read certain parts to us over dinner while skipping over other sections. Then she'd smile bravely and say something like "your father holds us all in his thoughts" or "we must all do our part in this hour of need."

Then a telegram arrived, not from Father en route, but from Galveston itself.

I happened to be upstairs reading *The Jungle Book* by Mr. Rudyard Kipling and was deeply immersed in the adventures of the "man-cub" Mowgli. (All right, technically it was Sam Houston's book, and I'd "borrowed" it when he wasn't looking, but he was no great appreciator of books, so why he got it for his birthday instead of me, I couldn't fathom.)

I heard crunching on the gravel drive and jumped up to see Mr. Fleming wobbling up on his bicycle. By the time he'd made it into the parlor, I'd gathered up as many of my brothers as I could find, and we stood waiting for him, along with Mother and Viola and SanJuanna. He bowed low and said, "Mrs. Tate. I got here a telegram from Galveston. I . . . I know you been waiting for this, so I brung it myself."

Mother tried to speak but could only nod her thanks. We held our collective breath as she opened the telegram with shaking hands. A moment later, she cried, "Thank God!" She burst into tears, and the paper fell from her hand. Viola helped her to her chair and fanned her with a piece of sheet music.

I picked up the telegram, written in the telegrapher's strange choppy diction.

"Read it, Callie," said Sul Ross.

"It says, 'Alive by God's grace, stop. House gone, stop. Living in tent on beach, stop. Love Gus Sophronia Aggie Finch, stop.' "

We stared at one another. Mother sobbed into her hand-kerchief, unable to speak. Viola fetched the bottle of tonic and a tablespoon, saying, "Miz Tate, you take this now. You had a shock to your system."

EVEN AFTER THE GOOD NEWS, Mother continued somewhat pale and worried, waiting to hear from two of her childhood friends, but really, the rest of us were bearing up pretty well and going about the business of our daily routines.

There were nature walks and field trips with Granddaddy. There were vetch seeds to germinate. There was Sir Isaac Newton, a black-spotted newt I'd found in a drainage ditch, who now lived on my dresser in a shallow glass baking dish with a mesh-wire lid. (My dresser was getting crowded, what with my precious hummingbird's nest in a glass box and assorted feathers and fossils and small bones.) I had to keep an eye on Sir Isaac, since he frequently tried to escape despite the fat flies I supplied him with. One morning I found him in the far corner under my bed, so covered in dust that I had to take him downstairs and wash him off at the kitchen pump.

Viola took one look and shrieked, "What in Jesus's name is that?"

"There's no need to pitch a fit. It's a black-spotted newt, also known as *Diemyctylus meridionalis*. Don't worry, he's completely harmless. This species is actually beneficial to man in that it eats flies and other pests, so—"

"I don't care what it is, you get it out of my sink!"

"I just need to—"

"Your momma see that thing in here, she'll have my job."

"What? Don't be silly." The thought of Mother firing Viola was beyond comprehension. She had been with us forever, since before I'd been born, since before even Harry had been born. The entire household would collapse without her.

"Nothing silly about it. Out of my kitchen. Now!"

Miffed, I took Sir Isaac out to the horse trough, where he splashed about happily enough.

And there was my budding friendship with Polly the Parrot, cemented for good the day I presented him with a whole peach of his very own. He practically purred with pleasure. He even liked the stone and kept it to sharpen his beak on.

I wondered if he would like a lady parrot to keep him company, and if so, how would we ever find one? Granddaddy had told me Polly could live to be a hundred. The thought of him doing so without one of his own kind made me sad, even though Mr. O'Flanagan took good care of him. He often carried him outside in warm weather and sprayed him with a hose; Polly spread his wings under the fountain and gyrated in ecstasy. Then Mr. O'Flanagan set him on his perch in the sun next to the old codgers in front of the gin who were still reliving the War on a daily basis. They would stop their ruminating long enough to engage in conversation with Polly, trying to teach him to say "The South will rise again!" But Polly would have none of it; he loved only Mr. O'Flanagan and would have no other master. I noticed that the bird now spoke with an Irish accent. When he dropped one of his foot-long crimson feathers, Mr. O'Flanagan saved it for me. What a treasure! I'd bet no other girl in Texas had one on her dresser.

One night after dessert, Mother pulled a letter from her bodice, saying, "Father and Harry have finally arrived at the coast. Tomorrow they board the steamship *Queen of Brazoria* to take them to Galveston. I know that all our thoughts and prayers are with them."

A solemn hush fell over the table except for J.B., the baby, who piped up with, "Dada's going on a boat? Can I go too?"

Mother smiled faintly and said, "No, little man. Not this time."

"But I *want* to, Mama, I *want* to."

Lamar muttered, "Oh boy, here we go again."

I shot him a dirty look and scooped J.B. from his seat as he was winding up for a full-scale conniption fit. I carried him out, saying, "Come on, J.B., I'll tell you a story. Won't that be nice?"

He checked his blubbering. "Will there be boats in it?" he hiccuped.

"If you like."

"I like boats, Callie," he said, smiling like an angel through his tears and snot.

As far as I knew, he'd never seen a boat, but I said, "I know you do, baby. Let's get you cleaned up, and then we'll have a story with lots and lots of boats. As many as you like." Then I said, "Who's your favorite sister?"

He giggled and said, "You are, Callie." It was our own little joke, and it never failed to tickle him.

That night while brushing my teeth, I tried to imagine the beach where the Finches now camped. I'd never laid eyes on the ocean, and it struck me as a baffling, mystical place from everything I'd read. What did it sound like? What did it smell like?

I was familiar with my own dear river, of course, but the thought of tides and waves, the thought of this massive, constantly changing body of water, befuddled and excited me. I'd put viewing the ocean on the list of New Year's wishes I'd made when the calendar rolled over from 1899 to 1900. (The same list that had included seeing snow.) I'd never traveled farther than Austin, only forty-five miles away. Even though my outer life was depressingly landlocked, my inner life was full of imaginary travel to exotic lands fueled by books, the atlas, and the globe. Most days it was enough. Some days it was not.

I HAULED MYSELF out of bed. It was a good half hour before sunrise but I was anxious to record my daily observations before my brothers could shatter the fragile peace of the morning. I opened the bottom drawer of my chest and reached in, but instead of a neatly folded chemise, there was a strange, coiled shape in the shadows. *Where there should be no strange shapes, especially not coiled ones.* My brain shrieked, "Snake!" and I flinched. The snake flinched too and opened its mouth, showing me an array of tiny teeth and a pale palate. It wasn't a very big snake as snakes go, but then, size doesn't really matter when you're dealing with a venomous animal. It was banded in red and black and yellow, which meant it was either the deadly coral snake or the harmless king snake. One could kill you; the other was a nonlethal imposter. My mind feverishly searched for the old rhyme about how to tell the two apart. How did it go? The snake gaped at me, inches from my hand. How did it go?

Okay, Calpurnia, now would be a really good time to remember, especially since your life depends on it. Okay, okay. The secret's in the order of the bands. Okay. Black on yellow—no, wait, that's not right, it's red on yellow. Red on yellow, kill a fellow; red on black, venom lack. Is that right? Please let that be right.

I stared wide-eyed in the gloom, straining to see, and there was a red band between two black bands. *Red on black.* I double-checked along as much of the body as I could see. The red bands were surrounded by black bands in every case.

Ha! Imposter!

It was a benign snake that had cleverly evolved over the eons to resemble a dangerous one, thus purchasing itself protection from predators. Granddaddy had once told me about certain tasty butterflies that had evolved to resemble bitter inedible ones, calling this process "mimicry." An interesting way for a species to get a free ride on the reputation of another. But wasn't this a form of lying? Question for the Notebook: Does Nature tell lies? Something to think about.

I relaxed and felt a lot more friendly toward the snake, which seemed to relax too; it tasted the air with its tongue. How had he ended up in my chest of drawers, so far from his natural home?

The poor thing was no doubt mighty confused. I'd have to repatriate him to his normal environment under a rotten log where he could make his living on mice and other small unfortunates. I reached for him, and he hissed at me. I pulled my hand back. No point in being bitten, even with tiny teeth and no venom.

I cast about for a bag or a sack in which to transport him. I pulled my pillow slip from my bed and turned back just in time to see the tip of his tail disappearing into a gap in the corner base-boards.

Oh, wonderful. I sincerely hoped he could find his own way out of the house, for even though I was no longer afraid of him, he wasn't my idea of the perfect roommate.

As I was drifting off to sleep the next night, I heard a faint scratching noise. I opened my eyes to see the snake gliding across the floor through a patch of moonlight, a tiny inert bundle in its mouth, possibly a mouse, scared stiff. My heart went out to the little creature, and for a moment, I entertained the idea of try-ing to save it, but the snake was only being a snake, after all, and deserved his dinner like the rest of us. This was an example of "Nature, red in tooth and claw," in the words of one Mr. Alfred Lord Tennyson, a famous writer whom Granddaddy often quoted. It meant that animals had to both eat and be eaten in turn on the great revolving wheel of life and death. And there was nothing to be done about it.

My next lesson served to point this out. Granddaddy called me into the library and told me it was time for my first dissec-tion. We would start with the large earthworm I'd been saving for this very lesson. He said, "Galen and the early natural philosophers thought you could understand anatomy and physiology simply by studying an animal's exterior. All nonsense of course, but this misguided notion persisted for centuries. It wasn't until the 1500s that Andreas Vesalius finally showed that the interior is at least as important and interesting as the exterior. His early dissections of man are still marvels of both Art and Science. Do you have your specimen?"

I held up a canning jar containing an inch of damp soil and the giant night crawler I'd been saving. Despite all my efforts to remain detached and objective, I did feel a little bad about killing this nice big worm. Living on a farm, I had of course seen plenty of plucked turkeys and skinned rabbits and butchered hogs, but Alberto generally dispatched these creatures. They were killed so we could eat them. Their demise was necessary for our own survival. And even though I was dissecting a lowly worm, and even though I had probably inadvertently killed and maimed hundreds of them beneath my feet over the years, I was now going to kill one intentionally to satisfy my curiosity. I felt that apologies were in order.

"Sorry, worm," I whispered, "but it's for Science, you know."

The worm had no vote in the matter and remained silent.

Granddaddy said, "There is no need for cruelty. Be sure you dispatch your subject as humanely as possible but in a way that will also preserve its architecture."

"How do I do that?"

"You will need to immerse it in a beaker of ten percent

alcohol for a few minutes. You will find what you need in the laboratory. Once you have done that, we will prepare your dissecting tray."

I carried my worm out to the laboratory and found bottles of alcohol and water. I mixed up nine parts of water to one part of alcohol and dropped in the worm. It twitched only once and sank slowly to the bottom. Granddaddy joined me a few minutes later. From under the counter, he pulled out a shallow metal pan and a package of wax. He led me through the slow process of melting the wax, adding some black soot to make for a contrasting background, and then pouring it into the pan.

While the wax cooled, he sat and read *Posner's Reptiles of the Greater Southwest* in his ancient shabby armchair with the stuffing exploding in all directions. I perched on my stool and read a pamphlet called "Dissection Guide to the *Lumbricus terrestris*."

The wax finally hardened, and we began. Granddaddy handed me a jar of pins and a magnifying glass and his pocketknife, saying, "You will need these."

I placed the worm on the wax and was about to make the first long cut when he stayed my hand. "Stop a moment. Let us begin with observation first. What do you see?"

"Uh, a worm?"

"Yes, of course." He smiled. "But describe what you see. Is one end the same as the other? Is one side the same as the other?"

"This end is different from that one," I said, pointing. I rolled the worm gently with my finger. "And this side is flatter than the other."

"Correct. The front end is indicated by the prostomium, and the back end by the anus. The rounder side is the dorsum, or back, and the flatter side is the ventral surface, or belly. Now take the magnifying glass and look at the ventral surface."

I squinted and saw many tiny bristles.

"Those are the setae, the means of locomotion," he said. "Now palpate them." I ran the pad of my finger over them; they felt slightly rough to the touch.

"Now carefully cut along the dorsal side."

I made a long cut from end to end along the back, then pulled the sides apart and pinned them to the wax as instructed.

We started at the head and worked our way along, examining the pharynx and the crop and the gizzard.

"Worms have no teeth, so after ingesting their food, they store it here in the crop. Right behind it is the gizzard, which contains fine grit that grinds up the food before it passes down the intestine. Your subject is drying out. Sprinkle it with a little water."

I did so, then asked, "Is it a male worm or a female worm?"

"It is both."

I looked up in surprise. "Really?"

"When an organism contains both male and female organs, it is called a hermaphrodite. Such an arrangement is not unusual in the flowering plants, mollusks, slugs, snails, and other invertebrates."

He led me through the rest of the dissection, pointing out the five aortic arches that served as five primitive hearts, then the reproductive organs, the nerve cord, and the gut. In this way I learned that an earthworm is essentially one long intestine through which passes soil, decaying leaves, and manure, emerging in an enriched state that promotes the growth of plants.

Granddaddy said, "We owe this humble tiller of the soil a great deal. Mr. Darwin hailed them as one of the most important animals in the history of the world, and he was right. Most plants on earth are indebted to the worm, and we in turn rely on the plants for our very existence. Think on the number of plants you ate at breakfast this morning."

I'd had flapjacks with syrup, so no plants there. I was about to say so but I could tell from his expectant expression that this would probably be wrong.

I stopped and thought. Flapjacks. Ah, made from flour, which came from ground-up wheat, so there was one plant. And the syrup came from tapped maple trees in New England, which we flavored with our own pecan extract, so there were two more.

"My whole breakfast was plants," I said, "except for a little butter, which comes from cows, who eat plants. So I suppose when we say the blessing, we should also give thanks to the worm, right?"

"It might be fitting," he said. "Without the lowly annelid, our world would change for the worse."

When we were through, I ran to Travis and showed him my work. "Look," I said. "Did you know a worm has five hearts? These little pale pink things right here are the main blood vessels. Isn't that interesting?"

He looked and said, "Uh . . . sure."

"And this is its brain, this little gray dot next to the mouth. Can you see it?"

Now, I admit it was rather dried out by that point and perhaps not the prettiest sight in the world, and maybe it smelled a little bit, but I didn't expect him to turn pale and back away.

I said, "Don't you want to see it? And look at these nerves, these tiny gray strings. Pretty interesting, huh?"

He turned paler and said, "Uh, I think I forgot to feed Bunny." And with that, he dashed away.

CHAPTER 8

A BIRTHDAY CONTROVERSY

A small sea-otter is very numerous; this animal does not feed exclusively on fish, but, like the seals, draws a large supply from a small red crab, which swims in shoals near the surface of the water.

OCTOBER, THE BIG BIRTHDAY MONTH, loomed ahead. We called it that because Sam Houston, Lamar, Sul Ross, and I shared it as our birthday month, and we all looked forward to it with breathless anticipation.

There was no forgetting the marvelous mayhem of the previous year when all four of our parties had been combined into one grand bash to which the whole town had been invited, with every kind of pie and ice cream known to man, and root beer floats, and pony rides, and croquet and horseshoes and sack races and prizes, and a towering cake aflame with forty-nine candles (the sum of our years), and birthday hats and crepe paper streamers, and even fireworks at twilight. A splendid day all around.

But there was still no news about when Father and Harry might return. Word came that they spent long weary days working like slaves from can't-see to can't-see, clearing the roads of debris, pushing the horses and themselves to exhaustion. They labored alongside volunteers and hired men who'd poured in from all over the South to restore some semblance of order. There was talk of building a seawall to protect the town from future floods. There was talk of raising every house still standing onto ten-foot stilts, an astounding feat of engineering never before contemplated in the entire State of Texas.

The newspaper headlines I sneaked a peek at read: Looting Controlled. Rebuilding Continues. Thousands Still Missing. Bodies Buried at Sea.

I resolved to read no more.

Despite the good news about our relatives, a pall of anxiety still hung over the house, causing me to worry that there might be no celebration this year. And if we took the unprecedented step of skipping birthdays, what about Halloween? And Thanksgiving? What about—oh Lord—what about *Christmas*? Could one possibly skip Christmas? Was that even *legal*? Gah. It was too depressing to think about.

But think about it I did, and I called a meeting on the front porch with the other celebrants, Sam Houston, Lamar, and Sully.

Lamar arrived late and demanded rudely, "What do you want? You're interrupting my reading."

("Reading," in this case, referred to dime novels, those cheaply printed books packed with lurid and predictable tales of derring-do involving a brave and strong young man saving the day for the Pony Express, or a brave and brawny young man saving the day for the Texas Rangers, or a brave and strapping young man saving the day for the Pinkerton Detectives. Endlessly enthralled by these stories, my brother could be accused of many things but not an excess of imagination.)

"Lamar, you really are the limit." I turned my attention to the others. "Has it not occurred to any of you birthday boys that maybe we won't have a party this year?"

I was not prepared for the level of general outrage this provoked.

"*What?*"

"Why not?"

"What are you *talking* about?"

"Why do you think?" I said, amazed at their obtuseness. Were all boys like this or just the ones I was unfortunate enough to be saddled with? "Mother is sad about Father and Harry being gone, and Uncle Gus and Aunt Sophronia losing their house, and her friends still missing, and all the people in town in mourning."

Sam Houston said, "That's true. She's drinking more than usual of her tonic. She takes her normal dose and then she takes another dose when she thinks no one's looking."

"But why should that mean no party?" demanded Lamar.

"Because you don't celebrate when people are in mourning. And because it's such a lot of work for Mother and Viola and everybody," I said. "I guess you were too busy having fun last year to notice how much work it was."

Silence fell. I could see we were all thinking the same thing but no one wanted to say it.

The pill finally said it: "So, what about it? How do we make sure we get a party?"

"And presents?" said Sam Houston.

"And cake?" said Sul Ross, who was about to turn nine and who always, *always*, got sick on cake.

They stared at me as if I had caused the problem.

"You can't blame me for this," I said. "I'm only bringing it up."

"What do we do?" Sam Houston asked. More silence.

Finally I said, "I'm not really sure there's any fixing it."

Sul Ross said plaintively, "Can't you talk to her, Callie? She's a girl and you're a girl, maybe she'll listen to you."

Lamar grunted. "Callie's a *dumb* girl—don't forget that part. And Mother's never listened to her before, so why should she now? I'll do the talking."

"No!" I shouted. "You'll botch it for sure."

"All right then, Miss Smarty, you fix it. And don't you botch it or I'll push you down in Petunia's sty."

"I'd like to see you try it."

Despite my brave talk, I wouldn't have put it past him to chuck me into the pig wallow. Lamar seldom thought of consequences, as in, for example, the endless heck to pay if he actually did such a thing.

We agreed to meet again in an hour, and I went to my room to gather my wits before facing Mother. I finally decided that the strongest pleading would be to point out how much the boys were missing Father and Harry (although, in truth, I didn't see that much evidence of it), and that it would cheer us all up to have a celebration. Now, this wasn't an out-and-out lie, but it wasn't really the truth, either. And the more I thought about it, the less like the truth it sounded, and the more insistently the nontruthful part of it elbowed its way into my conscience, filling it with a gloomy gray fog.

Buck up, Calpurnia. Time to locate your target.

I made my way downstairs. In the dining room I noticed, as if for the first time, the portrait of my parents taken twenty years before on their wedding day. I'd never paid much attention to the photo except to remark that the fashions of the time, especially Mother's ridiculous bustle, were now laughably out-of-date.

Now I stopped and studied the portrait. How tall and proud my father stood in his best suit, how beautiful my mother looked in her gown of Brussels lace, her crown of wax flowers, her long veil cascading all the way to the floor like a misty waterfall. Their expressions were severe due to the length of time they'd had to pose frozen in place, but still, there was something of hope for the future in their gaze, the anticipation of happiness in their newly entwined lives.

And they'd been happy, hadn't they? Why, look how they'd evolved and what they'd become: pillars of the community, parents of seven impressive offspring (all right, six if you didn't count Lamar), owners of a thriving cotton business and the biggest house in town, esteemed and respected by all. They'd found their own recipe for happiness, and it suited them. Didn't it?

I went into the parlor. Mother had fallen asleep in her chair with her mending basket at her feet, a torn shirt in her lap. With her chignon askew, she looked disheveled, an unusual state for a woman normally so smoothed down and buttoned up. I studied the deepening lines in her face and the new threads of gray in her hair and felt a surge of pity. When had she started to look so haggard? Her careworn appearance almost derailed me.

She gasped and woke up blinking. "Why, Calpurnia, I must have dozed off. You can do your piano practice now. You won't disturb me."

"I can do it later," I said. "I . . . I wanted to talk to you about everybody's birthday."

Her expression clouded over, which I did not find encouraging. Not at all. But I fumbled ahead with my prepared speech.

"You see, the boys are missing Father and Harry. I thought perhaps . . . that is, we thought . . . well, a big birthday party would cheer us all up."

She frowned. I hurried on. "It would give us all heart, don't you think, and we could—"

"Calpurnia."

"Invite only our closest friends. We wouldn't have to invite everyone in town like last year, since it was such a lot of work, I know it was, really, and we could—"

"Calpurnia."

Her voice, low, quiet, dispirited, stopped me in my tracks.

"Yes, Mother?"

"Do you think it right and proper that we should have a celebration when so many lives have been lost? Can you really stand there and tell me that?"

"Uh . . ."

"It would be unseemly in the extreme."

"Uh, well . . ."

"What with so many dead, and so many survivors living in wretched conditions, and poor Uncle Gus and Aunt Sophronia and Cousin Aggie having lost everything. It's beyond imagining, what they must have gone through. And think what your father and brother must be going through. Such a nightmare. So much sadness."

She didn't raise her voice. She didn't have to. Hives of shame popped up on my neck. "You're right, Mother. I'm sorry. You're right."

She picked up her mending, signaling the end of our parley. I crept away, feeling about three inches high. I clawed at the horrible prickles erupting on my neck and met the boys on the porch.

Lamar took one look at me and said, "You botched it up good, I can tell."

"I did my best."

"Well, it obviously wasn't good enough."

"You should have been there, Lamar. You should have seen the look on her face."

" 'The look on her face'? That's all it took for you to cave in? You're some kind of lousy negotiator. That's what we get for

sending a dumb girl to do a man's job. I'll do it myself next time."
He hawked and spat in the dust.

It was all so unfair I could have smacked him, but he wheeled
and stalked off. Sam Houston and Sul Ross looked back and forth
at us doubtfully and then straggled after him.

I yelled, "She said it was unseemly!"

They ignored me. And to top it off, I'd become a giant walking hive. At the horse trough, I pumped cool water onto my pinafore and applied it as a compress. I paced in circles and took deep
breaths, trying to calm down. This resulted in only partial sub-
sidence of the hives and my temper, so I decided there was only
one other treatment open to me: a soothing application of
Granddaddy.

I found him working in the laboratory with the burlap flap
pinned aside to let in light and fresh air.

He greeted me with, "Hives again? What is it this time?"

I stared at him and said, "Am I that predictable?"

"Generally not, but your dermis is, yes."

"Oh. Well, don't say a word, but I'm thinking about running
away from home." I smiled weakly to show him I was joking.
Mostly.

He received this bit of news with equanimity. "Is that right?
Where will you go? What will you do for money? Have you considered these things?"

"I've saved up twenty-seven cents."

"I doubt you can buy your independence with all of twenty-
seven cents."

"Yes." I sighed. "It's a pitiful sum to run away on. The train fare to Austin is more than that. But if I do save enough, will you come with me? I can't go without you, you know." I kissed him on the forehead, adding, "But you'll probably have to pay your own way."

"It's most kind of you to invite me, but I do most of my traveling in the library these days. A seated man can travel far and wide with nothing more than a globe and an atlas. And I find all the adventure I need at this stage in life through the lenses of the microscope and telescope. There is world enough for me right here with my specimens and books."

I thought about it and realized that I, too, was an explorer. Hadn't I crossed the wide ocean to England with Mr. Dickens? Hadn't I drifted down the great Mississippi with Huck? Didn't I travel in time and space every time I opened a book?

Granddaddy said, "What, may I ask, has precipitated this sudden desire to escape our town?"

"I didn't behave very nicely to Mother. But it wasn't all my fault. My brothers put me up to it."

"Brothers will do that," he said gravely, then listened to my tale of woe and agreed with me that life was not fair. Then he asked how old I was turning.

"Thirteen."

"Thirteen, eh? Soon you'll be a young lady."

"Please don't say that."

"Why not?"

"Because girls get to do little enough in this world, and, from what I can tell, young ladies get to do even less."

"Hmm, there's some truth in that, although I don't know why it should be so. It seems to me that any girl or young lady with a brain in good working order should be allowed to achieve whatever she might."

"I'm glad you feel that way, Granddaddy, but not everyone does, especially around here."

"Speaking of birthdays and travel, I have something for you in the library that I think you'll like. Come with me."

I took his hand as we walked to the house, glad that a girl can never be too grown-up to hold her grandfather's hand.

He unlocked the library door and pulled back the heavy bottle-green drapes for better light. Then he took a book from his cabinet, saying, "Before he wrote *The Origin of Species*, Darwin spent five years sailing around the world on a small ship, HMS *Beagle*. Five whole years, collecting specimens and exploring distant lands." Granddaddy stared into the distance, eyes agleam. The decades magically dropped from his face, and I could see the boy he once had been.

"An epic journey! Think of it! What I would have given to be at his side tracking the puma and the condor in Patagonia, observing the vampire bat of the Argentine, collecting the orchids of Madagascar. Why, look there, on the shelf."

He pointed to the thick glass carboy containing the bottled beast that Darwin himself had sent him years before.

"He collected that cuttlefish, *Sepia officinalis*, off the Cape of Good Hope. The voyage was arduous and short on creature comforts, and several times almost cost him his life, but it cemented his love of the natural world and started him along the path to thinking about evolution. I think you'll find this book smoother sailing than *Origin*."

He handed me the leather-bound book, *The Voyage of the Beagle*. "Happy birthday," he said, "and bon voyage."

Oh, the pleasure, the wonder, the anticipation of a new book. I thanked him with a hug and a kiss on his whiskery cheek, then hid it beneath my pinafore and ran with it to my room, for who knew what desecration Lamar might be capable of in a fit of rage?

I read well into the night, accompanying Mr. Darwin to the Galapagos Islands, Madagascar, the Canary Islands, Australia. Along with him, I marveled at the loud shocking click made by the butterfly *Papilio feronia*, a type of insect the world had previously thought mute. We watched the spermaceti whales leaping almost clear of the water, their splashes booming like cannon fire. Together we wondered at the *Diodon*, or puffer fish, a spiky fish that inflated itself into an inedible ball when threatened. (And although Mr. Darwin's description of this oddity was vivid, I yearned to see one in real life.) Together we hid from panthers and pirates, and dined with savages and grandees and cannibals, although not, one hoped, on human flesh.

My dreams that night were filled with the creak of the rigging, the swaying of the deck, the pressure of the wind. Not bad for a girl who'd never seen the ocean. A bon voyage, indeed.

CHAPTER 9

THE MYSTERY ANIMAL

In this northern part of Chile . . . an arrow-head made of
agate, and of precisely the same form with those now used
in Tierra del Fuego, was given me.

WE ENDED UP HAVING a birthday celebration of sorts, although
it was not the one Lamar wanted. Nor I, for that matter. Viola made
a fruit punch and I helped her make a pecan cake. Unfortunately, I
frosted it before it had completely cooled; the icing pooled in a
hollow on top and dribbled down the sides, giving it a truly pitiful look. Viola decorated it with a sparse handful of tiny candles,
rather meager and depressing, nothing like the conflagration of
the year before. Mother smiled bravely and made a short speech
about how we must all do our bit to support the refugees, even
those of us who stayed behind and whose part involved only
standing by. Her words filled us with such guilt that we smiled
weakly and pretended we were satisfied with our lot, even Lamar,
who'd never been blessed with much in the way of tact.

Our celebration may have been lackluster, but I did end up
receiving a once-in-a-lifetime gift on my actual birthday when
Granddaddy and I took the rowboat out for the day. We slipped

it loose from its mooring below the cotton gin and set off with a picnic basket, a butterfly net, and my Notebook. We took turns at the oars, but the work was easy and the current mild, and once we got away from the clatter of the gin, a great hush fell upon the river. We floated in complete peace downstream, talking about the passing flora and fauna on the way. The water was clear as glass.

We could see the silvery shiners and lively perch darting through the gently undulating star grass and wild rice. I even caught a glimpse of a great scowling catfish lurking under the bank.

About halfway to Prairie Lea, we landed on a gravel bar to eat our sandwiches and make some notes. The gravel and stones were worn smooth from the action of the water, but there was a jagged one that stood out from its fellows and caught my eye. I picked it up and realized from its triangular shape and beveled edges that I held a genuine Indian arrowhead in my hand.

"Look, Granddaddy," I cried. "It's an arrowhead from the Comanche wars." Each of my brothers had found one or two over the years but this was my first.

He examined it gravely in his rough palm. "I think," he said, "that you have found something much older, probably from the early Tonkawas. They served as scouts for us at the Battle of Plum Creek."

"Were you *there*?" I said. "Did you *see* it?" Plum Creek had been the early name for Lockhart, site of the last great fight against the Comanche. And only fourteen miles away. It had never occurred to me that a relative of mine had taken part.

He looked at me in mild surprise. "Oh yes, I was right in the thick of it. Have I not spoken of it to you?"

"Uh, no. You never have."

"Well, I suppose that's because it was not our finest hour, despite the public hailing us as heroes of the Republic. And it was not the Comanches' finest hour, either. In August of 1840, Chief Buffalo Hump and his warriors were driving a herd of almost two thousand horses and pack mules back from a raid on the pioneer settlements. They had been pillaging and burning in a great swath along the coast. Now they were headed for the Comancheria, their buffalo-hunting lands in northwest Texas. The mules were heavily loaded with iron, much prized for forging arrowheads, and a huge supply of dry goods plundered from a depot near Victoria. But the horses were the real prize."

I thought of Lockhart, with its courthouse and many stores and library, and even electricity. Our seat of civilization. "But why were you there?" I said. "How did it happen?"

"Ranger Captain Ben McCulloch had been following them for some days and realized that they would have to cross Plum Creek. He sent out some of his men to round up all the farmers and settlers in the area that they could, every single able-bodied man with a horse and a firearm. My father and I were plowing that day when one of the militia rode up with an urgent summons to arms. I was only sixteen, but like all sixteen-year-olds on the frontier, I knew how to ride and shoot, and that was all that mattered."

"Did you . . . did you kill any Indians?"

"I suppose I did."

This answer mystified me until he elaborated: "In the smoke and the dust and the chaos, it was difficult to be sure. We numbered perhaps two hundred, while the Indians must have had at least five hundred warriors, but Buffalo Hump at first did not wish to engage us in battle. Then it became clear they were trying to delay until the vast herd had passed safely by. They could not bring themselves to abandon the horses. And as for the other booty, they had taken yards of red cloth and decorated their warhorses with it, weaving long streamers of red ribbon into their tails. Some wore top hats; some carried open umbrellas. Oh, it was quite the spectacle. But then Captain Caldwell gave the order to charge, and we plowed into the great mass, firing our rifles. The herd panicked and stampeded. The overloaded pack mules got bogged down and were run over by two thousand frightened horses crashing into them. The Comanche were trapped by the very animals they prized so highly. Many were trampled and crushed by the horses; many were shot trying to escape. It was a terrible rout. And although Buffalo Hump lived to fight another day, their fatal weakness for horses spelled the beginning of the end of the Comanche in Texas."

"Were you hurt?"

"I was not hurt, and neither was my father. We suffered surprisingly few casualties. President Lamar was well pleased."

"And then you came home, right?"

"We all returned to our farms and families a few days later, but not before dividing up the enormous plunder. Since there was no way to return it to the original owners, my father and I returned with a mule laden with a bolt of red calico and a keg of brandy. My mother was glad to see that cloth, and I remember that for many years she dressed us all in shirts and pants of that same fabric, and used it for quilts and such."

I suddenly realized there were several blocks of faded red fabric in my winter quilt.

"Wait," I said, "is that the red material in my quilt?"

"Probably so."

I resolved to take better care of the quilt, which I'd never before given a second thought to. Gosh, here I'd been sleeping all this time under Indian spoils of war and never known it!

"Ah, me," he said, "the times I have seen. You might not realize, Calpurnia, that when I was born twenty miles from here, all this land was actually part of Mexico. Then I was just your age when Texas won its independence from Mexico and became an independent republic. I saw General Santa Anna, the defeated dictator of Mexico, led through the streets in chains. Five years after that, we fought the Comanche. Then, only four years later, we became part of the United States but had to fight another war with Mexico to make them accept it. Fourteen years after that, we tried to leave the United States, leading to the most terrible war of all, the only one we lost. We could not break up the Union. Now here I am, an old man, having survived four wars and lived long enough to see the age of the auto-mobile."

He stood up, saying, "That is more than enough reminiscing for one day. Let us proceed on our journey."

We tidied up the remains of our meal and climbed back into our little boat. A few minutes later, Granddaddy suddenly held his fingers to his lips and pointed over my shoulder at the high bank. A furry wedge-shaped face peered down at us from the shadows. Alert and inquisitive, the face was neither cat nor dog but something in between. Was it a baby black bear? There were still some *Ursus americanus* around but they were increasingly rare, what with the encroachment of civilization on their habitat. We studied it, and whatever it was studied us back; it seemed at least as interested in us as we were in it, maybe even more so. It stepped forward into a patch of dappled sunlight, and I could see that the muzzle was too short for a bear. It was a river otter. I'd heard about them but never before had the luck to see one.

And then the otter gave me a birthday show: It launched itself onto its belly and plunged headfirst down the steep bank on a narrow muddy slide, almost faster than the eye could follow, landing in the river only a few feet away from us with barely a splash.

I was so startled I nearly dropped the oars. "Gosh, did you see that?" I whispered hoarsely.

The otter surfaced and floated on its back, staring at us with palpable curiosity, giving us a good look at the bright eyes, the silky fur, the bristly whiskers. The creature was, in every way, enchanting. Deciding it had had enough of us, it suddenly dove and disappeared, leaving behind nothing more than a trail of small bubbles to prove it had not been a mirage.

"*Lutra canadensis*," said Granddaddy. "It's been years since I saw one in these parts, and I thought they'd all gone. They live on the river mollusks and smaller fish. Mark this sighting in your Notebook, Calpurnia. It is truly a red-letter day."

I dutifully marked it down, and added (most unscientifically) *Happy Otterday to Me!*

WELL, ONCE TRAVIS heard about my birthday otter, there was nothing for it but that he had to see it too. He nagged me mercilessly until we set off a couple of days later in the boat, provisioned with ham biscuits and a bottle of lemonade. We trailed the bottle behind us in the water on a length of string to keep it cool.

Rounding a corner, we surprised a great blue heron fishing in the shallows on its stilt-like legs, stabbing at passing minnows with its daggerlike beak. It uttered a sour croak, so at odds with its beautiful plumage, and flapped away, the sinuous neck folded into its chest.

When we reached the gravel bar, I told him Granddaddy's story of the Indian battle, and he looked deeply impressed. He said, "How come he tells you this stuff but he never talks to any of the rest of us?"

It was true. Granddaddy spoke so seldom to my brothers that I wasn't sure he could tell them apart. But Travis's question made me uneasy. I loved my grandfather with a deep, unquestioning love, and I knew he loved me. I also knew that part of our love for each other rested on our mutual love of Science and Nature. And if one of my brothers, for whatever reason, wanted to wiggle his way into Granddaddy's affections, that would be the logical way to do it. None of them showed any inclination to do this, and in fact they usually avoided him. But what if? Sharing him was more than I could stand. He was *mine*, mine alone.

"Callie?"

"Huh?"

"Are you okay?" Travis stared at me, his normally open, happy face creased with concern.

"I'm, uh, fine."

"I asked you why he never talks to us about the Indian Wars and such."

I pondered the consequences of my answer and sighed. "He will if you ask him."

"I dunno. He scares me. Doesn't he scare you?"

"He used to, but not anymore."

To my relief, Travis immediately lost interest in Granddaddy and moved on to an increasingly more frequent topic of conversation: Lula Gates. He prattled on about her many charms before I couldn't stand it one minute longer and declared it was time to pack up and go home.

"But we haven't seen the otter," he said.

"If it doesn't want to show itself, we can't make it. Don't expect me to pull an otter out of a hat. I'm not a magician."

We took turns rowing home and made it back by dusk. Just as we were tying up at the dam, something stirred in the bushes on the far side of the abutments. The creature, whatever it was, inspected us, and we—dismayed—inspected it back: a picture of abject misery, one weeping eye with the lid at half-mast; one ear mostly erect, the other mostly drooping; its flank peppered with lumpy scabs amid the matted reddish-brownish fur; the ribs standing out like a washboard.

Travis whispered, "Is that the otter? You never said it looked like *that*. I thought they were supposed to be cute. What happened to it?"

"I'm pretty sure that's not an otter."

"What is it, do you think?"

"It might be a coyote, or maybe a fox."

We stared at this mystery animal. I thought it was probably a fox, normally a shy species and of no threat to us, but you almost never caught sight of one in daylight.

"What's wrong with it?" said Travis.

"It's starving, and it looks like it's been in a fight. Whatever it is."

I looked at Travis out of the corner of my eye and waited for the inevitable, but he had finally met his match—the one animal on earth too awful to take home. Even so, I said, "Don't go near it. It's probably rabid."

"But it's not foaming at the mouth."

I displayed my superior knowledge by saying, "That doesn't mean anything. In the early stages, they don't foam."

Upon hearing this, the creature melted away into the underbrush. My brother and I walked home in silence, each absorbed in our own thoughts.

CHAPTER 10

FAMILY REUNION

If a person asked my advice, before undertaking a long
voyage, my answer would depend upon his possessing a
decided taste for some branch of knowledge, which could
by this means be advanced. . . . Even in the time of Cook,
a man who left his fireside for such expeditions underwent
severe privations.

FATHER AND HARRY had been gone for one whole month when
Mother, looking more chipper than usual, announced at dinner,
"I have some wonderful news. If all goes well, Father and Harry
will be home on Thursday evening."

We erupted in happy chatter, and Sam Houston, the oldest
boy present, led us in three cheers. Beaming, Mother allowed
this unusual boisterousness at the table. She said, "I want everyone bathed and pressed and looking their best. Lamar and
Sully, you see to the boiler. You'll need to bring in extra wood.
Callie, Aggie will be staying with us for a while until Uncle Gus
rebuilds the family home."

"She will?" This was interesting news. "For how long?"

"Several months, I expect."

"And where will she be staying?"

"In your room, of course. She will have your bed, and we will make you up a pallet on the floor."

"But—"

"I'm certain that no daughter of mine would refuse hospitality to her cousin in the hour of need." Mother gave me the gimlet eye. "Especially a cousin who has suffered such terrible losses, and now more than anything needs peace and quiet and loving care. I simply can't imagine that any daughter of mine would do that. Can you?"

I thought the question somewhat unfair but in truth I had no good answer. I stared at my plate and said in a small voice, "No, Mother."

"Good. I thought not." She sighed and then got that look on her face that often signaled the onset of one of her headaches. "Aggie needs our understanding and compassion. You will be good to her, won't you?"

In an even smaller voice, "Yes, Mother."

"Good. I thought so."

That night there was general restlessness in the house. I awoke at midnight to footsteps in the hall. Whoever was out there also took a couple of excursions up and down the stairs, oblivious to the noisy seventh step that always gave one away. None of the children would have made the mistake of touching that step when prowling about, so it had to be Mother pacing up and down. Unusual behavior for her, but I suppose she was keyed up about the return of her men.

On Thursday morning, I spotted a long-tailed butterfly, the skipper *Eudamus proteus*, drinking nectar from the black-eyed Susans. I got within a couple of feet before it fluttered away. With its shimmering blue body and twin tails, I would have liked it for my collection, but they were hard to catch and tended to collapse on mounting. Still, it was a special day and nothing was going to dampen my spirits.

Sam Houston chopped wood, and Lamar, who normally avoided hard work like the plague, actually stoked the boiler all day. We took turns in the bath. Mother changed into her sapphire gown, Father's favorite, the one that brought out the color of her eyes. She looked ten years younger. Granddaddy broke out a bottle of store-bought bourbon for the occasion. None of the children could keep still on a bet; we kept dashing to the windows and peering out, until finally Lamar cried, "They're coming! They're here!"

We poured from the house to greet them. Harry was on horseback; Father drove the wagon. A strange man sat beside him with his arm in a sling. In the back of the wagon, now empty of supplies, sat Alberto and a young woman of seventeen or thereabouts. She looked a bit like, well, me. Of course she did—she had to be my cousin Agatha Finch, with the map of our common ancestors written on her face. I wondered if I was destined to look just like her in a few years. Something to ponder.

Her print dress was faded, out-of-date, and laughably small, what with her knobbly wrists protruding and her pale shins on immodest display. Why was she wearing a pauper's dress? Then it came to me: She had lost everything in the storm. Mother had told me this but it hadn't sunk in until that moment, seeing the charity clothes. Calpurnia Virginia Tate, I chastised myself, you are a simpleton. And quite unkind to boot.

And what of the strange man, who was he? And why did they all look so dispirited and exhausted and downcast? This was supposed to be a joyful homecoming, a merry celebration. Our family was intact. The gaps at the table would be filled again.

Father climbed down from the wagon. The lines in his face and the stiffness of his gait shocked me. He embraced Mother, cupping her cheek lovingly in his palm as they whispered a few words to each other.

Harry dismounted King Arthur. He looked so dirty and ragged and thin that I ran to him and hugged him.

"Oh, Harry."

"Pet," he said quietly, "I'm glad to see you. Careful, now, you'll get all muddy."

"Doesn't matter," I said, squeezing him as hard as I could. "I missed you so much. What's it like? Was it awful? Is it true what they say, that so many people died? Is that Aggie? It's Aggie, isn't it? What's she like? Who's that man with you?"

Our conversation was interrupted by the others swarming around with shouts of welcome. The dogs, especially Ajax, went berserk and jumped on everyone, making a terrible nuisance of themselves. Father hugged and kissed us all. I felt oddly shy when he hugged me tight but was terribly relieved to find that although he looked different, he smelled just the same. The same old Father smell.

The stranger climbed down with difficulty. He was a big man, not young, with the thick chest and broad shoulders of a blacksmith. He was scruffy and badly needed a haircut. His right arm hung immobile in a grubby sling, the fingers strangely clawed. Despite his obvious fatigue, he smiled and bowed low over Mother's hand.

Agatha was helped down from the wagon, along with her luggage, consisting of one gunnysack and one tin case about the size of a hatbox but of a shape I'd never seen before. Was it a musical instrument? Maybe it was a concertina or bagpipes. Maybe we could play duets. But before I could ask her, she was delivered into the hands of SanJuanna, who whisked her off with strict instructions from Mother to feed her, bathe her, and put her to bed.

In my bed. But never mind.

After the men washed up, we all sat down to dinner. Father said an extra-long blessing, and it was both strange and comforting to hear his voice reciting the familiar words. Then he asked God's mercy on the people of Galveston and gave thanks for returning safely to the bosom of his family. A shadow passed over his face. "Truly," he said, "I am the most fortunate of men, to have my wife and children safe and well when so many others have suffered such grievous losses." He cleared his throat, forced a wan smile, and said, "Amen."

After our echoing chorus of *Amens*, we started asking about Galveston, haltingly at first, then peppering them with questions until Father held up his hand, saying, "That's enough. Galveston as we know it has gone."

Mother said, "Leave your father in peace. We will not speak further of it tonight. Lamar, pass him the potatoes."

You would naturally have thought the meal would be a festive occasion, but not so. Father and Harry were subdued. The stranger, who had been introduced as Dr. Pritzker, appeared to be in pain but gamely complimented my mother on her home, her lovely children (naturally), and her bill of fare. For some reason, he was wedged at the table next to me, taking up more than his fair share of space. Even though he was built like a blacksmith, there was an air of education and culture about him; he knew which fork to use and did not gawp at our chandelier like some country hick. But with his maimed hand, he fumbled awkwardly with his knife and fork, stabbing ineffectually at his beef. I nudged him. He looked at me quizzically, and I whispered, "I'll cut your meat for you if you like."

He whispered back, "I'd like that very much, young lady."

I was making a nice, precise job of it when Mother suddenly noticed and exclaimed, "Oh, Dr. Pritzker! I am so sorry. Let me get Viola to fix that for you."

"It's no problem at all, ma'am. I have a most capable helper here." He examined me. "Thank you, Miss . . . ?"

"Calpurnia Virginia Tate."

"Pleased to make your acquaintance, Miss Calpurnia Virginia Tate. I am Jacob Pritzker, late of Galveston. We shall shake hands properly once I am fully recovered."

Curiosity was eating me alive. I knew that Mother would consider it the height of bad manners to ask about his hand, so I waited until her attention was safely focused elsewhere. I leaned in close and said quietly, "Dr. Pritzker, what happened to your hand?"

He murmured, "I had to climb a tree to escape the rising waters. It was swarming with dozens of rattlesnakes."

"*No!*" I yelled.

The table fell silent. All eyes were on me. They were mostly curious, except for one pair, which were—predictably—furious.

"Uck." I coughed. "Uh, bone caught in my throat. Yes. But I'm fine now. Thank you for your concern, everyone." I cleared my throat ostentatiously.

J.B. piped up. "Can I see it? The bone?"

Mother glared at me and said, "No, darling," with ice in her voice.

I kept my head down and waited for conversation to resume. For the moment, camouflage and mimicry of the well-behaved daughter were called for. I contemplated the differences between my own lucky encounter with a snake versus Dr. Pritzker's unlucky one.

Mother said, "Callie, kindly do not monopolize our guest. Where are you from, Dr. Pritzker? Where are your people?"

"In Ohio, ma'am. Ohio born and bred."

"Ah."

Mother was too polite to say it but Lamar was not, and he burst out with, "A Yankee!"

There was a sharp intake of breath around the table—over Dr. Pritzker's origins or Lamar's bad manners, it was hard to say. Mother grimaced at Lamar while Father made his apologies.

"That's quite all right, Mr. and Mrs. Tate. Yes, I did serve in the War, as a hostler in the Ninth Ohio Cavalry. But that was thirty-five years ago, and I hope you will not hold such ancient action against me. In my defense, I have lived the last ten years of my life in Galveston, and I hope to spend the rest of my days in the great State of Texas."

Father announced to the table at large, "Dr. Pritzker is a graduate of the Chicago Veterinary College. I have persuaded him to set up his new practice here. I figure we have more than enough livestock in Caldwell County to keep him busy."

Various eyes lit up for different reasons.

"Ah," said Granddaddy with satisfaction, "a man who stands at the intersection of Science and Commerce."

"Indeed, sir. Your son has told me about your pursuits, and I look forward to many mutually beneficial discussions."

Travis and I grinned at each other. An animal doctor!

After cigars and brandy for the men, Alberto drove Dr. Pritzker and his few belongings in the wagon to Elsie Bell's boardinghouse, where he'd procured a room.

Travis and I walked alongside, burning with curiosity about his practice.

Travis said, "What kind of animals do you look after?"

"Most kinds, although my practice is predominantly made

up of the more useful farm animals. Mainly cattle and horses and pigs."

"Do you ever look after wild animals?"

"Well, young man, occasionally people will bring me an injured squirrel or raccoon or suchlike, but I generally prefer not to treat such animals. They're frightened and in pain, and they don't understand that you're trying to help. It's usually best to put them out of their misery."

I could tell Travis didn't like this. He said, "I had an armadillo once. His name was Armand. At least, we think his name was Armand, but maybe it was Dilly. Have you ever doctored an armadillo?"

Dr. Pritzker smiled and said, "No, and I've never heard of anyone doing so."

I chimed in with, "There's plenty of good reasons why not. I can't personally recommend them as pets."

Travis said, "Does it make you sad when the animals die?"

"You get used to it, like most things in life, and you try not to get too attached."

"Granddaddy always tells me the same thing," I said. "Can we come and watch when you doctor the animals sometime?"

Dr. Pritzker looked surprised. He thought for a moment and said, "If your mother doesn't mind, I suppose it will be all right."

I jumped in with, "Oh, she won't mind a bit," while shooting Travis a meaningful glance. He took the hint and kept quiet.

We dropped Dr. Pritzker off and waved him good night.

Travis and I chattered in excitement all the way home. An animal doctor! What could be better?

WHAT *COULD* BE BETTER would be sleeping in your own bed. By the time I got upstairs, my cousin was curled up in my bed, face to the wall, the lamp turned low. She even had my pillow, and you know how disconcerting it is to sleep on a foreign one. I'd been provided with a lumpy cotton pillow and a lumpy cotton pallet on the floor. At snake level. As I blew out the lamp, the tiniest sound issued from across the room. Was it the king snake on his nightly rounds? Or was it Agatha whimpering?

"G'night," I whispered, but there was no reply.

I thought about the two refugees the Galveston Flood had washed up on our shores. One of them was clearly a great prize. But the other? Well, she was still a question mark.

CHAPTER 11

AGGIE'S ORDEAL

An old man near Valdivia illustrated his motto, "Necesidad es la madre del invención," by giving an account of the several useful things he manufactured from his apples.

I AWOKE THE NEXT MORNING to find the question mark sitting on the side of my bed, hugging my pillow to herself, and staring at me. Just staring. How long had she been sitting there, and why was she looking at me like that? Had I been talking in my sleep? Snoring? Passing gas? She had such a strange look on her face that I wondered if she'd caught a glimpse of the snake. But never mind, she was a wounded dove who required tender care. I would help with her convalescence, gently coaxing her back to life. We would take long healing nature walks, and at night I would brush her hair the recommended hundred strokes for optimal health and beauty. We would share our favorite books. She would be the sister I never had.

"Uh, hello," I said.

No answer.

"How are you?"

No answer.

I studied her. She appeared to be of average height and figure, with medium brown hair and ordinary features. No beauty, but no gargoyle, either. All told, a middling girl. But as I reminded myself, one shouldn't judge another strictly on appearances, for although I myself might not be a great beauty, I was, nevertheless, an interesting person, was I not? And easy, pleasant company, was I not? Therefore I would withhold judgment for the moment.

There was, however, one unusual thing about her: the light of wary apprehension in her eyes, as if she were uncertain whether I'd bite or not.

I said, "I'm Calpurnia Virginia Tate, by the way, but you can call me Callie Vee. Do you go by Agatha or Aggie? I'm sorry about your house and all."

Still no answer. This was getting pretty uncomfortable, but I persevered. "Of course, we don't have to talk about it if you don't want to, Agatha."

"It's Aggie. And I don't want to." Her face crumpled, and she erupted in tears.

"Oh, Aggie, I'm sorry. We don't have to talk about it."

Well, of course we didn't *have* to—that went without saying. But I was bound and determined that at some point we actually *would*, because here was my very own flesh and blood, who'd survived the greatest natural disaster in the history of the United States. Not just Texas, mind, but the whole country. I'd have to wheedle the tale out of her eventually, even if it was only one small detail at a time, so as not to cause her too much pain. I was nothing if not considerate.

I fished my best lace handkerchief from the snake drawer and gave it to her.

"Here you go," I said. "I have to get ready for school. Are you coming with me?"

"No," she snuffled. "I've already got my diploma."

"So what are you going to do with yourself?"

"Do?" She looked puzzled. "What do you mean, 'do'? I'm waiting for Poppa to build a new house so I can go home."

"How long will that take?"

"They said just a few months."

Oh, good. Sleeping on the floor for "just a few months."

She stared off into space and wept some more. "But I don't want to go back there. After all the things I saw."

This piqued my interest. I whispered, "What did you see, Aggie?"

Suddenly the breakfast gong sounded, and she flinched violently. "What's that noise?"

"It's Viola telling us to come down for breakfast."

"Aunt Margaret said I could have a tray in my room."

It took me a second to realize that, first, she was referring to Mother, and second, that she was referring to *my* room.

On the way to school, I was joined by more than my usual quota of brothers, all of whom quizzed me about our cousin.

"Is she drippy like you?" said Lamar. "Or is she basically all right?"

I ignored the insult and replied, "Hard to say. She's really upset, that's for sure, so it's hard to tell if she's actually drippy or not. Maybe she's just droopy, being sad and all."

Sam Houston said, "Good one, Callie."

"Thank you," I said modestly. "I thought so."

By now the whole town had heard about Aggie. Our teacher, Miss Harbottle, interrogated me about her, and on finding that Aggie had earned her diploma, suggested that perhaps she'd volunteer to help out with the little kids' lessons.

"I don't know, Miss Harbottle. She's jumpy as a lizard on a hot rock."

"The poor lamb, but this might be just what she needs to bring her out of herself. I shall speak to your mother about it after she's had some time to recover."

At recess, Lula Gates asked me during hopscotch if Aggie played the piano.

"Why do you want to know?" I said, making the turn and hopping back, pretending that my foot hadn't—maybe—slipped over the chalked line the tiniest bit.

"I thought it would be nice to play duets with her."

Wounded, I said, "You don't like playing with me?"

"Whenever I ask you, you always have something else to do, or else you're going off with your grandfather to spy on insects or toads or something."

I had to admit the truth of this. Playing duets sounded like fun in theory but it meant you actually had to practice, something I often fell short on. But Lula was my best friend and a far better musician than I. She deserved a better partner, so I agreed to invite her over when Aggie felt up to it.

I arrived home to discover that Alberto had moved a small wardrobe into my room. I thought it was for Aggie, but then she took over the large wardrobe and my things were crammed into the smaller one. This seemed terribly unjust, as she had practically no clothes. She did, however, have the strangely shaped case that I still hadn't figured out.

She spent most of her time in bed with the curtains drawn, picking lethargically at the dainties on her tray, doing an excellent impression of an invalid with a wasting disease. She jumped at loud noises and sudden moves. Any little thing could set her off in fresh torrents of tears.

When I made gentle inquiries, she said, "I can't stop crying. Oh, I wish I could stop. What's wrong with me? I didn't used to be like this."

"Never mind, Aggie. I'm sure you'll get better." (Of course, I had absolutely nothing to base this on but it seemed like the right thing to say.) "Do you want me to brush your hair?"

"No. Leave me alone."

I left her alone.

A few days later, the magnitude of Aggie's misery was driven home to me. Passing the parlor door, I caught a glimpse of Mother, looking upset, slipping what appeared to be a letter into her sewing basket. Viola called her into the kitchen a moment later. The letter sat unguarded.

Calpurnia, I told myself, *don't do it. A letter is a private thing.*

I kept repeating this even as I tiptoed to the basket and extracted the letter, stealthy as a pickpocket. It was from Aggie's mother in Galveston, and read:

My dearest sister Margaret,

I am sending you this account of the storm in order that you may understand the ordeal that we survived by the grace of God. I fear that a severe shock has been impressed on Aggie's soul, and I fear that she may never fully recover from it.

Margaret, how I wish we had listened to your warning over the telephone! But our own weather bureau officials did not foresee any danger and raised no alarm that might have saved our city. Still, that morning there had been a strange orange light over the city that no one had ever seen before. Even as you and I spoke on the telephone, the skies darkened and filled with low black clouds, the temperature grew chilly, and the rains began. An hour later, I glanced into the yard, now under several inches of water, and was met by the strangest sight: hundreds—no, _thousands_—of tiny toads clinging to every floating thing. Where had they come from? I called to Gus to come and see this unprecedented sight but he was busy nailing boards over the shutters in the front yard.

Then the wind picked up. By lunchtime, most of the street was under two feet of running brown water.

The toads had all vanished. Now there were fish swimming in the gutters, and the neighborhood children laughed in delight at this amazing spectacle. By two o'clock, we saw driftwood floating by, washed all the way from the beach. At three o'clock, we stood on the porch and, to our horror, watched the water rise all the way up the front steps _in the space of seconds,_ driving us back inside. A moment later, we watched Dr. Pritzker splash—or rather swim—across the street to us, his house being only one story tall and having lost most of its roof to the wind. We took him in and huddled together in the parlor. A few minutes later, we were joined by the Alexander family from next door, Mr. Alexander having tied his wife and three children together with the clothesline, which he had then tied around his own waist. We pulled them half drowned from the waves and debris, all manner of common household goods, strange to behold. At four o'clock, we saw the first of many dead horses.

Sheets of water surged under the front door and we were forced to retreat to the stairs. Then the water drove us up the stairs to the bedrooms. By five o'clock, the whole island was underwater due to a great storm surge. We saw sofas, buggies, and even a piano floating by, to which a man and child clung. We sang hymns and prayed in an attempt to sustain our spirits. The windows shattered in the shrieking wind, forcing us to shelter under mattresses from the hail of broken glass. The water reached the top of the stairs, and we had to make the decision to climb on the roof and strike out for other shelter, or else ride out the storm with the house. An agonizing decision, with all our lives hanging in the balance. At that very moment, the whole house moved beneath our feet like a living thing; the groan of parting timber made our blood run cold, and the porch and the front of the house were torn away. Gus decided that we should abandon the house and try to reach the Ursuline convent, a three-story brick building a few blocks away. He begged the Alexanders to do the same, but Mr. Alexander would not, instead tying his terrified wife and screaming children to Grandmother's four-poster bed. With the next horrible shriek of cracking wood, the house broke apart around us. We, along with Dr. Pritzker, were cast into the water on our makeshift raft, straight into the teeth of the howling storm.

Several shutters lashed together floated by, somebody else's raft, now unoccupied, and we managed to haul ourselves partly upon it. I looked back to see the remains of the disintegrating house subsiding into the waves. We never saw the Alexanders again.

The water was freezing cold, and all around there was only blackness, but we clung to that raft as to life. The wind tore at our clothes, and the rain hit us with the force of bullets. Gus cried out that he could see a light in the distance, and he and Dr. Pritzker tried to steer us toward it. Halfway there, Dr. Pritzker was swept away into a tree where scores of poisonous snakes had sought shelter and sustained the injuries that are still evident.

At intervals the full moon appeared through thin clouds, lighting the scene of devastation around us. Gus pushed us toward the light, which we could now see was a lamp in the upper windows of the convent. A few minutes later, the light receded, and we realized we were caught in a whirlpool of debris that was now taking us away from our destination. When it carried us back nearer the light again, Gus, with a mighty effort, propelled our raft out of the whirlpool, but in doing so lost his grip and floated away from us. Oh, Margaret, I will never forget that moment, not as long as I live. I called his name in anguish, and a few seconds later, I heard his answering cry from out of the darkness. He was alive! But his calls slowly grew fainter and fainter, along with the hope in my heart.

We reached the safety of the convent, where the nuns and other refugees pulled us to safety through the upper-story windows. The good sisters gave us dry clothes, although I confess that at that point I no longer cared if I lived or died. I prayed for Gus's safety through that long black night.

The next morning, Sunday, the water had receded, and the convent stood alone amid the desolation of broken timbers and wreckage. A great and eerie silence descended. There was no keening, no lamenting, no wailing in grief as one would expect after misfortune of this magnitude. The survivors were all too numb to mourn properly. We picked our way through mountains of rubble toward the medical college, and there we were joyfully reunited with Gus, whom providence had sent a floating door to carry him to safety.

And now, Margaret, having laid out this tale of tragedy beyond measure, I resolve to never speak of it again. My dear sister, I remain forever,

Your loving Sophronia Finch

I put the letter back, my stomach heaving. No wonder Aggie could not speak of it. I realized I had been insensitive to her terrible trauma and resolved to treat her gently from then on. And I told myself I would never think of Galveston again. But of course the more you tell yourself you won't think of something, the more you end up thinking about it. Like it or not.

The next day I overheard a couple of worried discussions between my parents. Then Dr. Walker arrived, a tall, somber individual afforded great respect in our house and habitually clothed in funereal black. Typically we children scattered on his arrival like an ant colony when you poked it with a twig, as he invariably stuck some kind of cold metal instrument into your ears or mouth, or applied an icy stethoscope to your chest. (According to family lore, when I was afflicted with croup at age three, I asked to borrow his stethoscope to listen to my teddy bear's heart, which request he frostily declined. Since I have no memory of this, I can't defend myself one way or the other.)

The doctor and Aggie and Mother congregated in my room and shooed me out, shutting the door firmly in my face. I lingered at the keyhole for want of something better to do. From inside, I could hear a series of muffled commands.

"Open wide and say 'ah.'"

"Ahhhhh."

"Now take some deep breaths through your mouth."

Since I was not on the receiving end of the exam, I found it all much more interesting than usual. When I heard his bag snap shut, I knew it was time to skedaddle.

Mother and Dr. Walker walked downstairs to the parlor. Mother was wringing her hands and, in her distraction, did not notice me lurking in the hall.

"Calm yourself, Mrs. Tate," the doctor said. "I can find nothing physically wrong with her except a mild degree of anemia. This is easily treated by driving iron nails into several apples, letting them sit for a few days, and then making sure she eats one every day at breakfast. Do this for six weeks, and the anemia will be cured. No, the main problem here is a severe case of neurasthenia, also known as nervous prostration. Her nerves have borne a severe shock, and curing this will likely take months, not weeks. Try to provide her with soothing pastimes to calm her mind, such as sewing, and quiet music, and nonstimulating books. But I caution you not to give her novels—no, no, novels tend to excite the imagination and foment the mind, the exact opposite of the effect we are seeking in this case."

Really? Was this why Mother was always trying to pry Mr. Dickens and Miss Alcott from my hands, to replace them with knitting and sewing?

"No, no," he went on, "I find a steady, improving, educational biography to be useful in such cases, the longer the better. You will find such reading material to be just what the doctor ordered." He followed this remark with a strange rusty cough. It took me a moment to identify the parched sound as a laugh, the creaking laugh of a man with a dreadful sense of humor.

He went on. "I will provide her with a stimulating tonic of coca leaf tea for the mornings, along with a soothing draft of laudanum for bedtime. Be mindful that she does not reverse them. And now, I bid you good day."

Mother followed Dr. Walker out to his buggy, spouting effusive thanks.

I ran upstairs to my—our—room. Aggie was fully dressed and lying on my—her—bed. She stared unmoving at the ceiling.

"Am I dying?" she said listlessly.

"Aggie!" I was shocked to the core. "Of course not."

"What does the doctor say?"

"He says you have anemia, and we're to give you iron apples. He says you've had a shock, and he's prescribing dull biographies for you to read."

She propped herself on an elbow and stared at me with a flutter of curiosity. "Really? He sounds like a quack to me."

"No, no, he's the best doctor in town."

"That's not saying much. I'll bet he's the only doctor in town."

"Well, yes. But he's also prescribing you some medicine to make you feel better."

"Okay," she said, and flopped back on the bed.

I volunteered for apple duty. Mother was so pleased that I was "showing an interest" that I didn't correct her and tell her I was actually viewing the whole thing as a sort of experiment. Once a week I drove several large two-penny nails into seven apples, and every morning I extracted the nails from one of them, the pale pulp now stained a rusty brown. In the interest of Science, I filched a slice. It was like licking a cast-iron pipe.

Aggie slowly improved, but then we almost had a setback when she said one morning, "I had a terrible dream last night. I dreamed there was a coral snake in the room."

"It's not a coral snake," I said before I could stop myself. Oops. I clapped a hand over my mouth.

"What do you mean?" she said, looking at me curiously.

"Nuffin'."

Dr. Walker's tonics proved to be helpful, but then the most helpful thing of all happened: She received a letter from Galveston that improved her mood overnight. She didn't share the contents with us but we figured it had to be from her parents. Months would pass before we'd find out just how wrong we were.

The day following the letter, I got home from school and

found her up and dressed with her hair in a silly elaborate coiffure, taking a general interest in her surroundings.

"Hello, Aggie," I said, all politeness. "You look like you're feeling better."

"What," she said, "is that *thing*?"

"What thing?"

"That thing on the dresser," she said, pointing at Sir Isaac Newton.

"Oh. That thing, as you call it, is a black-spotted newt. He's an amphibium, as I'm sure you can probably tell, of the family Salamandridae, genus *Diemyctylus*."

"Why are you speaking that gibberish?"

This shocked and offended me. "Gibberish? It's hardly gibberish. It's Latin. It's what they call the Linnean Binomial Nomenclature. It's the way we Scientists classify the whole natural world."

She did not look impressed.

"Watch this," I said. "I'll feed him a fly. I've got some dead ones in a tin, and I tie them on a thread, which isn't easy, believe me, and then I dangle them over him to stimulate his appetite. He doesn't seem all that interested if they're not moving."

"That's disgusting. Get rid of it."

My goodness. A rapid recovery and a tart tongue to boot. "He's mine," I said, "and I'm studying him. You better not touch him."

"Never." She shuddered.

Poor Sir Isaac. What did the world have against him? And

with such an adverse reaction from Aggie, good thing she thought the snake was only a dream.

That night, after climbing into our bed and pallet, I said, "So what's in that funny-looking case in the wardrobe?"

"You better not touch it."

"Okay, but what's in it? Is it a concertina? It's some kind of musical instrument, right?"

"That proves how little you know. Be quiet and go to sleep."

"Not until you tell me what it is."

She sighed. "It's a type-writing machine, and you better not touch it. I'll tell your mother if you do."

"Gosh." As far as I knew, there was precisely one of these newfangled devices in town, owned by the *Fentress Indicator*, our local paper. You rolled a piece of paper into it and then tapped out your message on the keys, almost like playing the piano. The results were marvelous, the print as neat as a page in a book.

"Will you show it to me sometime?"

"No. Go to sleep."

"Why did you bring it?"

"Shut up and go to sleep."

Well, honestly, there was no keeping me away from it after that. The next day while she was taking a bath, I pulled open the wardrobe door and studied the position of the case to make sure that I—crafty Calpurnia!—could return it to the exact same spot. I lifted it out, amazed at its weight. Gad, it weighed a ton. Breathless with anticipation, I unlatched the lid. It had apparently survived the Flood in pristine condition, black and gleaming and complicated, with the name UNDERWOOD in handsome gold print across the top. Each letter of the alphabet had its own round key, but they were all out of order in a terrible jumble. How could you possibly find the one you wanted? The many complicated levers and dials made me afraid to touch it. Why had she brought it? Surely it worked, and surely she knew how to use it; nobody in their right mind would lug something so cumbersome all the way across the state if they didn't mean to use it. I carefully closed the lid and left it exactly as I'd found it.

The next morning, Aggie joined us at the breakfast table. J.B. stared at her with curiosity and said through a mouthful of flapjack, "Who's that lady?"

"That's your cousin Agatha," I said. "Please don't talk with your mouth full."

"What's a cousin?"

"Well, you know Aunt Sophronia and Uncle Gus?"

"No."

"Yes, you do. There's a picture of them on the piano."

J.B. stared at me blankly, and I realized that even the simplest explanation of genealogy was beyond his tender years.

"Never mind, J.B. She's going to stay with us for a while. A big wind blew her house down, and she has nowhere else to live."

He grew animated and said, "You mean like the pigs and the wolf?"

"It wasn't a wolf, J.B. It was a big wind, a storm. You know what a storm is."

But this news did not interest a six-year-old. He turned his attention back to his breakfast.

To celebrate his homecoming, and to make up for the fact that he had missed our birthdays, Father eventually called us into his room one by one. He made a short speech about his own good fortune, and how lucky he was to have a family, whole and safe and well, then quizzed us about our behavior during his absence.

"Were you a good girl, Calpurnia, while I was gone?"

"Uh, mostly, Father, yes."

"And did you do as Mother asked you while I was gone?"

"Uh, yes, Father, I mostly did."

He pondered my responses as if trying to make a decision. "In that case, I have a special present for this special occasion. Hold out your hand."

Instead of a nickel or even a dime, he placed a surprisingly heavy coin in my palm. I peered at it, and the coin shimmered with a warm light. It was a five-dollar Liberty gold piece, the head of the queen of Liberty on one side, the eagle and shield on the other, more money than I'd ever seen in my life. A fortune! And all mine!

"I don't want you to spend this frivolously," he said.

I immediately thought of the books I could buy and not have to beg from Mrs. Whipple at the Lockhart library, watching her face go all pruney whenever I requested something she deemed "inappropriate reading for a young girl."

Father said, "Think of it as an investment in your future."

I thought of all the scientific equipment I could buy, perhaps even a thirdhand microscope of my own.

"Save it now, and spend it wisely in the future," he said, "perhaps on your hope chest and your trousseau."

My what? Bridal linens? Clothes? Was he kidding? I searched his face for signs of joshing but there were none. I couldn't believe it. How had this happened? How could I be so misunderstood by my own father? I was a foreigner in my own home, a citizen of some other tribe, a member of some other genus.

He looked puzzled, waiting for some kind of response.

Words failed me. All I could stammer out was, "Thank you, Father."

"You're very welcome. Please send Travis in on your way out." I plunged the coin deep into my pinafore and left the room with a wounded heart. That he could know so little about his only daughter.

Travis, Lamar, and Sul Ross stood lined up in the hallway. Travis took one look at me and whispered, "Are we in trouble?"

"No, it's good news."

"So why do you look like that?"

"Never mind. He wants to see you next."

I retreated to my room and stewed in ambivalence, delighted with my coin and dismayed with my father. Had I been adopted? Had my rightful parents—whoever they were—slipped me into the Tate nest like a cuckoo's egg to be raised by others? Augh, the unfairness of it all. I could only console myself with

Granddaddy, and I thanked my lucky stars for him, wishing he were my father instead of my grandfather, who necessarily had a limited say about my life. I pondered the coin, a literal treasure, then wrapped it in a piece of tissue paper and stashed it in the cigar box under the bed.

A week later, Mother, relieved and gladdened that Aggie was emerging from her shell, suggested a trip downtown to the Fentress General Store. She asked me to come along, and I agreed; trips to the store were usually fine entertainment. I wisely left my gold coin at home so as not to be tempted to spend any of it. While they fingered the various muslins and linens and calicoes, I perused the latest Sears Roebuck Catalogue chained to the counter, good for at least a half hour's diversion. You could buy everything in the world through the catalogue, from overcoats to underwear, from wigs to watches, from pianos to tubas, from snakebite kits to shotguns. You could buy a Singer sewing machine (it's where we'd gotten ours), or you could buy blouses and skirts and other clothes already made up, saving you the trouble of sewing for yourself. Amazing! You could buy curtains and carpets; you could buy a tractor or even one of the newfangled auto-mobiles, and it would magically arrive on your doorstep a mere three months later. Talk about speedy service! You could also buy such mundane things as huge sacks of flour and sugar and beans. The company had been the savior of many a pioneer housewife living on the plains in some wretched sod hut, anxiously scanning the horizon daily for her delivery.

Mr. Gates, Lula's father, came in and bought some shotgun shells. He tipped his hat to Mother and said, "Mrs. Tate, you'd best keep an eye out and tell your husband that we're losing chickens. I can't tell if it's a coon or fox or what. I got a shot off the other night, and I thought I got it, but we're still losing chickens."

"Thank you, Mr. Gates. I will certainly pass that along to my husband."

We made our purchases, and with admirable efficiency, the clerk wrapped them in brown paper and secured them with coarse twine. We had turned to go when Mother said, "Oh, wait. I forgot to buy your needles, Calpurnia."

"My what?"

"Your number-three needles."

"For what?"

"Your Christmas knitting."

"My what?" I didn't like the turn this conversation was taking.

"Stop it. You sound like that wretched Polly. Thank goodness Mr. O'Flanagan took him off our hands. What was your grandfather thinking? No, I'm talking about your Christmas knitting. This year we move on to gloves."

My heart plummeted. The previous Christmas, I'd been forced to learn how to knit socks for all my male relatives, who seemingly numbered in the thousands. This painful exercise had kept me away from my nature studies for weeks, and I'd resented every minute of it. The results were lumpy, pathetic items that only vaguely resembled socks. Nobody ever wore them, and I couldn't say I blamed them. But now this?

"Why should I have to knit," I said, "when you can buy perfectly nice gloves from the Sears Catalogue?" In desperation I trotted back to the counter and started riffling through it. "Look, I can even show you the page. Why would anybody want my gloves, when you can have much nicer ones from Mr. Sears?" I stabbed frantically at the page. "Look at this: 'Available in all sizes and many pleasing styles and colors.' And look here: 'Your Satisfaction Guaranteed.' That's what it says, right here."

Mother's lips compressed, always a dangerous sign. "That is not the point."

"What *is* the point?" I said, a sudden flash of anger overwhelming my normally excellent judgment about not asking such insolent questions.

Noticing the clerk displaying an excessive interest in this exchange, Mother threw him a grim smile, took me firmly by the elbow, and pulled me out the door. I won't go so far as to say she yanked me into the street but it was pretty darned close. Aggie scuttled along behind with our parcels, a smirk on her lips.

"The *point*, my girl, is that you learn those domestic arts that are common knowledge for every young lady. That are *required* of every young lady. That is the point, and we shall speak no more about it. Agatha, I do apologize for my daughter's rudeness."

She wheeled into the store and returned a minute later with

a pair of needles. On the way home, I trailed behind and pretended not to know them, fuming and kicking viciously at blame-
less clods. They in turn chattered on about sewing and such and
pretended not to notice me sulking in their wake.

I thought I could make a dash for it when I got home, but
Mother herded me into the parlor before I had the chance to
escape.

"Sit," she commanded. I sat.

She handed me needles, a pattern, and a hank of navy blue
wool.

"Cast on," she said. I cast on and began to knit.

Aggie kneeled on the Persian carpet and cut out shirtwaists
and skirts; she and Mother discussed fashions and ignored me
some more. Which was fine with me. I wrestled with the pattern
and fought with the wool; I muttered and huffed and dropped
stitches, and generally worked myself into a fine snit, albeit a
quiet one. If they'd left me to my own devices, I'd have hurled
the whole sorry mess to the floor and run screaming for the
river.

By the time Viola rang the dinner gong, I had nearly finished
one tiny glove. Proudly, I held it up for inspection. Mother stared
in disbelief. Aggie squawked a harsh, jeering laugh, reminiscent
of the seagull and surprisingly cruel. I squinted at the glove, which
didn't look right. I counted up the fingers: one, two, three, four,
five. And six.

You'd think that would have been enough to get me out of
the glove business for life, but alas, not so. Mother merely demoted

me to mittens, which were really just socks for the hand, and a whole lot easier. I'm here to tell you that knitting gloves is devilishly hard, but on the other hand (ha!), mittens are a snap.

And as for Aggie, well, there was no friendship forged over books. ("I have better things to do than read.") There was no bedtime ritual of hair brushing. ("Get away from me with those newty hands.") She turned out to *not* be the sister I'd never had. Thank goodness.

CHAPTER 12

THE BANDIT SAGA

F. Cuvier has observed, that all animals that readily enter into domestication, consider man as a member of their own society, and thus fulfil their instinct of association.

ONE AFTERNOON Travis came into the parlor halfway through my piano practice, an unusual thing for him. Typically my audience consisted solely of Mother, acting more in the role of enforcer than music lover. (Although I have to say that she did enjoy Mr. Chopin's pieces whenever my teacher, Miss Brown, assigned one of them to me, particularly the nocturnes, all dreamy and pensive. It was a miracle I didn't put her off him for life, what with my sour notes and my style, which Miss Brown decried as "mechanical." Well, you'd play mechanically too, with a wooden ruler hovering inches above your knuckles, just waiting to show you the error of your ways.)

I watched the clock on the mantel like a hawk, determined to play not one second longer than my mandatory thirty minutes. Travis beamed and bounced and fidgeted with ill-suppressed excitement while I mangled Mr. Tchaikovsky's "Dance of the Sugar Plum Fairy." I doubted my performance was the cause, so something was up. He applauded politely with Mother at the end, and then urgently signaled me to follow him through the kitchen and out the back door. He trotted off to the barn, saying only, "Hurry up—you've got to see it."

"See what?" I said, trotting behind him.

"Come on. I've got a new pet."

Now, I knew that Travis's pets usually spelled a whole lot of trouble, but his obvious joy and enthusiasm were infectious. "What is it?"

"You'll see. It's in Armand's cage for now."

"Maybe you should tell me what it is first. To, you know, prepare me."

But he wouldn't answer. I followed him out to the barn. And there in a cage in a dim corner was a baby raccoon. She was about the size of a half-grown kitten, with a pointy nose, a bushy ringed tail, and the black mask that gave her the look of a mischievous child costumed as a burglar at Halloween.

"Isn't she cute?" he said. "I think I'll call her Bandit."

Bandit hissed in displeasure. She stared at us warily, her shiny black eyes exactly the size and color of Mother's jet beads that she wore on special occasions.

"Travis," I said, halfheartedly, "she's adorable, but you can't keep a raccoon. Father will be furious. He shoots them on sight. They raid the henhouse, and they tear up the vegetable patch, and they eat the pecans off the trees."

"Watch this," he said. He pushed a bit of lettuce through the wire, and she immediately grabbed it in her paw-hands, washed it carefully in the water bowl, and ate it like a miniature human at a picnic. No wonder they were called *Procyon lotor*, meaning "washer dog."

"And," I went on, "if Father doesn't shoot her, then Viola will. You know how she is about her garden."

He cooed at Bandit and fed her another lettuce leaf.

"And they grow wild as they get older. They don't make good pets. You know that, right?"

"I found her in the scrub. She was all by herself and crying."

"Was it near Lula's place? Her father says they've been losing chickens."

Travis did not answer.

Exasperated, I said, "Did you look for the mother?"

"What? Oh. Well . . . yes."

"Travis."

"She was starving! She was lonely! What could I do? You wouldn't have left her, either. Just look at her, Callie. She's cute as a bug's ear."

Bandit munched on her lettuce, turning it in her clever little hands, all the while gazing at us with alert black eyes. Yep, completely adorable. At least for a while.

"Besides," he went on, "nobody has to know."

"Do you really think you can keep a secret like this?" I said skeptically.

"Of course. No one has to know."

That night at supper, Father said to Travis, "So, young man, Alberto tells me you are keeping a coon in the barn. Is that right?"

Travis gaped. He obviously hadn't had time to work up a good story and had been caught flat-footed. Alberto was the hired man, and Father paid his wages. Of course he would report such goings-on.

Father said, "You know how I feel about coons and such. Varmints, all of them."

"Yes, Father," he said, head bowed. "I'm sorry." He raised his head and mustered his arguments: "She's an orphan, you see, and she was starving when I found her. I couldn't just leave her there. And I promise to take good care of her. I'll keep her away from the henhouse, I promise."

Father looked at Mother, who sighed deeply but had nothing to add, having no doubt been worn down by variations of the same argument over the years.

"All right," said Father grudgingly. "But if there's any trouble, any trouble at all, I'll shoot it myself and feed it to the dogs. Is that understood?"

"Yessir." Travis beamed his heartbreaking smile, which even drew a half smile from Father, so potent was its force.

Thus began the saga of Bandit. What made her more troublesome than Armand and Jay put together were her boundless curiosity and her busy little paws. They were more like hands than paws, really, in that she could open anything. Travis put a puppy collar on her, and she had it off within five minutes. He made a tiny harness for her from leather scraps, and she had it off within ten minutes. Then he hit on the idea of putting the buckle between her shoulder blades, the one place she couldn't reach. Yet. He put her on a leash and tried to take her for walks, which so infuriated her that she leaped and thrashed like a hooked trout to the point of exhaustion. He figured out that he could coax her to follow him for a few feet with bits of cheese, discovering along the way that she would eat anything—literally anything— that could remotely be construed as edible. Potato peels, kitchen scraps, garbage, rotting fish heads—she relished it all. After carefully washing it, that is; her fastidiousness about the disgusting things she put in her mouth amused us both.

"She's what's called an omnivore," I said, "an animal that's somewhere between an herbivore that only eats plants and a carnivore that only eats meat. Granddaddy says it's a survival mechanism that allows such creatures to adapt to all sorts of habitats. Coyotes are the same. They can live practically anywhere."

And she could escape practically anything. There was no cage that could hold her for more than a day or two. She quickly became attached to Travis, chirruping in distress when he locked her up at bedtime.

"I hate to leave her by herself at night," he said. "She gets so lonely and unhappy." He cast his eyes at me sideways.

"You must be joking," I said. "You can't possibly take her in the house."

"Well . . ."

"Absolutely not. I'll do some research on what we can do to calm her down. But you have to promise—*promise*—not to even think about taking her inside."

"Okay. I sure hate to see her sad."

"Doing some research" sounded much grander than the reality, which was that I went and talked to Granddaddy, the font of all knowledge when it came to kingdom Animalia.

He listened gravely and said, "The kits are admittedly appealing. They are gregarious creatures when young and can be tamed if caught early enough. But the adults rarely make satisfactory pets, and when they reach adulthood, their temperaments change. They are no longer in need of human company, and are, in fact, capable of biting the hand that feeds them."

"So they really do turn mean later on."

"Quite so. As for your question about how to keep the animal content in a cage, I suggest you read the *Guide to Texas Mammals* for suggestions."

I pulled down the volume and read that baby raccoons are social creatures that become distressed when separated from their family and are happiest when sleeping in a pile of their siblings. And yes, the book confirmed Granddaddy's pronouncement about the adults.

But when I told Travis that Bandit might turn on him someday, he merely pooh-poohed the idea, saying, "Look at that sweet little face."

We both looked at Bandit who, at that opportune moment, as if understanding we were discussing her future, sat on her hind legs, cocked her head, and held out her paws as if begging.

"Awww," my brother and I said together.

We ended up giving her one of J.B.'s old stuffed toys to sleep with, a teddy bear about her size, and she took to it immediately, snuggling with it and trying to groom it, gently exploring the plush fur for fleas and ticks. Having a "littermate" definitely calmed her down and improved her behavior. She grew fat and playful. She and the barn cats cautiously investigated one another, and as they grew accustomed to each other, she even began lining up with them at the twice daily milking of our cow Flossie to have warm milk squirted into her mouth straight from the teat.

After a while, Bandit even gave up on the tug-of-war and submitted to the leash. Then she and Travis began to take actual walks together. Ajax, who knew a varmint when he saw one, charged her on one of these walks. She scampered for her life up the nearest object, which happened to be Travis, climbing up him at great speed, all the way to the top of his head, where she perched, growling and hissing, her claws digging into his scalp. It would have been amusing except for Travis's cries of pain. I ran to the rescue and hauled the excited dog away. When I scolded him, he looked terribly confused, and why wouldn't he? He'd been encouraged to chase varmints his whole life; in fact, raccoons were one of his specialties.

Bandit grew, if anything, even more adorable. And she kept us busy figuring out how to secure her cage. Finally we hit upon the perfect combination of latches and levers, all wired shut, and stood back to admire our escape-proof cage.

I said to Travis, "You misnamed her."

"What do you mean? Bandit's the perfect name."

"You should have called her Houdini."

Two days later, Bandit/Houdini escaped from her "escape-proof" cage. Travis ran to me and begged for help.

"We have to find her. The dogs will get her, or some farmer will shoot her," he said, fighting back tears. We searched for her everywhere, even going into the scrub, but I knew that if she'd made it that far, we'd never see her again.

Travis was bereft. Lamar mocked his grief and called him a titty-baby well out of earshot of our parents, which was fortunate, as they couldn't hear Lamar yelp when I kicked him in the shins.

When Travis went out to feed Bunny early the next morning, there was Bandit sitting on top of her cage, waiting for breakfast. I wasn't witness to the poignant reunion but I heard all about it in detail. The sun returned to Travis's face and stayed there, at least until the next time she disappeared. This became her pattern: disappearing for a while, returning for a while; happy to see Travis and accept a handout and just as happy to slip away again. Her absences gradually grew longer, as Granddaddy had predicted they would.

Unfortunately, they didn't grow long enough. One Sunday after returning from church, my parents went upstairs to rest before lunch. Travis was grooming Bunny in the barn when he heard a terrible ruckus in the henhouse, and there crouched Bandit, at her feet a dead hen covered in blood, its neck awry. Travis flew into a panic, knowing she had called a death sentence down upon herself.

Aggie was out for the afternoon, so I was upstairs reading

on my comfy old bed instead of the lumpy pallet for a change. He burst into my room without knocking, something he'd never done before, eyes wild, stark terror in his face. For one terrible moment, I thought that someone in our family had died.

"It's Bandit," he choked. "She's killed one of the hens. You've got to help me!"

"Help you what?" I said, leaping to my feet, wondering what on earth could be done.

We ran out to the henhouse, where the hysterical inhabitants milled about Bandit in fear and confusion. Her paws and muzzle were smeared with blood, and there was a crazed look in her eyes. I realized she was nearly fully grown and impossible to control. A feather dangled clownishly from the corner of her mouth. Now there were two dead hens instead of one.

"What'll we do?" he cried.

"Go in there and *stop* her, Travis." I ran to the barn and retrieved a stout canvas sack. By the time I got back, Travis had cornered Bandit away from the hens and was trying to entice her within reach, his voice shaking. She looked like no one's pet; she looked like a wild animal.

I hissed at him, "If you calm down, then she'll calm down."

He got himself under control and spoke to Bandit in low, soothing tones. I retrieved a newly laid egg from one of the nests and broke it open on the ground. She was so busy trying to scoop up the runny mess in her paws that she didn't notice me sneaking up behind her. I flung the sack over her, and she screamed in fury. I held the sack closed but knew I couldn't contain the boiling raccoon within it for long. It was like grabbing a tiger by the tail.

I wheezed at my brother, who stood there wide-eyed and useless. "Get some rope or some baling wire. Hurry!"

The urgency of my words got through to him, and he jumped into action. A few moments later, he returned from the barn with a length of twine. We tied the neck of the sack, then paused to catch our breath. Travis had streaks of blood on his hands. I was sticky with egg yolk. The sack on the ground chittered and writhed.

We stared at each other, and the light dawned simultaneously that our troubles, far from being over, were in fact multiplying. What swamp of trouble had he mired us in?

In anguish, he whispered, "They'll kill her if they find out."

For a split second, I wavered. I could do the responsible thing, the *adult* thing: go to Father, and thereby break my brother's heart. Or I could cast my vote with Travis, and we could face the fire together.

I said, "First we have to get her out of sight. Help me."

Together we lifted the thrashing sack and carried it into the barn. We hid Bandit near her old cage and then regrouped. Hauling a thirty-pound raccoon around was harder work than you'd think.

I grabbed a shovel and said, "We've got to bury the evidence."

We returned to the pen, where the hens, calmer now, were starting to investigate the bodies of their former sisters. I thought about burying the corpses right there, but we were in sight of the back porch. Better to get them out of there and bury them later. While I spaded dirt over the blood, I ordered Travis to take the dead hens into the barn.

He said, "I . . . I don't think I can."

"Oh, for goodness' sake, this is no time to be queasy." I handed him the shovel and grabbed both hens by the feet and carried them, necks flopping, into the barn.

The next order of business was to clean ourselves up. We went to the trough and took turns scouring each other with my wet handkerchief. Having no mirror, I wiped the blood from his cheek (without telling him what it was), and then he rubbed the egg from my chin. We inspected each other and, although we were somewhat disheveled, decided we could pass cursory inspection.

"Now what do we do?" he said.

"We have to take her as far away as we can. Far enough so that she won't come back."

"We could put her in the wheelbarrow and take her down the road to Prairie Lea."

Although this wasn't the best plan in the world, I was relieved that he was at least now thinking on his feet.

"We could do that," I said, "but we'd probably run into someone we know, and it might get back to Mother and Father. I think we'll have to go downriver on one of the deer paths." Lucky for us, Sunday afternoons were relatively relaxed, a time of loosened supervision. I figured we could get away with a few hours' absence.

"Stay here," I said. "I'll tell them we're going on a nature walk."

I ran to the back porch, took a moment to smooth myself down, and went into the kitchen, where Viola was cooking lunch. The second she laid eyes on me, she said, "What is it? What's wrong?" There was real worry in her face, so apparently I didn't look as normal as I thought. Her concern, along with the stress roiling within me, was almost too much. How easy it would be to break down in tears right then and there, but this was a luxury neither I nor Travis could afford. For better or worse, my brother's happiness depended on me.

I got a grip and said, "Will you please tell Mother that Travis and I are going on a nature walk? We won't go far, and we'll be back by supper." I ran out the door before she could quiz me further, and before I broke down.

Travis spoke soothing words to Bandit, who uttered sporadic protests. I was grateful that the sack was made of thick canvas, but with her wily brain and dexterous paws, I worried about how long it would hold her. She was probably plotting her escape at that very moment.

"Come on, we have to hurry. We'll take the path to the inlet." Neither of us owned a watch, but I reckoned by the sun that we had about four hours, maybe five at the most.

I took the two dead hens. Travis lifted the sack to hissing and muttering; we set off, alternately trotting and walking through the scrub. At the inlet I dropped the two sad corpses into the shallow water, where the assorted wildlife would be grateful to receive them.

We pressed on, taking turns with our unhappy burden. If you think it's easy carrying a grumbling, thrashing sack of raccoon for miles, think again. Sometimes we lugged her between us, and sometimes we slung the sack over our backs like Santa Claus toting the world's most uncooperative gift. Often we had to stop and rest. We had not a crumb of food between us and nothing to drink but river water. At one point, Travis proposed we open the sack and give Bandit some water too, but hastily retracted his suggestion when he saw the look on my face.

We struggled on, branches whipping us in the face, thorns tearing our legs, sweat bees and no-see-ums adding to our torment, but thankfully, we saw no one and no one saw us. Finally, when we could go no farther, we collapsed in a heap. I judged we were about halfway to Prairie Lea.

Travis panted, "Thanks, Callie. I guess I owe you one."

"Wrong. You owe me about a million. Now open the sack."

I watched his face change with the realization that the moment of farewell was at hand.

He had barely loosened the rope when Bandit's sharp, impatient nose protruded and she shoved her way out, more than ready for her freedom. She scampered off a few yards and then sniffed the ground, sniffed the air, turned, and sniffed at us. Then she ambled back to Travis and gave him one of those expectant, where's-my-dinner kind of looks.

I said, "Go on, Bandit, go away," and stamped my foot. She ignored me. "Travis, we have to go. Turn away, don't look at her. Come on and follow me. Right now." I headed back down the trail.

"Bye, Bandit," he said, and I heard the agony in his voice. "Be a good girl. Have a nice life and be a good girl." He dashed the tears from his eyes and followed me.

And Bandit followed him.

"Stop," I cried, and waved my arms at her. She barely glanced my way.

"Travis," I said in mounting desperation, "you have to make her go."

She stood up on her hind legs and put her paws on his knees. Tears streamed down his face and fell into her fur. He reached down to pick her up, and I screamed, "Don't, you're killing her! If she comes back, they'll shoot her. You know they will."

Stricken, he said, "Go 'way, Bandit." Then more sternly, "Scoot!" He pushed her off his knee, and she looked at him with, I swear, puzzlement.

"Yell at her," I said. "Chase her off."

He raised his voice and flapped his arms. "Scoot, Bandit!"

"Louder," I said. "More."

He screamed at her, and she looked uncertain. He charged at her, and she backed away.

Then he did what I'm sure was the hardest thing of his young life: He picked up a handful of stones and started throwing them at her, weeping and yelling the whole time. "Go away, you stupid raccoon," he screamed. "I can't love you anymore."

The first stone whizzed over her head, and she turned to look at whatever it was behind her. The second one struck the ground in front of her paws, and she flinched. The third rock struck her on the flanks with a faint thunk. It wasn't a very big stone, only a pebble, and it probably didn't hurt, but I couldn't tell who was more shocked, she or Travis. The hair on the back of her neck stood up. She growled like a dog at her former lord and master, turned tail, and disappeared into the bush.

Sobbing, Travis wheeled and ran down the trail toward home. I followed him, helpless, filled with pity and admiration, sending up a silent prayer to the raccoon gods that none of us would ever set eyes on Bandit again.

IF THE TRIP OUT had been miserable, the trip home was excruciating. Scratched, sunburned, hungry, weary, and burdened not with a raccoon but a heartbroken brother.

When we stopped to rest, I hugged him and said, "You did a brave thing. You saved her, you know."

He only nodded and sobbed. He managed to cry himself out and wipe most of the grief from his face by the time we got home, for which I was grateful. We did our best to tidy ourselves before going inside but still were met with quizzical looks at the table. Lamar spoke to me in a voice carefully calculated for me (but not Mother) to hear: "You look like someone dragged you through the cactus patch backward and beat you with buzzard guts. Har."

I was too tuckered out to come up with a smart retort. Travis and I managed to hold it together through the meal, and I was proud of both of us. But there was one thing we'd forgotten. How to explain the loss of two hens out of fourteen? If I'd been thinking more clearly, I'd have torn an "escape" hole in the corner of the pen to explain their disappearance.

Viola noted their absence the next day when collecting eggs for breakfast. She must have guessed that we had something to do with it but she never brought it up. She must have figured that we had paid a high enough price—whatever it was—for the goings-on, whatever they were.

A week later, the scab healing over Travis's grief was ripped open again when we discovered what we figured was Bandit's former den, a dry hole in the riverbank where she'd been living before he found her. The rank hole was littered with chicken bones and fish guts and even a filthy scrap of cloth that turned out to be part of a man's shirt, filched, no doubt, from some housewife's clothesline.

Travis paled and said, "It's too close to home. If she comes back here, she might come all the way back to the house."

Our discovery caused him several sleepless nights but—thank goodness—we never saw that raccoon again. I sympathized with Travis as best I could until I had to face an animal trauma of my own.

CHAPTER 13

DR. PRITZKER IN ACTION

Many of the remedies used by the people of the country
are ludicrously strange, but too disgusting to be mentioned.

DR. PRITZKER WAS NOW OFFICIALLY in business, with Viola's
nephew Samuel as his newly hired assistant. He had rented an
office off Main Street that shared a corral and stable with the
blacksmith, an arrangement that would increase business for them
both. Our opportunity to see the doctor in action came soon
enough. The draft horse King Arthur had gone lame and was
getting worse. Our family owned six heavy horses, four riding
horses, and Sunshine, the vicious elderly Shetland pony that most
of us were now too big or too smart to ride, what with her propensity for trying to take a chunk out of your leg and hanging
on like a snapping turtle.

Dr. Pritzker and Samuel pulled up in a cart drawn by a buckskin mare. Samuel unloaded a big clanking canvas bag and carried it to the barn. Travis and I trailed along behind, interested
in how a veterinarian with only one usable arm could possibly
manage.

"How is your hand, Dr. Pritzker?" I said.

"It's getting a little stronger, Calpurnia. Nice of you to ask. I have a ball of India rubber, and I squeeze it as hard as I can for ten minutes every morning and evening. The exercise improves the muscles, you see." He held up his clawed hand and tried to waggle the stiff fingers.

"I see," I said doubtfully. It looked about the same to me.

We followed them into the cool depths of the barn where stood King Arthur, a great gentle dapple-gray Clydesdale with feathered hooves and a mild personality much at odds with his intimidating physique. If you wanted to, you could fit half a dozen children along his back. And unlike Sunshine, he wouldn't even blink, let alone try and take a hunk out of you.

Arthur stood on three legs, the left front leg canted off the ground. His head drooped; his eyes were filmy. He looked the very picture of an unwell equine.

Samuel and Dr. Pritzker each put on a leather apron and entered the stall. Samuel secured a rope to Arthur's halter, smoothing his forelock and gently rubbing the long face.

Travis said, "What's wrong with him, Dr. Pritzker?"

"You see how he's standing? He doesn't want to put any weight on that hoof, which means it's either founder or an abscess. Let's hope it's an abscess."

"Why?" Travis said.

"Because founder is hell—uh, difficult to treat, unlike an abscess, which is easy to fix."

"How do you fix it?"

"You'll see. Snub him up tight now, Samuel."

Samuel looped the rope through a tie-down ring and then gently lifted the leg, cradling the hoof in his hands. Dr. Pritzker produced a strangely shaped tool that looked rather like a medieval instrument of torture. Being used to Granddaddy's lessons, I expected him to tell me its name and its uses. But he said nothing, merely started pressing it against various parts of Arthur's hoof.

I spoke up impatiently. "What *is* that thing?"

He glanced up and seemed surprised. But why? Was I just supposed to stand there being decorative? What about learning something new? Granddaddy always said that life was full of opportunities to learn something new about the world, and one should glean all one could from an expert in his field, no matter what that field might be.

Dr. Pritzker said, "It's called a hoof tester. You compress various parts of the hoof with it, and it tells you where the pain is." He tapped gently. Arthur flinched and whickered and tried to toss his head against the rope.

"Abscess, I think." He pulled a long curved knife from his tool bag and said, "I'm not sure you should watch this."

"Why not?" I said.

"Well, it's not a sight for those of delicate constitution."

Me? Delicate? What a laugh. I said, "I only look delicate, but I'm not. Really."

"Well, I doubt your momma would approve."

"She doesn't care," I lied. I had no idea what he was referring to but I knew for a fact that anything Mother didn't approve of would probably be really interesting.

"I suspect she'll care about this. Better stand back."

We took a small step back.

"A bit more."

We took another small step back. He looked as if he was going to order us back again, so I said, "We have to be able to *see*, you know."

"Don't say I didn't warn you," he said wryly. I barely had time to think, *Warn us about what?* when he inserted the point of the knife into the bottom of the hoof and twisted it. A great gout of foul-smelling black fluid erupted from the hoof; it fountained all the way across the stall and splattered on the far wall, missing us by inches.

"Yow!" I'd never seen anything like it. It was dumbfounding . . . disgusting . . . amazing. I turned to Travis. "Did you see that?"

He didn't answer. He was breathing heavily and had turned an interesting greenish hue.

I said to Dr. Pritzker, "What *is* all that stuff?"

"That's the pus and blood from the infection. He'll start to feel better now that it's out."

"And he's been carrying all that stuff around in his hoof? Why does it smell like that?"

"That's the smell the germs make when they're breaking down the tissues of the body. That's what produces pus."

Lucky it had missed us. I could imagine Mother's reaction if I showed up covered in horse pus. Black horse pus at that. She'd never let me out of the house—no, out of my room—ever again.

Never ever in my whole life. (Actually that might not be so bad, as long as I could have all the books I wanted, and not just Aggie's dull biographies.)

Samuel left to get a bucket of hot water and Epsom salts from Viola. Travis leaned against the stable door.

"Are you all right?" I said.

He gulped. "Yep. Fine."

"Are you sure? You don't look so good."

"Fine."

I turned my attention back to Dr. Pritzker and watched him run his good hand over Arthur, checking his teeth and withers and fetlocks and hocks.

"He's a grand horse otherwise," he said. "Should be good for many years of plowing yet."

Far from bearing a grudge, Arthur actually looked better already and seemed to enjoy the knowledgeable hand moving over him. Samuel returned with the bucket, and the two of them maneuvered it under the infected hoof. Arthur sank his leg into the bucket, sighing in what sounded like relief. I glanced at Travis and noted that his color was improving.

"The heat will draw out the rest of the infection," Dr. Pritzker said. "Then we'll put a bandage on it to keep it clean."

"You know what?" I said. "Granddaddy says the days of the horse are numbered. He says that soon we'll all be using automobiles to plow. I can't see it myself. But he's generally right about such things."

"Well, I think he's right about that. They're using steam

tractors in some parts of the country, although I'd hate to see these old fellows go, myself." He offered Arthur a palm full of grain and thumped his thick neck affectionately.

"All right," he said, "now we'll put the bandage on." He pulled a square of chammy leather from his bag while Samuel lifted the foot from the bucket and dried it with a clean cotton rag. He and Samuel secured the leather, finishing up with a binding of thin rawhide cord to hold it all in place. I watched closely and said, "Why are you doing that?"

"It's important to keep it all clean until it heals up. We don't want other germs getting in there where they don't belong. We'll check on him tomorrow."

That evening Travis and I took a stroll through the barn and stopped at the patient's stall. To my dismay, Arthur was tugging at the cords around his hoof and had managed to pull the bandage halfway off.

"Oh, Arthur," I said, "you bad horse. What are we going to do with you?"

Arthur gave no answer, but Travis said, "Should I run for Dr. Pritzker?"

"We could send for him, or . . ." Longish pause while I thought furiously.

"Or what?"

"I could fix it."

"Really?" Travis sounded impressed. "You know how to do that?"

I couldn't back out now, so I slipped into the stall. "I saw them do it today. It's just a bandage. I can do it. I think. But you'll have to help."

Arthur stood eighteen hands high and weighed about two thousand pounds, but I would rather have dealt with him than Sunshine the Shetland, shorter of stature and fouler of temper. Better the gentle giant than the nasty midget, to my way of thinking. Arthur nudged me in a friendly way, no doubt thinking of the many apples I'd brought him over the years. Good. I wanted him to remember those apples, every single one of them.

I tied his halter rope short and then tried to pick up his foot. Nothing happened. I leaned against his massive shoulder and pushed. Nothing. I took a deep breath and threw myself against his side. Still nothing. I made a fist and punched him. He took no notice. I might as well have been a gnat.

"Travis," I wheezed, "get me something sharp."

"Like what?"

"I don't know, something sharp. A hatpin will do."

"A hatpin? In the barn?"

"Something, anything, and for goodness' sake, hurry up."

He ran to the tack room and returned a moment later with a screwdriver. "Will this do?"

I grunted and took it from him. He said, "What are you going to do with that?"

I wondered if, despite Arthur's placid nature, I was taking my life in my hands. I wondered if he would pound me into oatmeal and I would live out my days in the Austin Home for Crippled Children.

"Oh boy," I muttered, "here we go. Forgive me, Arthur." I drew my arm back and then let fly, poking the muscular shoulder with a good hard jab, enough to startle him but not enough to break the skin. Travis cried out. Arthur snorted in surprise, pulled away, and . . . lifted his foot. I dropped the screwdriver, threw all my weight against him, and pulled at the dressing, centering it over the hoof and retying the cords. It was fiddly business and had to be done quickly. It took me only a few seconds but it felt like an hour and I broke out in a light sweat.

"Whew," I said, easing my weight off his shoulder. Arthur put his foot down in the straw. The bandage did not move.

"Hey, Callie, that's pretty good. Maybe you could be an animal doctor."

I didn't pay him much attention. I was still breathing hard, happy to have survived my first horse doctoring with all my limbs intact.

The next day was Saturday, so Travis and I hung about until Dr. Pritzker and Samuel returned to check on their patient. Samuel led Arthur out of the stall so that we could observe his gait. The bandage was intact and he walked with barely a limp. Dr. Pritzker picked up the foot and frowned over it.

Uh-oh.

"These are not my usual knots," he said as I edged away.

Surely somebody in the house needed me for something. Had I made my bed? Had I fed my newt?

Dr. Pritzker went on, "Did Alberto do this? It's nice work."

I stopped in my tracks. Travis piped up proudly. "We did it. It came off, so we put it back on."

"You did this?"

We both nodded.

"Well, little man, I am quite impressed. You've done a very tidy job. Perhaps you could be a veterinarian yourself one day."

What? I couldn't believe my ears. The "little man" stood there and grinned. I poked him with my elbow.

"Ow." He turned to me and remonstrated, "I did help, you know." He saw the look on my face and added, "A bit." Then he fessed up: "Callie's really the one that did it. She's good at that kind of stuff."

Dr. Pritzker looked at us doubtfully, as if we might be telling tales.

"So," Travis went on, "maybe we could both be animal doctors, right?"

"Hmm," Dr. Pritzker said.

I expected not doubt but praise, and prompted him with, "Couldn't I be a veterinarian too?"

It had never seriously occurred to me to consider such a goal, but now that I'd said it aloud, I rather liked the sound of it.

"Well," he said, "I've never heard of such a thing. It's dirty, heavy work, and too much for a lady. I spend half my days wrestling a steer in the mud and the other half getting kicked by a mule. Can't exactly see a lady doing that, can you, Samuel?"

"No, sir, not hardly." They both enjoyed a lonnnnggg rich laugh at this fine joke. I could have smacked them both.

Dr. Pritzker went on, "But take Travis here. He could go to veterinary college if he wanted to. Have you thought about that, young man? It's a fine career for someone who loves animals. But you'd have to work hard for two years, and the tuition costs quite a bit of money."

What about *me*? Why was he ignoring *me* and talking to the boy who couldn't face worm guts? I wheeled and stormed into the house and was heading upstairs when Mother called from the parlor, "Time for your piano."

Drat. I should have headed for Granddaddy's laboratory, but too late. The daily half hour of practice was inviolate. I stomped my foot in frustration, and Mother called, "You'd better not be stomping your foot. Come in here at once."

I went into the parlor, made note of the time on the mantel clock, and sat down for thirty minutes—not one minute more— my mood blacker than horse pus. I attacked Mr. Gioacchino Rossini's "William Tell Overture" with unprecedented ferocity, which, coincidentally, is exactly what the piece called for.

Mother said, "My goodness, you're playing with such verve today. Why don't you play like that more often? It's a definite improvement. Miss Brown will be so pleased."

Ah, yes, Miss Brown, our aged piano teacher. She of the menacing ruler and a tongue sharp enough to lance a boil. (No need for a vet, just call Miss Brown!) It was important to keep the old bat happy, for even though I'd talked my way out of having to perform at the annual recital, I was still stuck with weekly lessons until I turned eighteen. A lifetime away.

Then it was time to change into a clean pinafore for dinner. At meals, everyone except Granddaddy was expected to make polite chitchat and keep up their end of what Mother called "the art of conversation." Even J.B., only six years of age, was expected to contribute. That evening his contribution was, "Today I learned how to spell *cat. T-A-C.* That spells *cat.* Did you know that, Mama?"

"Uh, well, dear, perhaps we'll work on that some more tomorrow. Travis, what about you?"

He popped up with, "Yesterday, me and Callie got to see Dr. Pritzker open King Arthur's abscess, and a whole bunch of pus came out. It was like a regular fountain. You should have seen it."

"Excuse me?" said Mother.

I kicked him under the table.

"Yeah," he went on, "and Dr. Pritzker said that I could be an animal doctor. Do you think I could, Father? He says it's two whole years of study, and it's a lot of hard work, and it costs a lot of money."

Father studied Travis thoughtfully before saying, "Well, the population of Texas is growing, and the demand for beef is growing. It seems to me that the need for veterinarians must surely grow as well. You'd have a good steady income to support yourself and your future family." He smiled and said, "My boy, I think it's a fine occupation to pursue. And don't you worry about the cost. I'm sure we'll find a way to manage."

Travis glowed with pleasure, then looked at me and said, "Callie changed King Arthur's bandage, and the doctor said she did a good job. She'd make a really good vet too."

The table fell silent. I suddenly realized that the moment and the stage were mine. I took a deep breath and said, "Maybe Travis and I could go together."

Mother and Father looked startled. Even Granddaddy snapped out of his usual mealtime reverie and regarded me with interest. Father glanced at Mother, cleared his throat, and said, "Well, Calpurnia, we might be able to, uh, send you to college for a year. That should be long enough for you to earn your teaching certificate, I should think."

I couldn't believe what I was hearing. One year. Not two.

"And who knows?" he went on, looking at Mother for help. "You might, heh-heh, meet a young man and get married in the meantime."

One year. Not two. One. Which meant I would be allowed exactly half the education of Travis. The injustice of it overwhelmed me. Then what popped into my head was the question that—the moment it came to me—I realized I'd been waiting to ask my whole life.

I said, "How is that fair?"

Father and Mother stared at me as if I had sprouted another head.

"Indeed," murmured Granddaddy, "an excellent question."

"Do you think I'm not smart enough? Is that it?"

Mother looked uncomfortable and said, "It's not that, Calpurnia. It's just—"

"Just *what*?" I snapped.

She shot me a warning glance to let me know that I was perilously close to crossing the line into unacceptable behavior. "This is not the time or place for this discussion. Let us say that we've always had other plans for you and leave it at that. Sully, please pass the gravy to your father."

A red mist descended over my vision. Hives of fury erupted on my neck. Here we were in a brand-new century. And here I'd been thinking of myself as an example of the modern American girl. What a joke! My throat constricted but I forced out the words: "What about *my* plans, *my* plans for me? What about that?"

Lamar snickered and said, "Why should *you* go to college? You're only a girl. You don't hardly count."

Father frowned and said, "Lamar, you will not speak to your sister in that tone."

And even in my rage, I registered the difference between what my father was saying and what he was not saying. He was not saying that Lamar was wrong. Only that he was rude.

I tried to muster a suitable retort for Lamar and a convincing argument for my parents, but to my mortification, I burst into tears. Everyone gawked at me. Their gaze felt so hot on my skin that I could not bear it a moment longer. I shoved myself away from the table and ran upstairs and threw myself on my miserable pallet. No one came to offer comfort; there was only me to comfort me. I wiped away my tedious tears and realized that, for the first time in history, a Tate child had left the table without being excused. I had thus achieved the world's tiniest victory. Not enough. Not enough.

An hour later, Aggie came up to get ready for bed. I stewed in a volcanic mood, alternating between fits of rage and sorrow.

"Boy," she said, "you sure put your foot in it."

"Oh, shut up," I snapped. "Who asked you?" And with that, I rolled over to face the wall.

This apparently shocked her into silence. In truth, it shocked me too. I'd never said those words to someone older, not even Lamar.

It seemed to me that everything boiled down to one question that kept repeating in my head: Am I not as smart as my brothers? The answer was no. No, I was not.

I was smarter.

And if I had to make my own way in the world, so be it. I would find that way.

CHAPTER 14

MONEY TROUBLES

Captain Fitz Roy seized on a party of natives as hostages
for the loss of a boat, which had been stolen ... and some
of these natives, as well as a child whom he bought for a
pearl-button he took with him to England. ...

IT WAS SATURDAY, a cold, rainy, miserable Saturday, and I had
been ordered to perch on a hassock in the parlor and knit yet
another mitten. I was improving, but did I care? I did not.

Mother and Aggie worked on their stitchery. J.B. stacked
wooden blocks in the corner, chortling and murmuring some
nonsense tale to himself that only he could follow. A cheery fire
of pecan logs popped and sputtered in the grate against the dreary
weather and my equally dreary mood.

The doorbell rang, signaling a reprieve from my labors. I
sprang to my feet, crying, "I'll get it." It was my teacher, Miss
Harbottle, come to discuss matters with Aggie and Mother. I
took her soaked pelisse and dripping umbrella and parked them
in the hall tree. With her plain black clothes and bedraggled
hat, she displayed all the charm of a wet crow.

"Are you keeping well, Calpurnia?"

"Very well, thank you, Miss Harbottle," I said, dropping a small curtsy, which seemed to please her. "And yourself?"

We exchanged the usual pleasantries. For someone such as myself, who was often accused of being pert at school (and who spent an inordinate amount of time in the Corner of Shame as a consequence), I felt oddly shy around my teacher outside of school. School was her natural environment, and I always experienced a mild shock of discomfort running across her in "the outside world." It felt a bit like finding a snake in my chest of drawers or an armadillo in Travis's bedroom.

I escorted her into the parlor, where Mother and Aggie rose to shake her hand and make polite inquiries about her health. Mother turned to me, saying, "Callie, please ask Viola to bring us tea and refreshments."

I skipped to the kitchen with a light heart. Refreshments for such an important visitor would no doubt include Viola's chocolate layer cake, a sublime confection surpassing all others, and normally available to us children only on special occasions. I figured I could cadge a slice by sticking around to pass the teacups (and cake), and generally imitating a model child.

I interrupted Viola, who was peeling—what else?—spuds.

"Mother says tea. Oh, and chocolate cake for four." I didn't include J.B. That would be pushing it, and besides, I could probably keep him quiet with a single forkful of mine.

Viola paused in her labors and squinted at me. "The good china?"

"Yep, it's Miss Harbottle."

Viola changed into a clean apron and got down the tea tray. I left her to it and returned to my hassock in the parlor.

The conversation meandered through various topics that did not much interest me—who was ill and who was well, who had married, who had died. The talk was . . . desultory. Yes, that was a good word, one of my new ones. I'd have to teach it to Travis.

Viola bustled in with the tea tray. I sprang up to help her and count the slices of cake. She retreated to the kitchen, Mother poured, and I passed around the plates and cups. We were about to tuck in when Miss Harbottle arrived at the point of the visit.

Looking first at Mother, she said, "I wonder if Agatha would like to be an assistant at the school? Since she has her diploma, she could be a great help in teaching the little ones their ABCs."

I took my first mouthful of the miraculous cake. Oh, heaven. I chewed slowly, determined to extract every molecule of pleasure. So entranced was I, so busy concentrating on my treat, that at first I did not notice something amiss.

But what?

The murmuring ebb and flow of conversation had stopped. Silence reigned. Then lengthened. I glanced at Mother, who was regarding Aggie with an encouraging expression, the kind of look a mother gives a baby to get her to eat her peas. Aggie in turn ate her cake thoughtfully. What had I missed? The silence lengthened some more. Even J.B. looked up from his blocks.

Mother said, "Aggie, did you not hear what Miss Harbottle said?"

"Oh, I heard," said Aggie. "I was just waiting to hear about the pay."

"Pay?" said Mother, as if she were unfamiliar with the word. "Pay?"

I'd always been taught it was a dreadful faux pas for a lady to discuss money matters in public. Things were getting really interesting.

Miss Harbottle looked shocked and then miffed. "Well, I don't know about that. We were hoping for a volunteer. But I suppose I could go to the school trustees and ask them to pay you a salary of, say, twenty cents an hour."

I did the arithmetic rapidly in my head: six hours a day, times five days a week, times twenty cents an hour, came to . . . six whole dollars. A magnificent sum. I looked at Aggie with new admiration. I guess it hadn't occurred to any of us that she would expect payment for her labor, but the more I thought about it, why not? After all, it was a new century, and surely a girl's labor should now count as much as a boy's. Why, during the last cotton harvest, I'd sulked until Father gave me a nickel to look after the colored children while their parents toiled in the fields. A whole nickel for a whole day. And I'd been thrilled to get it.

Then Aggie did something that flat-out amazed us all. She put down her fork, genteelly dabbed her lips with her napkin, and uttered three words I'd never heard before from girl child, young woman, or grown lady:

"It's not enough."

Goodness! Our mouths flopped open at her audacity. Not simply mentioning money but asking for more! What a fascinating development. The atmosphere was electric. Mother flushed a bright red; Miss Harbottle spluttered and coughed, apparently having inhaled a crumb down the wrong pipe in shock. I ran to the kitchen and pumped her a glass of water, which she gulped down in relief, alternately fanning herself with her hankie and patting her bosom.

Aggie sipped her tea, cooler than any cucumber. "I will need thirty cents an hour."

"Well, I never," huffed Miss Harbottle.

"I do have my diploma, you know. That should be worth another ten cents an hour."

Mother said, "Agatha, you leave me speechless. Where does this mercenary attitude come from? Why this talk of payment? It would be an honor for our family to have you volunteer to teach. Do we not provide adequately for you?"

"You do, Aunt Margaret, and I'm terribly grateful. But I have to do my part to help rebuild our house in Galveston. I want to send money home to Momma and Poppa, you see."

"Oh," said Mother. "Of course. Of course you do."

"Ah," said Miss Harbottle. "I see. A laudable goal, my dear. In that case, I will see what I can do."

And just like that, the weather in the room swung from stormy to fine.

A week later, Aggie found herself the newest employee of the Caldwell County School District at the princely sum of thirty cents per hour. Nine dollars per week. Her temperament—at least at home—improved even more.

School, however, was a different matter, and there she pretended we weren't related and would not return my smile when our paths crossed. We even had to address her as Miss Finch until we got home. She turned out to be a humorless teacher and a firm disciplinarian (not much of a surprise there), and her pupils learned quickly not to misbehave. She taught the ABCs to the young ones, guiding them as they stumbled their way through the tedium of the *McGuffey Reader* with such exciting tales as this one: "The cat. The mat. Is the cat on the mat? The cat is on the mat." Not much of a story, but I suppose we all had to start somewhere.

WATCHING AGGIE COLLECT her weekly pay, I began to think that saving money might be a good idea, although I didn't have any particular goal in mind. Maybe one day I'd have enough to buy train tickets for me and Granddaddy to go to Austin. Maybe one day I could buy my own microscope. Beyond that, I had no real plan. Exercising supreme willpower, I allowed myself to spend only one penny per week on candy, trading with my brothers to achieve a nice, balanced assortment. After receiving my allowance each Friday afternoon, I indulged in the small but satisfying ritual of counting my pennies and nickels and admiring my gold piece before rewrapping it in its bed of tissue paper and replacing the box under the bed. I was up to the remarkable sum of $5.42.

On this particular Friday, I thanked Father for my nickel and raced to my room. I opened the cigar box. The moment I touched the wad of tissue, I knew that something was wrong. I unwrapped it in disbelief.

Gone.

My world tilted and spun. Miss Liberty, my favorite coin, with her sunny complexion, reassuring heft, and promise of the future, was gone. Stunned, I scrabbled through the contents of the box—the lesser coins, the smaller treasures, the scraps of paper—knowing, even as I did so, that I would not find it.

Gone.

All right then, gone. Time to get a grip and accept it. Time to apply my superior brain power to getting it back. I inspected the box. One of the corners was frayed as if something had nibbled at it, but it looked too small to squeeze the coin through. Who or what had been under my bed? Mice, for sure. The snake, probably. Had it been attracted like a magpie to the coin's shiny surface and taken it off behind the baseboards? No, that struck me as too far-fetched. Sir Isaac Newton had been under the bed; I had found him there before encrusted with dust. But I checked and he was floating in his dish, inert, the wire cover anchored with a rock.

I moved on to human suspects. One of my brothers? Father would kill them if he found out. None of them would dare, although Lamar might be a possibility. How about SanJuanna, our maid of long standing? Trustworthy as the day is long, I'd heard Mother once describe her. And Viola, who had been with us since before Harry was born? Unthinkable. So that left . . . Aggie.

Of course, the most obvious of all. Grasping, driven by money, she had the means, the motive, and the opportunity. And she was no sibling, no sister, no "first-degree" relation. Our attenuated blood ties might allow her conscience to steal from me. Thinking like Sherlock Holmes, I felt it all click into place. It had to be her.

And right at that moment, "her" came in, tossing me—the wronged individual, the wounded party—the coolest of glances.

"What are you doing?" she said casually without any trace of guilt. Oh, ice water ran in her veins, all right. She sat in the dresser chair, took off her hat, and smoothed her hair.

And that's when I charged her and pushed her from the chair. She yelped and sprawled on the floor in a most unbecoming posture, her skirt hiked up to show her petticoat.

"Are you *crazy*?" she said.

I stood over her, panting, my hands clawed in rage, and although she was four years older and a foot taller, fear flickered in her thieving eyes. She clambered awkwardly to her feet, her clothes and hair in disarray.

"Give it back," I choked.

"What's wrong with you? Have you lost your *mind*?"

I advanced on her, and she backed into the corner.

"Give. It. Back."

"What are you talking about?"

"My money. Give it back."

"Don't come any closer." She held up both hands to stiff-arm me away. "I have no idea what you're talking about."

Her expression was so wholly incredulous that a glimmer of uncertainty arose within me. It also occurred to me that if she wanted to, she could probably best me in a fight. I stopped advancing on her and said as calmly as I could, "My coin. The five-dollar gold piece you took from me."

"I took nothing from you. You're crazy."

And this time I believed her. She shoved past me and ran downstairs, leaving me to slowly deflate like a sad balloon. Now I was in for it.

Sure enough, one minute later, Mother's voice rose from the bottom of the stairs, angrier than I'd ever heard her: "Calpurnia! Come down here at once."

I knew that the loss of my money was nothing compared to the trouble I'd made for myself by assaulting my cousin. Ach. I trudged down the stairs, trying to concoct some kind of defense, but I knew I had none.

I entered the parlor and took the place on the Turkey carpet traditionally reserved for children in trouble. I'd stood there many a time before, head bowed, so I was well familiar with the intricate pattern.

"Well?" demanded Mother. "Is it true? That you attacked Aggie and pushed her to the floor? Tell me it can't be true."

This seemed an odd way to put it. Was it an invitation to lie? I peeked at her and quickly looked away. I'd never seen her so furious.

"Sorry, Mother," I whispered, meek as a mouse.

"What was that? Speak up!"

"Sorry, Mother," louder this time.

"It's Aggie you should be apologizing to, not me."

"Sorry, Aggie." I ground my toe into the small bare spot in the pattern, the bare spot I'd helped my brothers wear away over the years.

Mother shrilled, "Look her in the eye when you say it!"

"I am sorry, Aggie, truly," spoken this time in heartfelt tones. "I . . . I thought you'd stolen my gold coin."

"Hmpf," Aggie sneered.

Offering up my excuse did not have the desired effect of calming Mother down. Her voice grew louder and shriller. "The gold your father gave you? You've lost it? How *could* you be so careless?"

"I didn't lose it. Someone stole it."

"Nonsense! No one under this roof would do such a thing. Father gives you a ten-dollar gold piece, and what do you do? You lose it of your own carelessness."

I blinked at her in confusion. "Uh, you mean a five-dollar piece, right?"

She stared at me in equal incomprehension. "*Ten* dollars, not *five*. Is this another example of your ingratitude, you wretched girl?"

Incipient hives prickled my neck. "I . . . I don't—"

She snapped, "The ten dollars Father gave you. And now you've *lost* it. Out of my sight. Go to your room. No, wait, go outside. Allow Aggie some peace and quiet. You're to stay out of your room until bedtime, understand?"

"But I—"

"*Understand?*"

"Yes, Mother. And I truly am sorry, Aggie. I hope you'll forgive me."

She said only, "Hmm . . . well."

I went out the front door and stood on the porch, scratched at a hive or two, and promptly burst into tears of rage and confusion. What was going on? What could she be talking about? Sam Houston and Travis appeared at the far end of the drive, but rather than allowing them to view my humiliation, I dashed into the scrub and headed for the river.

Arriving at the inlet, I sat down on the bank and cried over the injustice of it all. And my own stupidity. I had violated Granddaddy's instructions in observation, analysis, and judgment. I had jumped to a conclusion without a proper foundation, and look where it had landed me: in record-setting trouble, probably for the rest of my life. And I was no closer to solving the theft. I dipped my hankie in the cool water and bathed my face, never mind that I was applying untold numbers of *Volvox* and *Paramecia* to my skin. As my complexion gradually cooled, so did my temper. Could I have misplaced the money? It didn't seem possible. Thinking about where it might have gone made my head hurt. Instead, I concentrated on applying my vaunted intellect to the question of five dollars versus ten. Either Mother was mistaken or she was correct. There was no way I'd approach either her or Father to ask, so I'd have to figure it out. Well, the older boys got a dime allowance; the younger boys and I only got a nickel. Father, using the same reasoning, must have given the older children ten dollars and the younger ones five dollars. But I did not know this for a fact. Which of the older boys would tell me? Perhaps Harry would know, even though I didn't remember him lining up in the hall that day. Approaching Lamar, with his maddening superior ways (for which I could see no justification) would be my last resort. So that left Sam Houston, and he seemed like a pretty good candidate. We mostly got along all right, except for those times when he fell under Lamar's sway. Sam it would be.

I heard Viola ring her bell on the back porch to signal dinner. I dried my face and hands and headed home with my plan in place.

Dinner was a tense affair. Mother was quiet; Father regarded me with consternation; Harry looked at me as if I were some kind of species he'd never seen before; Aggie's expression was studiously blank. My brothers, who had obviously heard the news, cut sideways glances at me as they spooned up their soup. I spoke not a word and mostly kept my head down, peeking up every now and then like a turtle in its shell. Travis telegraphed silent sympathy by waggling his eyebrows. Only Granddaddy and the baby seemed oblivious to the stormy atmosphere in the dining room. J.B. filled up the unaccustomed void in conversation by prattling on about his good Confederate toy soldiers and how they'd killed all the bad Yankee soldiers and how he'd fired his pop gun, and how he'd learned how to spell *dog*: *D-O-O-G*.

Mother in her distraction murmured, "That's nice, dear."

SanJuanna cleared the main course and spooned out bowls of cherry cobbler drizzled with fresh cream. She placed a bowl in front of me, causing Mother to come awake with a sharp, "No dessert for Calpurnia. And none for the next two—no, make it three—weeks."

There was a sharp intake of breath around the table at this unprecedented punishment, and although draconian in the extreme, I was in no position to protest.

Travis murmured, "You can have some of mine, Callie," to which Mother posted the immediate addendum: "And no one is to share with her!"

I sat with my hands in my lap while Lamar ostentatiously smacked his lips and said, "Gosh, this is the best cobbler ever."

So like him.

On the way upstairs to bed, I ran into Travis and Sam Houston on the landing. Good. An older brother and a younger one.

"Sam," I said, keeping my voice low, "when Father came home from Galveston and he gave us all some money, how much did he give you?"

"Ten dollars in gold. Why?"

"I just wondered." Then I turned to Travis and said, "He gave you five, right?"

My younger brother looked puzzled and spoke the few words that would break my heart. "No. He gave me ten, but he said not to talk about it. He gave each of us ten."

"Each of us ten," I repeated dully. So ten for the older boys and ten for the younger boys. But not for me. I pushed past them and ran to my room, where I flung myself on my pallet and let loose another torrent of bitter tears. I cried over my lost fortune and the unfairness of being blamed for it. I cried over my future. I cried over my prospects, shrinking rather than expanding as the years slipped by, hemmed in on all sides by the dismal expectations of others.

Aggie came in to prepare for bed. She ignored me and lit the lamp and changed into her nightgown. She brushed and braided her hair, continuing to ignore me.

Finally she said, "Oh, stop crying." She fished a hankie out of the snake drawer and shoved it at me, saying, "Here. I'm not mad at you anymore. Now, get ready for bed so I can turn out the light."

But I couldn't stop. And I couldn't tell her I'd put our fight behind me. I couldn't tell her that I wept over the hard fact of being a half citizen in my own home.

CHAPTER 15

THANKSGIVING

It has always been a mystery to me on what the albatross,
which lives far from the shore, can subsist; I presume that,
like the condor, it is able to fast long; and that one good
feast on the carcass of a putrid whale lasts for a long time.

THE DREARY WEEKS wore on, and Thanksgiving approached,
although I myself could see little to be thankful about. It was my
turn to be in charge of raising the turkeys that year. We always
raised three: one for the family, one for the help, and one for the
poor at the other end of town. Travis had raised them the year
before and had, naturally enough, befriended his charges, going
so far as to name them Reggie, Tom Turkey, and Lavinia.
Disastrous, really, if you considered their ultimate fate, so I discouraged Travis from accompanying me to the turkey pen. For
once this was not difficult. He'd learned the hard way that one
couldn't afford to become fond of creatures bound for the dinner table.

I had named my turkeys but I'd called them Small, Medium,
and Big, a classification system with nothing personal about it
(although perhaps it would have been more appropriate to call

them Dumb, Dumber, and Dumbest). I fed and watered them twice a day but kept my heart cold and aloof.

Question for the Notebook: What is the point of the male turkey's wattle? Is it strictly for looks (gah), or temperature control, or what? I'd seen the green anole lizards, *Anolis carolinensis*, who lived in the lilies along our front walk inflate and deflate their pink neck pouches to entice females and repel males. But the turkey's appendage struck me as so singularly ugly that I wasn't convinced that even a lady turkey could find it attractive.

Two days before the holiday, I was pressed into making apple tarts under close supervision; Aggie volunteered to make what she grandly called her "specialty," a pie of peach preserves in brandy with blackberry compote drizzled on top. The day before the big meal, we were all shooed out to allow Viola and SanJuanna to get down to it. Their preparations were massive, and even Mother joined in, her sleeves rolled up, her hair bound in a kerchief. She fortified herself with periodic headache powders and Lydia Pinkham's, and looked tired but happy.

Father, concerned about her delicate constitution, cautioned her, "Be careful not to overtax yourself, my dear."

The Day of Thanks dawned. We all ate a meager breakfast in anticipation of the huge meal that lay ahead. In consequence, by lunchtime I was practically starving, but the kitchen, filled with alluring smells, clouds of steam, and the cacophony of clanging pots, was off-limits.

Nevertheless (and knowing better), I girded my loins and stuck my head around the door. Viola juggled pots and platters madly like a master conjuror, every move a marvel of practiced efficiency, and even though I did not aspire to her talents, I nonetheless had to admire them. Her lower lip, distended by the plug of snuff that she inevitably took under such exhausting conditions, gave her an intimidatingly pugnacious look.

"Viola," I said in my meekest voice, "do you think I could—"

"*Out!*"

"But I'm hun—"

"*Out!*"

What a grouch, but I really couldn't blame her. I consoled myself with a stale macaroon I'd stashed away in my room for just such emergencies, sparse comfort in light of the enticing smells wafting through the house.

At two o'clock, we lined up for our baths, and at three o'clock, Mother went upstairs to change into her sapphire evening gown and sparkling jet choker. At four o'clock, our honored guest, Dr. Pritzker, arrived as Aggie and I were setting the table with the best china and crystal (always a dodgy idea with the little boys around).

While waiting for dinner, Dr. Pritzker and Granddaddy and Father entered into an animated discussion of the spread of tick fever across the Rio Grande, along with blackleg and foot-and-mouth disease, bovine maladies that were wreaking havoc on the Texas economy. I lurked on the edge of their conversation and was proud of Granddaddy's fund of microbiology knowledge and the deference paid him by Dr. Pritzker. They debated the merits of dipping cattle in solutions of arsenic and tobacco and sulfur. Dr. Pritzker said, "There's been talk of using electricity to treat the ticks. One of the students at A&M College rigged up an electrical current to the dipping vats and sent a charge into the water as the cattle went through."

Granddaddy, a forward-thinking man, responded with enthusiasm. "An intriguing idea. And what were the results?"

"Unfortunately, the cows dropped dead on the spot. The ticks, on the other hand, all lived to swim away in search of a new herd."

"Fascinating," said Granddaddy. "I imagine some adjustment in the dosage of electricity is called for."

Mother, overhearing this engrossing news, shuddered and turned to Aggie with a bright false smile and inquired after the latest news from her parents. Mother did her best to emulate the grand salons in Austin; tick fever was probably not the kind of polite parlor talk they engaged in there.

I pondered the marvels of electricity and longed for its presence in our lives. The thought of doing away with candles and lamps, and flipping a switch for light, was almost beyond belief. I knew it would never happen in our little part of the globe, sad to say.

At the magic hour of five, Viola sounded the gong at the bottom of the stairs, and we took our seats. I had hoped to be seated next to Dr. Pritzker, but instead he was seated between Travis and Aggie. Was I the only one who noticed the slight frown on her face about this?

Father said the blessing and included a special thanks that our kin had survived the tragedy of the Flood. I peeked over my steepled hands to note that Dr. Pritzker, while appearing attentive and polite, did not bow his head. Strange. And Aggie looked sour for no reason that I could tell. Then we tucked into the massive meal, all shoveling forks and discreetly jostling elbows, eating like farmhands who hadn't seen food in weeks. Dr. Pritzker praised Mother lavishly on the feast, and she glowed under his compliments. There was enough to feed Coxey's Army.

We opened with turtle soup, followed by an appetizer of creamed mushrooms on toast points. Then the turkey I'd raised was brought in to applause, now roasted crispy brown and dressed with currant jelly. I suspect it was Big (also known as Dumbest) but I couldn't be sure. Father stood at the head of the table, sharpened his knife on the steel, and proceeded to carve. There was also a brace of ducks caught with Ajax's help. Although the duck was flavorful, I avoided it; I'd once almost broken a tooth on a hidden shot.

We had roast potatoes, sweet potatoes, green beans, lima beans, corn fritters, glazed squash, and creamed spinach. We all had seconds, and some of us had thirds, and just when we thought we couldn't eat another bite, it was time for dessert. Everyone oohed and aahed over Aggie's pie, as if it were something really special. Nobody made much of a fuss over my tarts, but did I care? I did not.

Travis quizzed Dr. Pritzker so avidly about the care and

feeding of rabbits that Mother had to finally rescue him from this engrossing topic.

Aggie ended up with the coveted wishbone, but I suspect that Mother had craftily orchestrated this with Father's help. Aggie could have pulled it with Dr. Pritzker, but she turned away from him and pulled it with Travis. She got the long end and looked thoughtful, mulling over her wish for so long that the table grew restive.

"Oh," she said, snapping out of it and looking around at our expectant faces. "Well, I wish that everything goes well for Momma and Poppa and our new house and all our dear friends in Galveston." We all applauded politely, but there was something about this that struck me as, well, a little too pat. But how could you possibly object to such a selfless wish? She had come so far and suffered so much.

After dinner the adults retired to the parlor for a glass of fizzy wine, although how they could swallow even one mouthful was beyond me.

We children were strongly encouraged to go outside and play. A few of the boys attempted a halfhearted game of soccer but were too stuffed to do much more than stagger about in slow motion. A couple of the others went upstairs to lie down on their beds; I thought about my pallet with yearning but figured that, once down, it would take a block and tackle to raise me to my feet again.

The thankless task of cleaning up fell to SanJuanna, who'd brought in two of her grown daughters to help, such was the chaos left behind. Mother gave Viola, who had outdone herself, an extra silver dollar for her efforts.

Wisely, I snagged Travis to take a short constitutional walk with me in aid of digestion. It was one of my favorite times of day—the light going purple in the deep autumnal silence, broken only by the faint call of straggling late-migrating geese. We were both too full to make much conversation but we went ahead and made a small wager (three jujubes) on who could spot the first star.

Travis spotted a faint light in the west and chanted, "Star light, star bright, first star I see tonight—"

"That's not a star," I said. "It's the planet Jupiter so it doesn't count."

"*What?*" he said, outraged.

"See how the light is steady? It's not twinkling, so that means it's a planet. Granddaddy told me all about it. It's named after the Roman king of the gods."

"You're just saying that to get out of paying up."

"Travis," I said, furiously scanning my memory, "have I ever lied to you?"

"Well . . . no. At least, not that I can ever tell."

"All righty, then. Even though it *is* the first light in the sky, it's technically not a star. I'm willing to call it a draw, so no jujubes are owed either way."

The most agreeable of my brothers agreed to this, as usual.

We walked to the gin. The workers had all been given the day off, and the absence of the familiar machinery clatter made the place seem eerily quiet. We sat on the dam above the turbines that powered the gin, and I spotted a water moccasin, thick as my arm, coiled in one of the dry spillways. It too was basking in the quiet.

Travis shuddered when I pointed the snake out to him, but Mr. O'Flanagan tolerated their presence as they helped keep the rats down, a perennial problem, gnawing their way as they did through the leather drive belts that ran the machinery. Mr. O'Flanagan had brought in a batch of half-grown kittens once, but the deafening noise had apparently been too much for their sensitive systems, and one by one, they'd decamped for parts unknown. Then he'd brought in Ajax, who'd spent an enthusiastic but unproductive hour sniffing excitedly in the corners, too big to track the rats into their lairs. I wondered if Polly, unchained from his perch, would do the job? I didn't know if he'd eat a rodent or not, but any rat that caught sight of those claws would scuttle for the county line lickety-split.

Travis and I sat in companionable silence, broken only by the loosing of a discreet belch every now and then (perfectly understandable under the circumstances). A handful of bats flitted along the river and charmed us with their acrobatics. They were evidently dalliers storing up bugs for their imminent migration south, or had decided to winter over, in which case folklore held that there would be no snow.

Apropos of nothing, Travis said dreamily, "What do you want to be when you grow up?"

Not one single person in the whole world had ever asked me

that before. Such a huge question, posed so innocently by someone whom I loved and who loved me in turn. And who didn't know any better than to ask it. My heart knotted inside me. A world of choices lay at his feet, but not at mine.

He went on, "I think maybe I really would like to be an animal doctor."

"Really?" I remembered how the sight of my earthworm's innards had so affected him. "You know that you'd have to see, uh, blood and guts and things like that. You do know that, right?"

He thought for a moment and said slowly, "I suppose. How come that stuff doesn't bother you?"

Truth to tell, things like that *did* bother me sometimes but I'd never admit it aloud, especially to a younger brother. I fibbed and said, "It's because I'm a Scientist."

"But how do you stand it? Can you teach me?"

"Um, well, I'm not sure. . . ."

He looked crestfallen, then said the one surefire thing guaranteed to enlist my help: "But you're smart as a tree full of owls, Callie Vee. Can't you figure out a way?"

"Hmm. I'll think on the problem. And maybe I'll talk with Granddaddy about it. If I can't figure it out, maybe he can think of something."

We digested some more in silence. Then to our surprise, a small four-legged figure stepped onto the embankment downstream from the dam.

"Look," Travis gasped.

It was the mystery animal, still alive against all odds, and even looking a little better than before. Its weepy swollen eye had healed, but it was still terribly thin and covered in dark scabs. Despite the falling darkness, I could see that it did not have the delicate, graceful, light-boned build of a fox, but rather its chest was thicker and legs more stumpy, making its appearance more doglike than foxlike. The more I stared at it, the more it looked like a half-grown dog.

The pathetic creature gave its tail a half wag, confirming that it was not in fact vulpine, but canine.

"It's a dog," I said. "I think."

"It can't be. Are you sure? What kind is it?"

"It's what they call a mixed breed." That was certainly an understatement. It looked like someone had taken dollops of several breeds, dropped them in a sack, given it a good shake, then poured out . . . this.

"Do you think Dr. Pritzker would—"

"No. You've got to face facts. You can't save every living thing, even though I know you want to."

The dog gave us another half wag, and this time I could swear I saw a flicker of yearning in its mournful gaze. It had clearly been a domesticated dog at some point—not feral at all. A feral dog would have melted away into the undergrowth at our first approach; it would never have let itself be seen, much less given us a pitiful half wag of its tail. Anger washed over me. Who was the heartless master who had betrayed it, driving it away, abandoning it to cruel fate, expecting it to fend for itself?

The answer came to me in a flash. I wondered how I'd been

so stupid to miss it before. "I know what it is!" I whispered hoarsely. The answer seemed both obvious and a near miracle.

"Shhh, you'll scare it away."

"I've got it now. It's one of Maisie's pups. Can't you see, Travis? It looks a lot like what you'd get if you mixed a terrier with a coyote."

Travis gaped at me. "No, no, it can't be. Mr. Holloway drowned them."

"I know, but we never saw the sack, remember? This one must have gotten out somehow, or maybe it ran away before he drowned the others. It's probably been living on fish guts from the dock and garbage from the dump." A less happy thought suddenly occurred to me: "And stolen chickens." Oh, dear, that could be a problem. "But," I went on with excitement, "it's a genuine coydog: half coyote, half dog."

"Gosh." Travis raised his voice and chirruped, "Here, doggy."

Looking vaguely startled, the creature backed into the bush and disappeared.

I spoke sternly to my brother. "No naming it, no taking it to the doctor, no bringing it home. After Bandit, we agreed: no more wild animals."

"But he's not really wild, he's only half wild. The other half is tame."

"Father would have a fit. He'd shoot it, you know he would. And you mustn't try to touch it. It's probably carrying worse diseases than Armand. You promise?"

"All right," he said dully.

"Promise?"

"Promise."

We were mainly silent on the way home, each lost in our own thoughts. I pointed out a couple of true stars along with the planet Saturn in an attempt to take our minds off the coydog. It didn't work too well.

CHAPTER 16

THE SCRUFFIEST DOG IN THE WORLD

The shepherd-dog comes to the house every day for some meat, and as soon as it is given him, he skulks away as if ashamed of himself. On these occasions the house-dogs are very tyrannical, and the least of them will attack and pursue [him].

THE NEXT MORNING I woke well before sunrise and tiptoed down to the kitchen. I was busy in the pantry tearing scraps of meat from the turkey carcass and wrapping them in wax paper when Travis crept in, scaring half the wits out of me.

"What are you doing here?" I whispered.

"No, what are *you* doing here?"

"I suspect the same thing *you* are. Hurry, there's not much time. Viola will be here in a minute." I glanced out the back window, and sure enough, I saw Viola striding in the dim light from her quarters to the chicken pen. Her day began well before everyone else's: There were eggs to be gathered, the stove to be lit, massive meals to be cooked.

"She's coming," I whispered, and we crept out the front door, easing it shut behind us. We bolted down the drive and, once we'd rounded the bend in the road and were safe from view, slowed to a walk. The predawn air was cool, and neither of us had thought to bring a coat. We could see our breath, a welcome signal of cooler weather to come. The smells of autumn filled the air. Matilda, the neighbors' bloodhound, gave her early morning cry as she did every sunrise, a peculiar strangled yodel you could hear all over town. Instead of a steam whistle or community clock, Fentress had dozens of roosters and Matilda to signal the dawn.

The gin was still dark as we crept past it and down the bank to the dam, mindful of the water moccasin. There was no dog in view.

"Oh no," said Travis. "What are we going to do?"

A terrible thought occurred to me: Maybe the dog had died in the night.

As if reading my mind, Travis said, "Do you . . . do you think it died?"

Maybe we were a day too late, which suddenly struck me as a terrible thing. Maybe in dire straits it had gone after the moccasin and been bitten. Maybe its bloated corpse lay caught in the snarl of half-submerged tree limbs downstream at the bridge. Maybe—

"Look! There it is!"

I followed his pointing finger, and sure enough, a little brown face poked out of the tangle of vines and undergrowth twenty feet away on the far side of one of the dam's concrete abutments and regarded us with . . . hope?

I felt a sudden surge of gratitude that we—and the dog—had been given another chance.

"Whatever you do," I said, "don't touch it."

"Never." Travis unwrapped the turkey and spoke kindly. "Good doggy. Here's some breakfast for you."

The dog drooled and licked its chops but would not approach.

"Throw it," I said.

He pitched it underhand, but the dog, no doubt reminded of rocks and bottles thrown its way, flinched and yelped. A moment later it wheeled and staggered off.

Travis cried, "Oh no! Doggy, come back. It's food."

"It'll be okay. Pitch it over there, and he'll find it."

"How do you know for sure?"

"It's a dog—sort of—so it lives by its nose. It'll smell that turkey and be back for it the minute we leave."

He tossed it over and made a pretty good job of it, most of the scraps landing within a few feet of where it had disappeared. We sat in silence for a minute as the sun warmed the horizon, but the dog did not return.

We walked through the front door as Viola was beating the gong in the front hall for breakfast. After the din died down, we followed her into the kitchen to wash our hands, where she said, "You feeding something?"

"No," I said before Travis could open his mouth, which of course he did, saying, "How did you know?"

" 'Cos I planned to get another dinner off that turkey, but now it's only good for soup."

"Well," I said, "soup is good."

"Tchah," she said in exasperation and flapped a dish towel at us. "You-all scoot. I got work to do."

On our way home from school, we approached the gin from the other side of the dam to see if we could spot the dog. No luck. But to our dismay, we found the uneaten turkey meat where we'd left it, swarming with ants. So that was the end of that.

EXCEPT THAT IT WASN'T. I could not put the pitiful creature out of my mind. It preyed on my conscience with its mournful brown eyes and cringing expression epitomizing every dog ever used and abused by man, the "evolved and enlightened" species, the supposedly superior being.

I sneaked back to the gin at dusk three days later and sat quietly scanning the underbrush. A few minutes later, my patience was rewarded by the sound of an approaching animal. The dog lived! It was not too late. Hardly daring to breathe, I listened to the cracking of twigs until out of the bushes stepped . . . Travis. We stared at each other.

"Have you seen it?" I said.

"No. But the turkey's gone, so that's a good sign, right?"

"Maybe. Or maybe a fox got it, or a coyote, or the ants hauled it off."

Travis frowned. "Ants couldn't have carried off all that meat."

"They can carry up to fifty times their own body weight, making them one of the strongest animals on Earth. You'd think they'd get more respect for it, but they don't."

"What should we do?"

I sighed. "I think we should go home."

He said, "I had a dream about that dog last night."

"Me too, but I'm all out of ideas."

As we turned to go, I caught a small movement along the inlet from the corner of my eye. I turned in time to see the very tip of a pointy nose withdrawn into a hollow in the embankment, partially hidden by an ancient, lightning-blasted pecan tree. Right at the site of Bandit's den.

"Travis," I hissed, "look over there. I think it's in Bandit's den below the dead pecan."

"Really?" He lit up like the sun.

"Maybe it was never Bandit's den at all. Maybe it's always been the coydog's den. Stay here and be quiet. I'm going to look for food. Don't move a muscle, don't make a sound."

He nodded, his face the picture of perfect happiness. I flew to the gin, where Mr. O'Flanagan was getting ready to lock up, chucking Polly under his chin (or chucking him where his chin would be if parrots had chins).

"Mr. O'Flanagan, can I please have some of your crackers?"

"Sure, darlin', take as many as you like."

I thanked him, scooped the contents of the bowl into my

pinafore, and ran. He called out behind me, "Goodness, darlin', do they not feed you properly at home?"

It occurred to me for the first time that he probably found me a most peculiar child.

I slowed down to a stealthy creep as I approached the bank. No need to sound like a charging elephant. We'd probably frightened the thing enough for one day.

I showed the crackers to Travis, who looked dubious. "Will it eat those?"

"At this point I'm pretty sure it'll eat anything." I scouted the lay of the land. "Here, you hold on to the tree, and I'll hold on to you."

I crabbed partway down the bank, clutching Travis's hand tightly, then took careful aim with a cracker and landed it close to the hollow. I repeated the process, pitching each subsequent cracker a couple of feet farther away, making a trail I hoped would draw it out. Travis hauled me up the bank, and we sat down to wait.

A muzzle emerged, the scuffed nose twitching so furiously I could almost read the dog's mind: Was it edible? Was it a trap? And even if it was a trap, might it not be worth the risk for a mouthful of food?

It stepped halfway out, sniffing all the time. Travis and I sat frozen in place.

It lunged feebly at the cracker and bolted it down, then immediately withdrew into its den. We sat patiently while the beast decided whether the cracker had been worth it or not.

Evidently so, as it emerged a minute later all the way out of its hole. In this way, we got our first close look at the poor creature, both repugnant and heartbreaking. The round scars and scabs across its hide looked to be birdshot. Was this the chicken thief that Mr. Gates had been buying shotgun shells for? It stared warily at us; I rated its mood as somewhat anxious but no longer completely terrified by our presence. It limped to the next cracker and wolfed it down, then the next cracker and the next, glancing at us all the while. When it had finished, it investigated the scrub for more without luck.

Slowly, we rose to go, careful to make no sudden moves. The dog watched us but did not bolt for its den. Travis spoke to it in the encouraging sing-songy tones in which one addresses a pet or the very young or the very stupid: "Good doggy, there's a good doggy."

He was rewarded this time with a full-fledged wag, this way, then that, just like a real dog.

THE FIRST PERSON to figure out that Travis was still feeding an animal was, of course, Viola, the person in charge of the pantry. Travis and I knew the dog couldn't subsist on crackers for long, and if we actually wanted to improve its health, we'd have to snag it some meat. But this was not easy since Viola spent most of her time in the kitchen and we had to slip past her to get to the pantry. She always knew exactly how much meat and milk and bread, and how many eggs, she had on hand at any given moment, what with having to stay at least one meal ahead of three adults, seven growing children, a transplanted cousin, herself, and two hired help.

Travis and I debated the issue. I said, "I think the easiest thing to do is to ask for another half sandwich in your lunch pail. Then you can stop at the gin on the way home from school and feed him. Since you're taking food to school, it probably won't occur to her that you're feeding a dog."

"Gosh, Callie, you're so smart. And sneaky."

"Why, thank you."

We approached her during one of her rare moments of leisure between meals, sitting with a cup of coffee at the kitchen table.

Before I could even open my mouth, she squinted at us and said, "What do you want? What kind of critter you feeding now?"

"*What?*" I said, stunned at her prescience.

"How did you know?" burst out Travis, before I could muster a denial.

"Whenever I see *you*"—she pointed at me—"and *you*"—she pointed at Travis—"together in this kitchen, I know you're up to something. I know every crumb what's in this house, so don't think you can pull a fast one on *me*, you hear?"

We both stared at her. Maybe I wasn't so terribly smart or sneaky after all. Or maybe I was. I thought furiously about what tools were at hand, what pressures could be brought to bear.

"Okay," I said, "you caught us. It's for a starving cat at the gin."

Travis gaped at me, and I prayed he wouldn't give the game away.

Viola's face softened as I hoped it would. "A cat, huh?" She glanced at Idabelle, her dear companion, asleep in her basket.

"An awfully thin cat."

I looked at Idabelle.

She said, "Why don't it go after all them rats they got at the gin? Your daddy's always complaining about them rats."

"It's too weak to hunt. If we don't feed it soon, it's going to starve to death."

"Yeah," said Travis, "starve to death from, you know, not enough food. For a *cat*. To *eat*."

Ugh, what a terrible liar. I cut him off before he could say anything even more stupid. "And if questions ever came up from, um, anyone, the fact is that Travis is a growing boy, and you know how growing boys get hungry. An extra sandwich at lunch would tide him over, you know."

Viola cast another fond glance at her feline friend. "All right, starting tomorrow. Maybe sardines, maybe roast beef, we'll see. Now, scoot."

We scooted while we were ahead of the game.

The next day, Travis found an additional wax paper parcel in his lunch. Good thing it was roast beef instead of supremely smelly sardines, or no one would have sat next to him at lunch, probably not even Lula.

We stopped at the gin on the way home from school and

climbed down the bank. Travis called softly, "Here, doggy, good doggy," and to our great satisfaction, the dog stuck its head out. I pitched the food, and it withdrew for a moment, then reappeared. It limped to the sandwich and wolfed it down.

Thus began Travis's new routine. I left him to it, with strict instructions to save the creature only until it got back on its feet, but otherwise leave it alone. Occasionally he ran into Father coming or going but Travis pretended he was exploring and playing along the bank; Father waved at him and went about his business. Most of the time, Travis spied the dog, although occasionally it was missing, causing him to worry that it had sickened and died. But it always showed up the next day. It slowly gained weight and recognized Travis's soft call of "Here, doggy, good doggy."

Then because I had so many other things to do, I stopped paying much attention. Honestly, you would think I'd have known better, given Travis's history with animals.

CHAPTER 17

THE TRAVAILS OF IDABELLE AND OTHER CREATURES

The Gauchos differ in their opinion, whether the Jaguar
is good eating, but are unanimous in saying that cat is
excellent.

I FOUND VIOLA stirring a pot of venison stew and frowning at
Idabelle the Inside Cat, who was crouched in her basket next to
the stove.

Viola said, "Take a look at that cat. You see anything wrong?"

"What do you mean?"

"She's hungry all the time, but she's losing flesh. I think she's
poorly."

Viola doted on Idabelle, who subsisted on mice and was generally a dab hand at catching more than enough to keep herself
fat and happy.

Viola added, "I worry about that cat. She cries all the time."
As if on cue, Idabelle rose, stretched, and began shuttling around
my ankles in figure eights, yowling dolefully.

I picked her up to comfort her, and she felt lighter than expected. Oh no, not another sick animal. "I do think she's

thinner," I said, feeling the ribs through the fur, which admittedly seemed to have lost some of its luster.

Viola looked distressed. "You think that animal doctor can help?"

Now, here was a novel idea. Veterinarians looked after the large animals and livestock that produced income. I'd never heard of a sick dog or cat getting professional attention; I doubted that anyone in the county would have dreamed of spending one thin dime on a pet. The animal would either get better on its own or die, and that was that.

I said, "I'll ask him. Maybe he will."

"You tell him I don't have no money but I can cook for him. You tell him I'm the best cook in town. Your momma will vouch for me. So will Samuel."

I retrieved the rabbit hutch from the barn that had housed Armand/Dilly. Travis was nowhere to be seen. I wondered if he had gone to the dog's den without me.

Trusting and placid, Idabelle had no idea what lay in store, and I was able to push her into the hutch and latch it before she could react. She sniffed delicately at the floor of her cage, no doubt picking up traces of its former inhabitant. Then she hunkered down and glared at me. I picked up the hutch, and she howled.

And kept on howling all the way to Dr. Pritzker's office, a good ten minutes away. Together, the hutch and cat were heavy, and I was sweating by the time I arrived at his door to find a note affixed: *Gone to McCarthy's farm. Back at noon.*

So I could wait a whole hour or trudge back with my unhappy

burden. I tried the door, not expecting it to open but it did. The room was clean and furnished simply with a desk covered with papers, two straight-back chairs, a filing cabinet, and a glass-front cabinet filled with jars labeled with intriguing names: Nux Vomica, Blue Vitriol, Hemlock Water, Tartarized Antimony. There were a wooden exam table and a zinc counter where he apparently mixed and measured his drenches and elixirs and purgatives. And there was also a shelf full of fat books bound in worn leather.

I put the cage on the floor and sat down to wait. Idabelle's howling subsided to an occasional soft mew of hopelessness. There was nothing for me to do except speak soothingly to her and twiddle my thumbs for a whole hour. I kept this up for a good five minutes, staring hungrily at the books all the while. Then, well, the hard wooden seat got the better of me, and I had to get up to stretch my hindquarters. And then, well, the thick inviting books whispered to me, *Come over here and take a look, Calpurnia. Just a look. Nothing more. Really.* So I got up and examined the titles: *Diseases of Cattle, The Complete Guide to the Domestic Sheep, Hog Fundamentals, Advanced Equine Husbandry.* But nothing about cats or dogs, and certainly nothing about coydogs. Maybe Dr. Pritzker didn't know anything about felines or canines.

An hour later, I had learned that baby lambs often arrived in twos and sometimes even threes, and frequently got mixed up together in the birth canal, and it was the vet's job to sort out the tangle of three heads and twelve hooves all jumbled together.

This required a gentle touch to avoid killing the ewe in the process. I was deep in the discussion of breech deliveries when the door opened, the bell clanged, and I jumped about two feet straight in the air, almost dropping the precious book.

Dr. Pritzker, covered in dust and manure, said with amusement, "So, Miss Calpurnia, are you learning something useful?"

"Uh, sorry, Dr. Pritzker, I—"

"No need to apologize. Your grandfather tells me you have a positive thirst for knowledge." He glanced at the rabbit hutch and said, "What have you got there? It looks like some new breed of rabbit I'm not familiar with."

"This is Idabelle, our Inside Cat. She's losing weight, and she cries a lot. Will you take a look at her? I can pay," I added hastily. "But if it's more than forty-two cents, I'll have to go on the installment plan."

"Don't you worry about that. The trouble is, I sent Samuel off for his lunch. We'll have to wait until he gets back."

"I don't see why," I said. "I can help. She's only little."

He hesitated. "What would your parents say?"

"It's fine, really it is. I look after our animals all the time," I said stoutly, stretching the truth but only a tad.

"All right, but don't blame me if you get scratched."

"She'd never do that," I said. But looking at the normally calm and affectionate cat crouched miserably in her cage, a gleam of desperation burning in her eye, I felt a pang of doubt.

"What are her symptoms? Runny eyes? Runny nose? Vomiting? Diarrhea?"

"None of those, but she's losing weight, and she cries a lot."

"Right," he said. "Put her on the table and we'll take a look."

Now that the time of reckoning had come, Idabelle decided she didn't want to be dislodged from the hutch; she clung to it like a limpet, her claws firmly hooked in the wire. Unhooking all four limbs and keeping them unhooked simultaneously proved to be a major operation in itself.

I placed her on the edge of the table and held her by the scruff. Dr. Pritzker started up at the head. He looked in both ears, which she didn't like, and I feared for his good hand. But she did me proud and did not hiss or bite or scratch. Then he pulled down each of her lower lids.

"What are you looking for?" I said. "You have to tell me what you're doing."

"Right. First you check in the ears for sores or any black material, which is a sign of ear mites. Then you check the eyelids to see if they are pale or not. See, she has a pink color to the conjunctiva, which is this membrane here. If it were pale, that would indicate internal bleeding or anemia. And the pupils are of equal size, so that's good."

"What if they were different? What would that mean?"

"It's a sign of being struck on the head, of damage to the brain. Also, the third eyelid, the nictitating membrane, is retracted. If it were visible now when she's fully awake, it would usually be a sign of ill health. You typically only see it in a sleepy cat. Now for the mouth. Pull her head back for me and hold it so."

I did as he told me while he pulled up Idabelle's lip on each side. She liked that even less.

"See here," he said, "the gums are pink and healthy. No abscess, no broken teeth. So far there's no reason she shouldn't be eating. Now we'll check the glands in the neck."

He ran his good hand under the cat's jaw. "Nothing there. If her glands were big, it would be a sign of infection." Then he felt her belly and pronounced it free of tumors. He ran his hand up and down each limb and the tail and pronounced her free of fractures.

"Hold up the tail," he said, and peered closely at her backside. "No diarrhea. No visible parasites. Now open that drawer and get me the stethoscope. It's the instrument with the black tubing."

"I know what it is," I said, slightly offended. "Dr. Walker comes to the house and listens to our lungs with it when we have a cough. But that's only if the cod-liver oil doesn't work." I shuddered at the thought of Mother's favorite nostrum.

I pulled the instrument from the drawer and handed it to him. It smelled of rubber.

He struggled to put it in his ears, and I reached up to help him. He smiled his thanks, then pressed the scope to Idabelle's chest and listened intently. After a moment, he tried to pull the earpieces out, and I helped him again. He handed me the instrument, saying, "Her heart and lungs sound completely normal. There's nothing there. You can put that back in the drawer."

I took the stethoscope from him and hesitated. I had often laid my ear against Idabelle's warm fur and heard the rapid faint pitter-patter of her heart, far-off and practically inaudible. Here was my chance for a real listen with a real instrument.

"Can I please try it?" I said. *"Please?"*

He apparently found this amusing but said, "All right. Put the bell right here." He pointed to a spot behind the left foreleg. It seemed a funny place to listen to a heart, but then he was the expert, right?

I put the earpieces in and pressed the bell to her fur, not expecting much. To my surprise, a thunderous tympany filled my ears, almost too loud to bear, and so rapid that it seemed like a rolling kettledrum. Idabelle's valiant little heart beat like mad, and I listened for a good long time before I could make some sense of it. What sounded like a continuous thrumming was actually two distinct sounds (that I later learned were the "lub" and the "dub," the sounds made by the closing of various valves in the heart). I could also hear a loud, whistling wind and realized that it had to be air moving through her lungs.

"Gosh, that's amazing," I said.

He smiled and said, "Do you know what's wrong with this cat?"

"What?" I said with trepidation.

"Absolutely nothing. She's fine. And now we'll do the final test." He went into the back room and returned with a small flat tin of sardines, saying, "You'll have to open this. I can't manage it."

I opened the tin with the key, and the reek of oily fish filled the room, all too reminiscent of cod-liver oil.

"Try her with that," he said.

I placed it in front of Idabelle. She sniffed it once and then grabbed a sardine and bolted it as fast as she could, then attacked the others, tearing through them at great speed. She finished up by licking the can dry and looking around for more. Her belly bulged comically.

Dr. Pritzker said, "See? She's hungry, that's all."

"Really?" I was incredulous. "That's it?"

"Nothing wrong with her. How often do you feed her?"

I had to think about this. "I don't really know. We keep her inside for the mice, but I don't know if Viola gives her other food or not."

"It looks like your mouse population has decreased for some reason. You don't have traps set out in the house, do you?"

"I don't think so."

"No poison?"

"No, sir."

"And she's not competing with any other cats?"

"No, the other cats are all Outside Cats."

"Well, you'll have to supplement her food until the mice come back. Give her some sardines every day but not so much that she stops hunting."

I thanked him profusely and stuffed her back into her cage, anxious to get home and give Viola the good news. Idabelle immediately started howling again, at even greater volume.

Although it nearly killed me to say it, I said it anyway, speaking up over the heart-rending noise. "Will you please send me your bill, Dr. Pritzker?"

He looked amused and gestured at the mass of papers on his desk. "I might, if I can ever catch up on my accounting. Or, I tell you what—you can run a few errands for me, deliver a message or two. Sometimes I'm stuck sending Samuel, which is a great inconvenience. Deal?"

"Deal! Oh, and do you ever look after dogs? I didn't see any dog books on your shelf."

"I have doctored a few cattle dogs and hunting dogs in my time. The principles of care are essentially the same. Do you have a sick dog?"

"Uh . . . no. But I might. One day."

He gave me a peculiar look but I figured there was no point in explaining. Even if I could somehow bring the coydog to Dr. Pritzker, I knew that he would recommend the standard treatment for such a beast: a quick and merciful bullet through the brain. And even if not, the bill to fix such a wreck would probably come to the huge sum of twenty dollars.

I cast one last longing glance at his books and turned to go. He said, "I leave my door open during business hours. You can come and read whenever you like."

"Gosh, thanks!" This was turning into my lucky day.

"Although, come to think of it, some of that material is not appropriate for young ladies, so you'd better get your mother's permission."

Well, maybe not so lucky after all.

I carried Idabelle home with a light heart and pondered where the mice had gone. And then it came to me in a thunderclap. How could I have been such an idiot not to see it sooner? Poor Idabelle. She was losing out to the king snake.

I took the cage into the kitchen, where Viola jumped up, tears welling in her eyes. "What's wrong with her? Is she dying?"

I'd never seen Viola so upset. The tide of our family affairs ebbed and flowed around her while she maintained, on the whole, a perfect state of equilibrium (albeit a low-grade grumpy one that applied to everybody and everything with the exception of Idabelle). I'd never seen her shed a tear before. And although she had scores of nieces and nephews, including Samuel, she had no children of her own, so I guess that made Idabelle her baby.

"She's fine," I said. "She's hungry because there aren't enough mice about."

"Hungry? That's all? Praise Jesus!"

"Dr. Pritzker said you should feed her sardines every day until she gains some weight and the mice come back."

She wiped her eyes on her apron, saying, "I'll get her a can right now."

"No, no, she just ate a whole tin. Wait until tomorrow or I swear she'll pop."

"Praise Jesus," Viola whispered, and clasped the cat to her bony chest. "My baby girl's home," she crooned. Idabelle kneaded at her apron and purred at full volume.

Viola said, "What's wrong with the mice?"

Without thinking, I said, "It's the sn—oops."

"The snoops? What's that?"

"Oh, nothing. It's just, uh, the natural fluctuation in the population."

"I never knowed this to happen before."

"Got to go," I said, and left them to their joyful reunion.

Question for the Notebook: It sure is nice that *Felis domesticus* purrs, but what about lions and tigers, do they purr, too? And how would you ever find out?

That night "the snoops" reappeared in a most unpleasant way. Sir Isaac Newton had once again escaped from his dish, but this time had the bad luck to run into the snake, a primeval foe. I walked into my room to discover an epic battle taking place in the middle of the floor: newt versus snake, with the newt losing fast, being halfway down the snake's gullet at that point. Now, a fair fight doesn't offend me, but this? Newts being retiring and soft-bodied, the whole thing was a pretty one-sided affair that really got my dander up.

I leaped forward and grabbed Sir Isaac Newton's hind half and pulled. The snake pulled back. I yelled, "Gimme my newt, you rotten snake!" The snake refused and kept pulling, so I did the only thing I could think of: I reached over and flicked it on the snout. It recoiled and spat out its limp victim, then high-tailed it for the baseboards. Sir Isaac stirred groggily as I wiped the snake spittle from him with my handkerchief. I spoke encouraging words to him and stroked him under his chin. He shook himself and, after a moment, looked none the worse for wear, so I slid him back into his dish and secured the lid. Good thing Aggie was at the general store getting a soda. If she'd been there she'd have croaked. Completely croaked.

Honestly, the drama in my life.

CHAPTER 18
GRASSHOPPER GUTS

[W]e observed to the south a ragged cloud of dark reddish-brown colour. At first we thought that it was smoke from some great fire on the plains; but we soon found that it was a swarm of locusts.... [T]hey overtook us at a rate of ten or fifteen miles an hour. The main body filled the air ... "and the sound of their wings was as the sound of chariots of many horses running to battle:" or rather, I should say, like a strong breeze passing through the rigging of a ship.

AND SPEAKING OF DRAMA, I gave a fair bit of thought to the "problem" of Travis's queasiness in the face of blood and guts, and how to fix it. I cornered Granddaddy in the library and posed Travis's dilemma to him.

"So, as I understand it," he said, "you want to help, uh . . . Travis? Which one is he again?"

"You remember, Granddaddy. He's the one who raised the turkeys last year and got so upset about killing them."

"Ah, yes. Quite the charade, as I recall."

"Yep. I mean, yes."

Travis had been so wrought up about us eating his pets that the night before they'd met their doom, Granddaddy and I had altered their appearance with paint and scissors to convince him that we had traded with the neighbors for different birds. The turkeys had not been happy about their transformation, and I still bore a small scar on my left elbow as a souvenir. (The things we do for the brothers we love! I wouldn't have done it for Lamar in a million years.)

"And you want to help him get over his, shall we say, squeamishness? Do I have that right?"

"Yessir."

"May I inquire exactly why?"

"He wants to be a veterinarian, so he needs to be able to work with innards and blood and things like that. But he's not at all tough like me. He got nauseated when I showed him my earthworm."

"Did he, now?"

"Yes, but it didn't bother me. I have a cast-iron stomach, you know."

"Indeed you do."

I practically glowed under this high praise.

He thought for a moment. "An interesting conundrum. I suggest we expose him to progressively more vivid and complex examples of dissection. In this way we can slowly accustom his nervous system to greater degrees of explicitness, so as not to cause too great a shock. At the same time, this will offer you a good opportunity to learn more about anatomy. We shall proceed upward through the invertebrates to the vertebrates and perhaps finish with some small mammal. I leave it to you to instruct him from there. Tomorrow we shall work on the American grasshopper, *Schistocerca americana*."

The next day, I caught a big yellow grasshopper in my net. I took it to Granddaddy in the laboratory, where we euthanized it humanely in a killing jar. As we began, he said, "We are dissecting an insect at the top of the invertebrate ladder. Observe. Describe. Note. Analyze."

I did so, remarking on the two large compound eyes, the three minuscule simple eyes (so small as to be almost invisible), the two sets of wings, the three sets of legs. The large eyes gave the insect a wide field of vision that made it difficult to creep up on; without the long-handled net, I'd never have snagged it.

Under his instruction, I dissected and pinned the various parts. There were no lungs but rather spiracles, a set of tiny holes along the abdomen that acted as bellows to draw air directly into the body. There was also an open circulating system where blood flowed freely through open body cavities rather than a closed system with the blood contained in blood vessels. (As in, for example, man.) I made a few sketches and took careful notes.

When finished, I covered my dissecting tray with cheesecloth and carried it out to find Travis. I tracked him down at the pigpen, where he was scratching Petunia between the ears with a stick.

"Look," I said, pulling back the cloth and showing him the

bright yellow shards strewn across the black wax. "This is the grasshopper we did this morning."

"Uh," he said.

"Travis, you have to look. Granddaddy says this will help you."

"Uh."

Now, I'll admit that to a beginner the sight of a dismantled grasshopper might be a little disconcerting, but really, the boy needed some grit. And how was he to get it without my help?

"Stop scratching that pig and take a look."

He reluctantly stopped, glanced over briefly, and swallowed hard.

"You can touch it," I said in encouraging tones, stirring around a couple of the large muscular hindlegs. "It won't bite, you know."

He took a deep breath through his nose and turned pale.

"See how this set of legs is specially adapted for jumping? And look at these big eyes here—that's one reason they're so hard to catch. Here, hold the tray."

"That's okay, I can see from here."

"Take. The. Tray." I shoved it at him.

He took it but averted his gaze. His hands trembled a little.

"Do you want to be an animal doctor or not?"

He gulped. "I do. At least . . . I think I do."

"Then you're going to stand here and look at that thing. I'm not kidding."

"I don't think I can do it, Callie."

"Yes, you can do it, because I'm going to stand right here beside you. All right?" No answer.

"I said, 'all right?'"

"I guess."

"Look, here are the maxillae and mandibles for crushing food."

"Uh-huh."

"And here are the antennae, and here are the cerebral ganglia. They're a sort of primitive brain."

"Yep."

"And look at the pattern of the veins in this wing. Every species of grasshopper has its own unique arrangement—did you know that?"

"Nope."

He kept glancing away, and I reminded him each time to stay focused on the tray. The tremor in his hands finally subsided but the color did not return to his cheeks. We must have stood there for a good five minutes before I finally said, "That's enough for today."

"Okay, thanks!" He shoved the tray at me and bolted for the barn, no doubt to hug Bunny and sink his cheek deep into the soft white fur, his standard ritual of comfort.

I looked at Petunia and said, "I'm not sure he can do it. He's already having trouble with a *grasshopper*." The pig grunted sociably in reply, but I couldn't tell if she agreed with me or not.

———

AND SPEAKING OF TRAVIS and dilemmas, he confessed to another on our way home from school when I asked him, "Has the coydog finally run off, or are you still feeding it?"

"You mean Scruffy?"

Uh-oh. "Travis, we agreed you wouldn't name him. Right?"

"Well, I figured it couldn't hurt. And everybody needs a name. Come and see him with me. He's looking real good, better and better all the time."

He led me down the bank, calling softly, "Scruffy, here boy, good doggy."

Out of the bushes came not the wreck that I remembered but something that looked in the main like, well, a dog. The eyes were bright, the nose moist, the expression happy. He still limped, but less than before. Yes, I had to admit it, he looked like your usual *Canis familiaris* of the small-to-medium, brownish-reddish variety. He approached Travis with his ears folded submissively and his tail wagging, but stopped in his tracks when he saw me.

"It's all right, Scruffy," said Travis. "We've brought you your lunch."

Travis put down a sandwich, and Scruffy, deciding I was not a threat, approached us and wolfed it down. I studied him. Up close, he actually looked more like a coyote than a dog, with a long, narrow snout and a bushy coyote-like tail. He finished his food, licked his chops, and looked at us expectantly.

"That's all there is today, boy. I'll bring you more tomorrow." Travis turned to me and said, "Hey, Callie, watch this." He turned back to the coydog. "Scruffy, sit."

Scruffy sat.

My mouth flopped open. Then Travis did something else. He patted Scruffy and was rewarded with a lick on his hand.

"You shouldn't touch him," I warned. "Who knows what kind of diseases he has?"

"Oh," he said airily, "if he had any diseases I would have caught them a long time ago. He lets me pet him and pull the ticks off, and he loves it when I brush him."

So much for warnings from a concerned sister.

"Do you want to pet him? He won't hurt you." Travis beamed at me with the full force of his happiness, before which so many were powerless.

I held out my hand to Scruffy. He sniffed it carefully and then rewarded me with a small lick. I tried not to think about the possible germs involved and gave him a pat on the head.

"See?" said Travis. "He's just as tame as can be."

I looked at my little brother and decided that, painful as it might be, I had to speak up as the voice of reason. "Look, Mother says we have too many dogs, and Father only wants a purebred hunter. And your history with Armand and Jay and Bandit means your reputation with wild pets is at an all-time low."

"But he's not wild. He's only half wild."

"I know, and if you want to keep feeding him, that's one thing. But you can't bring him home. They'll never accept him, not in a million years."

He sighed, a deep shuddering sigh hauled up from the depths of his being.

"So let him stay right here," I said. "He has his den to live in and you to feed him. You can visit him every day. He can be your secret pet."

Travis scratched behind Scruffy's ears and finally said, "Okay. I guess."

"And be sure you feed him enough so he's not hunting chickens. That's the last thing either of you needs. Come on, I have to get home for piano practice."

He reluctantly hugged Scruffy good-bye, and then turned to wave at him from the top of the bank. I worried about that boy. And his coydog.

CHAPTER 19

NAVIGATING THE INNER AND OUTER WORLDS

While sailing...on one very dark night, the sea presented a wonderful and most beautiful spectacle. There was a fresh breeze, and every part of the surface, which during the day is seen as foam, now glowed with a pale light. The vessel drove before her bows two billows of liquid phosphorus, and in her wake she was followed by a milky train. As far as the eye reached, the crest of every wave was bright, and the sky above the horizon, from the reflected glare of these livid flames, was not so utterly obscure as over the vault of the heavens.

IN BETWEEN MY SCHOOLWORK, my nature studies with Granddaddy, knitting mittens, and piano practice, I ran to Dr. Pritzker's whenever I could. Sometimes he gave me a nickel or even a dime for my help.

That particular day, I arrived at his office bearing a fragrant basket of fried chicken from Viola, along with a warm apple crumble. The doctor was pulling jars from the shelves with his good hand and pouring ingredients into a mortar while Samuel pulverized them with a pestle.

Dr. Pritzker looked up and said, "My, that smells good. I hope you've got something in there for me."

"Yessir," I said. "It's from Viola in payment for Idabelle. And, Samuel, there's a bundle in here for you too. Viola says to stop by before you go home—she has a message for your momma."

Samuel, who could not read or write, poured the finished powder into a clean jar while Dr. Pritzker fumbled at his desk with a paper label. His clawed, withered right hand looked no better to me. He wrote laboriously with his left hand and examined the results.

"Blast. That looks flat-out terrible."

It did look terrible, like something J.B. had done.

"Uh, Doctor?" I said. "I could write that for you, if you like."

After a moment, he replied, "Of course you could. That would be a great help. I don't know why I didn't think of it sooner."

He handed me a fresh label and a pencil. I decided to play it safe and print in block letters rather than write in cursive. I worked slowly and carefully: MAKE A POULTICE OF TWO LEVEL TEASPOONS IN HALF-PINT OF TEPID WATER AND APPLY TO TORN EAR THRICE DAILY.

"Much better," he said.

"Do you want me to deliver it?"

"I surely would appreciate that. It needs to go to McCarthy's farm, and we've got to make a call on a sick heifer in the opposite direction."

I walked off eastward while the doctor and Samuel headed westward in their buggy. McCarthy's farm was a good twenty minutes away, and I poked along, looking for life in the drainage ditch and taking note of the flora and fauna on the way.

Mrs. McCarthy, a thin, weatherworn housewife, met me at the farmhouse door and pointed me in the direction of the barn, where her husband was tending a heifer with a badly wounded ear.

I handed over the medicine to Mr. McCarthy. To my surprise, he drew a nickel from the depths of his baggy overalls and handed it to me, saying, "Here y'are, missy."

"Oh no, Mr. McCarthy, I can't take that."

"Sure you can. Go buy yourself a so-dee at the store."

I stammered my thanks and hurried off, clutching my windfall. My brothers often made a little money here and there doing all sorts of things, whereas the only money I ever earned was tending the colored children for the week their mothers picked cotton. By the time I got back as far as the Fentress General Store, I'd made up my mind: a "so-dee" from the fountain sounded good, but the thought of adding to my cigar box treasury of $2.67 sounded better. And the thought of not telling my brothers about a potential new source of income? Better still.

After a few afternoons with Dr. Pritzker, I noticed that he prescribed a half dozen or so of his mixtures over and over again.

I said, "Dr. Pritzker, while I'm here, do you want me to write a whole bunch of labels? I could do them for the arnica, the mustard seed, and the spirits of turpentine. I notice you use them a lot. If I made several of them right now, you'd have them ready for when I'm not here."

He grinned first at me and then at Samuel. "By golly, we've got a real brain in our midst."

Well, that puffed me up quite a bit. I took extra care with my work, and as I was leaving, he gave me a whole quarter.

I pondered his situation and mine. I thought about the turtleback mound of bills and correspondence sliding off his desk. I thought about my cursive handwriting that was no great shakes. And I came up with a plan.

Interrupting Aggie at her mending, I said, "You're not using your writing machine, so why don't you teach me to type?"

Startled, she looked up. "Why would I do that? You don't need to type-write."

A child of lesser fortitude might have been discouraged by this and retreated, but I was made of sterner stuff. And I knew what made Aggie tick. I said, "I'll pay you."

She considered this. "You'll pay me to teach you?"

"Yep."

"Why?"

"So I can make money."

A crafty look crept over her. "Oh, I get it. You want to work for that dirty old Jew, right? Although he does have nice manners for a Jew, not like some I've met. I have to give him that."

"Dr. Pritzker?" This puzzled and offended me. "Well, of course he's dirty *some*times. You would be too if you worked in the stables and sties and such, but he always washes up afterward. He carries his own bar of soap in his bag. I've seen it. And he's not *that* old."

She barked a harsh laugh that set my teeth on edge. "You don't know anything at all."

"That's not true! I know plenty of things."

"Right. You know all kinds of things about stuff nobody cares two hoots about. Newts and bugs. Who cares about that?"

Rage and incredulity flared within me. "How can you say that? All those things are important. Granddaddy says so."

"Another old loon," said Aggie. "Why you pay any attention to someone like that is beyond me."

I could have punched her at that moment and would have willingly faced the infinite maternal consequences. But then I'd never get what I needed from her. Something important. I marshaled every ounce of self-control in my being and forced myself to calm down.

I said, "If you teach me, I can make some more money."

"So you want to spend money to make money."

When she said it aloud like that, I had to admit it didn't sound all that smart.

"So what'll you pay me?"

I'd thought carefully about this ahead of time. "A whole dollar. Cash money."

"That's not very much. I'll need two."

My mind raced through the rapid mental calculations for which I'm justly famous. What could I threaten her with? How about the snake? He'd be perfect, but then she'd run to Mother, and Mother would send Alberto to trap it and kill it. It didn't seem right to involve an innocent snake in matters of pure Commerce. Perhaps I could play on Aggie's sympathy, but she didn't seem to have any. Since I couldn't come up with anything else on the spot, I'd have to resort to the truth.

I gulped and said, "A whole dollar is a lot for me, Aggie. Maybe it's not an awful lot to you. But it's an awful lot to me."

She examined me shrewdly, and I could tell she was running her own calculations.

"A dollar fifty."

"Okay," I said, and we shook on it. It was more than I wanted to pay and less than she wanted to make. "When do we start?"

"As soon as you give me the money. Oh, and you have to buy your own ribbon. I won't have you wearing out mine."

So even though it about killed me, I took two dollars out of my cigar box, gave a dollar fifty of it to Aggie, and ordered a type-writing ribbon for fifty cents from the Sears Catalogue. And even though Mr. Sears was famous for his speedy delivery, I knew I was in for one of those annoying lessons in patience until it arrived.

For want of something better to do, I threw myself into my lessons. At school we were studying the great explorers, Christopher Columbus and Ferdinand Magellan and Captain

Cook, valiant men who had set sail from Europe and headed for parts unknown at a time when some people still believed that the Earth was flat with dragons lurking at the edge, waiting to gobble up the plunging ships. Miss Harbottle told us they navigated great distances "by the stars," but when I asked her to explain further, she ducked the question; I had the distinct feeling she didn't know much about it.

Of course I went to Granddaddy.

"Ah," he said, taking the globe from the shelf and placing it on his desk. "Notice these lines running parallel to the equator. They are called lines of latitude. These other lines running from pole to pole are lines of constant longitude. These imaginary lines divide up the Earth in an especially useful way. Taken together, they can specify any position on the planet."

"But how can you tell your latitude and longitude by the stars?"

"I'll show you tonight. But first you will need to build a mariner's astrolabe. Gather together the following items: a good-sized piece of cardboard, a protractor, a length of string, a cardboard tube, and a heavy nut or bolt. Then come back after dark, and we will navigate the old-fashioned way."

It took me only ten minutes to gather the cardboard, the tube, the string, and the nut. Now, where was I to find a protractor? Then I realized with a sinking heart that the only one I could think of belonged to that pill Lamar. Ugh. He'd received it last Christmas, along with a compass and a steel ruler in a handsome leather case. (Meanwhile, I got a book called *The*

Science of Housewifery. There was no justice in the world.) To go back to Granddaddy without the protractor was unthinkable. He often told me I was a resourceful girl, and I didn't want to damage his opinion of me.

I examined my options. It might be simplest to ask Lamar but I could just hear him saying no in that sneering voice of his. Or perhaps I could "borrow" it without him knowing. What could be the harm in that? (Other than the never-ending heck to pay if he caught me.) I considered the ever-shifting allegiances and loyalties and alliances that constantly formed and re-formed between my brothers at a dizzying pace. Sometimes it was hard to keep up with who was on the outs with whom, but there was one boy who was always loyal to me.

TRAVIS SAID, "What do you want it for, Callie?"

"Granddaddy and I are going to make a mariner's astrolabe, and I can't do it without a protractor."

"What's an astrolabe?"

"It's a scientific instrument, and I'll show it to you later. So will you do it?"

"Why don't you ask Lamar?"

"*Travis*, don't be a dolt. He'd never lend it to me in a million years." Really, the boy's propensity for thinking the best of everyone got on my nerves sometimes.

"Oh. Do you want me to ask him for you?"

"No. I want you to . . . get it. And don't say anything to him about it."

"You mean, steal it?"

"It's not stealing, it's only borrowing."

"And then we'll give it back?"

"Absolutely."

I expected further protestation but he merely said, "Okay."

After dinner, he sidled up to me in the hall and said in a stage whisper, "Here it is." He handed me the cool metal instrument, and I hid it in my pinafore pocket before seeking out Granddaddy in the library, where we were guaranteed privacy from the prying eyes of certain nosy brothers.

Under his direction, I cut the cardboard into a half circle. Then I used the protractor to draw marks along the edge of the circle every five degrees. I punched a hole in the center of the flat edge of the cardboard, threaded the string through it, and tied the string to the nut. Finally, I glued the tube across the flat edge. The finished astrolabe looked like this:

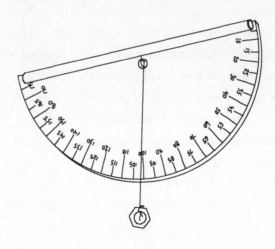

When I was finished, Granddaddy inspected my handiwork. "A primitive instrument, but workable. Shall we go outside and locate the North Star? We will need a little light, but not so much as to obscure the stars."

He lit a lamp, and we walked out to the middle of the front lawn. The crickets hushed their creaking song as we approached. It was almost bedtime, but Mother had a natural reticence about approaching Granddaddy, and I could usually eke out an extra half hour working on a project with him before she called me to bed.

He turned the lamp down to a tiny firefly-size flame, and the crickets resumed their chorus. Matilda the hound yodeled once in the distance. Otherwise the night was silent.

Granddaddy said, "Show me the North Star."

I knew the major compass points—everybody did—so I could at least point vaguely northward. "It has to be somewhere over there."

Granddaddy sighed, no doubt at my shocking ignorance. "Let us start from the beginning. Can you find Ursa Major? Also known as the Big Bear or the Big Dipper?"

"Oh yes, I know that one." I proudly pointed to it. There was no missing it, with its shape exactly like a dipper. "But it doesn't look like a bear."

"I agree. Nevertheless, the ancients called it such. Now, look at the dipper bowl and locate the two stars at the end of it. Do you see them? Then follow the line those two stars make until you find a fairly bright star, which turns out to be the last star in the handle of the Little Dipper, also known as Ursa Minor, the Little Bear."

"Got it," I said.

"That is Polaris, also called the Phoenician Star, also called the North Star. The other stars appear to wheel around it in the night sky due to the Earth's rotation, but that star remains in a nearly constant position. If you were to stand at the North Pole, it would be almost directly overhead. The axis around which the Earth rotates happens to point almost directly at this star, which explains why the star does not appear to move as our planet turns, once every day. Shakespeare wrote in one of his plays three hundred years ago, 'I am constant as the northern star.' Once you know where north is, you naturally know where the other directions are as well. In the southern hemisphere, sailors cannot see the North Star and must use the Southern Cross instead. So no matter where in the world you are, no matter how lost you may be, these stars will guide you home. Sailors have always considered them lucky; this is where we get the expression 'to thank one's lucky stars.'"

I thought of the Phoenicians and Egyptians and Vikings, brave men who had steered their ships by the very same star. It was as if their hands and hearts and voices reached across the centuries to a girl in Fentress, Texas, who had never seen the sea and probably never would. I felt a part of history and also, truth to tell, a bit sad.

"Now," said Granddaddy, "the North Star does more than tell you the four cardinal directions. Sailors have used it for two thousand years to find their position at sea. But now we will measure our latitude. Look through the tube at the North Star."

This was a bit tricky, what with the tube so narrow and the star so easy to lose from the wobbling aperture. Finally I had it.

"Good," said Granddaddy. "Now, being very careful to hold still, keep the tube immobile while you read the angle marked by the string."

I did as instructed and saw that the string hung at an angle of thirty degrees as marked on the cardboard. This meant that the angle between the horizon and the North Star was thirty degrees.

"We'll double-check our work," he said. I measured the angle again.

"Yep, thirty degrees."

He gave me a look, the one that meant: I know you know better.

"Uh, I mean yes. It is thirty degrees. But what good does that do us?"

"I'll explain inside."

As we walked back to the house, a soft breeze sprang up and stirred my imagination. For a moment I was a pilot, sister to the many brave pilots of the past centuries, balanced on the prow of my ship, facing leeward through the endless black nights on the vast indigo sea, the freshening wind behind me, sailing the bounding main with only pinpoints of light to guide me. Stouthearted explorers all!

We returned to the library, and he showed me on the globe

that we were in fact 30 degrees north of the equator. And if you set sail eastward across the Atlantic at this latitude, you would land in the Canary Islands, five thousand miles away. Granddaddy handed down his *Atlas of the World*, and I spent a few happy minutes reading about the lives of (what else?) canaries in the Canary Islands (surprise!).

"So, Granddaddy, what about longitude?"

"Solving the problem of longitude is considerably more difficult. It requires the use of an accurate timepiece. These days we take clocks for granted, but none existed a few hundred years ago. People told time by sundials or estimating the angle of the sun in the sky. The great sailors of the time were the Dutch and the Spanish and the Portuguese. However, the British government offered a vast sum of money to any inventor who could devise a timepiece that would keep accurate time under the difficult conditions at sea, thus solving the longitude problem. It took Mr. John Harrison more than thirty years, but he did it, giving the English a marked advantage on the seas. Just think: If Portugal had invented the clock a little earlier, we might well be speaking Portuguese at this moment instead of English."

An interesting thought, but it was time for bed.

At breakfast the next morning, I happened to glance at Lamar as he gobbled down his oatmeal and realized with a jolt of fear that I still had his protractor. What if he needed it for his schoolwork? He'd raise such a stink about it being missing. If he suspected Travis, it was all over, as my younger brother would collapse like a house of cards with the merest breath of pressure from him. Fortunately, Lamar stalked off to school with his satchel and did not have to solve any geometry problems that day.

After school, Lamar and Sam Houston and some of their chums got together for a rousing game of baseball on the lawn, using old feed sacks filled with cottonseed hulls to mark the bases. They were short a fielder, so they enlisted Travis, whom they normally would have scorned. They hollered mild insults at each other and kept up an annoying rapid chant of *batter batter batter* whenever someone came up to bat. I figured that as long as I could hear their shouting, I'd be safe.

I ran to my room to retrieve the protractor. Aggie was down in the parlor sewing more blouses. I slipped down the hall to the room Lamar shared with Sam Houston, looked this way and that to guard against potential witnesses, and crept inside.

I figured he'd keep the protractor in the tin trunk under his bed with his allowance and candy and other assorted treasures. I peeked out the window and, sure enough, they were thick in the middle of an engrossing play, shouting contradictory suggestions to Travis about where to throw the ball as Sam headed for second base, head down, arms pumping.

I pulled the trunk out, feeling guilty as a felon the moment I touched it. Meddling with one of the younger boys' things was deemed a misdemeanor, but interfering with Lamar's stuff would be a hanging offense. At least in his book.

The shouts on the lawn continued.

I opened the trunk. Before I touched anything, I took a moment to study the position of everything *in situ*, as Granddaddy called it, so that I could replace each item exactly as I'd found it. There were a cigar box similar to mine, two chocolate bars, and a small paper sack filled with cinnamon red hots. A pocket dictionary, a pen with a fine steel nib, a bottle of blue ink. An eagle feather, a broken windup clown from younger days, its innards now turned to rust, and the leather case containing his compass and ruler. I slipped the protractor into its slot and was closing the whole thing up, when I paused and considered the cigar box. Well, seeing I was here. . . .

I opened the box. There were a few scattered pennies and nickels. There were a couple of dimes and quarters. There was the ten-dollar gold piece Father had given him. And, right next to it, gleaming up at me, a five-dollar gold piece.

I froze in shock. My mind reeled. Was it mine? It had to be mine. Whose else could it be? But how could I tell for sure? I examined it closely, cursing myself for not having made some kind of scratch in the soft metal to mark it positively as my own. And unmarked, there was no telling for sure. Did that really matter? Of course not. He'd *stolen* it from me. But would Lamar commit such a heinous crime? *Don't be silly, Calpurnia, and stop concerning yourself with niceties. He did it and you're looking at the proof. The only real question is: how to make him pay? Right?*

I suddenly realized there was silence outside. Uh-oh. The front door slammed below me, and I nearly jumped out of my skin. Go! Without really thinking, I grabbed both pieces, restored the box and trunk to their previous positions, and ran down the hall to my room, clutching a heavy coin in each sweaty palm.

Back in my room, I looked around wildly for a secure hiding place. I couldn't put them in my money box under the bed. That was the first place Lamar would look if he indeed came looking. And the last place? Why, under the gravel in Sir Isaac Newton's dish, of course. No one—but no one—would think to look there.

FOR THE NEXT TWO DAYS, I lived in a miasma of fear and guilt (with, I confess, a dash of glee mixed in), wondering when Lamar would open his trunk. The burden of thievery was a heavy one and weighed me down with anxiety. But then, I kept telling myself, it wasn't thievery to steal your own property back from a thief. If it was your own property. Which it was. It had to be.

Lying awake at night, I plotted various ways of restoring Lamar's money to him—not that he deserved it, the louse. Some of these schemes involved returning it anonymously; others involved tipping my hand so he would know—*he would know*—it was me. But the choice was ripped from me when he charged down to lunch on Saturday, nostrils flaring like a bull, casting about wildly for the culprit. You could almost see the steam coming out his ears. He glared at each of us in turn. I screwed up my courage and struggled to maintain a neutral expression, refusing to quail beneath his frightful gaze. Prickles zinged across my skin. *Calpurnia*, I told myself strictly, *you will not break out in telltale hives and give the game away. You. Will. Not*. And amazingly, my skin calmed down.

Mother turned to Lamar. "Something the matter, darling?"

He was caught in a terrible bind and so choked with rage he could barely speak. Did he dare fess up? He spat out a vicious "no!"

We all gasped, and Mother recoiled in shock. Father thundered, "Lamar Tate. You will not speak to your mother in that tone of voice. Leave the table at once, sir. I will deal with you later."

Lamar scraped back his chair and stormed from the room. Father said to Mother, "What's wrong with that boy?"

She murmured with a catch in her voice, "I have no idea," and for one awful moment, I thought she might cry. In an attempt to restore order, we went back to our chicken and dumplings, which now tasted like ashes. Then someone asked someone else to pass the rolls and was asked in turn to pass the gravy, and slowly, ever so slowly, we resumed a conversation about nothing at all. The only one eating with gusto was Granddaddy, and he, the sharpest observer at the table, regarded me thoughtfully as he chewed.

Lamar, banished to his room, had no dinner that night, and also suffered three hard licks across the palm delivered by Father with a leather quirt. Travis felt sorry for Lamar and asked me if we should smuggle him some food. When I said no, Travis no doubt thought me mean, but I couldn't let on that I knew about the chocolate bars in Lamar's trunk.

I wisely stayed out of Lamar's way, worried that my facade of innocence would crack if he attacked me. But what could he do? He was stuck in a trap of his own devising. To finger me to the authorities (in this case, Mother and Father) would only give himself away as a bigger thief than me.

I did feel a little bad for him and thought about how to return his money now that he'd been punished, even if that punishment had been not for the theft itself, but rather the indirect consequences of it, his awfully cranky behavior.

For three days, I schemed and plotted and brooded like Napoleon in exile on Elba, and then I had it.

I enlisted Travis as my lieutenant and dispatched him to bring Lamar to me behind the barn next to Petunia's pen. (And lest you accuse me of violating the rule against naming food animals, J.B. had christened her, thinking it a great joke to name a mud-slathered beast after such a pretty flower. This particular Petunia was really quite a nice pig and enjoyed having her poll scratched with a stick; I had to admit I was going to be a bit sorry to see her go. Even though named, she was destined for the oven, the pot, and the smokehouse, to be replaced by yet another smaller, younger Petunia the following year.)

I leaned on the fence, tossing her potato peels, one of her favorite between-meal snacks. She grunted in appreciation and even caught a few of them on the fly like a pet dog. Lamar approached, Travis trailing behind and looking apprehensive; I'd told him he had to stay and witness the proceedings.

"Whaddya want?" Lamar growled, ever the ray of sunshine.

"You might try being nicer to me, Lamar," I said, tossing Petunia some more peelings. She rooted in the muck and snorked her appreciation.

"Why should I be nice to you? You're only a stupid girl. I got no reason to be nice to you."

"Oh," I replied, all sweetness and light, "I think you do."

He scoffed, "Gimme one good reason why."

"All right, I'll give you one," I said, reaching into my pinafore pocket. "In fact, I'll give you ten."

I held up the coin so that he could see it clearly and no mistake. His frown turned momentarily to pale confusion, then to red stupefaction as he registered what it was, and then to purple rage as he realized how I'd got it. The rapid progress of expressions—and colors—across his face was one of the highlights of my life.

"Give it back," he choked. "Give it back, or I'll tell Father."

"You can't," I replied, all calm and collected. "Because then I'll tell him you stole my money first. How many licks will that be worth, d'you think? The five you stole? Or a full ten? Or maybe he'll add them up to make fifteen. What d'you reckon?"

The look on his face was priceless. Strangely, the more perturbed he grew, the more calm and collected *I* grew. Travis, our witness, twitched in anxiety.

Lamar, thinking himself cunning, switched tactics. "Come on, Callie," he pleaded. "There's no reason to be like that. Won't you please give it back? Please?"

"Well," I said, "since you put it like that, okay. Here it is." And with that, I tossed the coin high into the air. Time magically slowed, and the three of us watched the coin sailing, sailing, sailing over the fence, gleaming majestically in the sun. And just for that moment, I was transformed from a half citizen into a full citizen—no, a soldier—no, an *entire army*—of justice and vengeance for all the other half citizens in the world.

The coin landed with a plop in the middle of the pigpen. In a large pool of semiliquid dung.

Petunia, alerted to the sound of something potentially edible, ponderously turned around and lumbered toward it, determined to root it up and swallow it, whatever it was.

"Hurry up and fetch it, Lamar!" I cried. "Or it's going to get a whole lot worse."

I wheeled and ran for the house, fleet of foot, faster than I'd ever run in my life, no longer an army but the wind itself. There'd be no catching me that day.

It was months before Lamar spoke to me again. Do you think I cared? I did not.

CHAPTER 20

AN ASTONISHING
SUM OF MONEY

Some of the Fuegians plainly showed that they had a fair notion of barter. I gave one man a large nail (a most valuable present) without making any signs for a return; but he immediately picked out two fish and handed them back on the point of his spear.

WE NEGOTIATED OUR WAY through another holiday season, the quietest Christmas and New Year's ever, the festivities still muted due to the Flood. Mother's two girlhood friends had been swept away, their bodies never found. Still, I could tell she was doing her best to bear up and not look too sad, at least in front of the younger ones.

Even though I knew better, I prayed for another miraculous snowfall. But there was no snow. There was only rain. I gave everyone the mittens I'd made, and they at least pretended to like them in varying degrees. (Oh, all right, they weren't the best mittens in the world; there was the occasional dropped stitch and skewed row, but if the recipients didn't care for them, well, they could order their next pair from Mr. Sears.)

On New Year's Eve, we followed the family tradition of announcing our resolutions. The year before, I'd had a long list that included seeing snow as well as the ocean, but this year I had only one. When my turn came, I stood up, took a deep breath, and said, "I want to go to college. Not for the teaching certificate—that's only one year. But for a whole degree. I know that takes more years."

My parents fell silent. Finally Mother said, "Well, dear, perhaps we can talk about this later. When you're a bit older."

I said, with more boldness than I felt, "What's wrong with now?"

J.B. piped up with, "What does that mean? Are you going away, Callie?"

Then Granddaddy, bless him, spoke up. "An excellent plan, don't you think, Margaret?"

Mother dared not actually glare at Granddaddy but there was definite ice in her mien. She turned to Father for support.

Father cleared his throat and said, "Yes . . . well, we shall just have to see. It's far too early to be thinking about such things. Perhaps we'll discuss this again when you're sixteen."

Three whole years away! I gaped at him, trying to rally some kind of supporting argument. Before I could come up with something, he said, "Travis, I believe it is your turn. Tell us your resolutions."

And we moved on around the circle, just like that. J.B. climbed in my lap. He gave me a sticky kiss and whispered, "Where are you going? Don't go away. I'll be sad."

"Don't be sad," I whispered back. "It looks like I'm not going anywhere. Maybe never."

"That's good," he murmured, his breath warm on my cheek. Except that it wasn't good. I hugged him and rocked him, but really it was myself I was trying to soothe. I looked around the circle. Everyone's attention was now on Travis—except for Granddaddy, who gave me a small nod of approval.

So we got through the rather flat holidays. And then, ten days later, on January 10, 1901, a gusher came in at a place in east Texas called Spindletop. A roaring black geyser of oil jetted 150 feet into the air for nine days straight before it could be contained, setting in motion the oil boom that would spell the rise of the auto-mobile and the end of the horse, and usher in transformative changes in everything else, including our own home, the whole country, the entire world.

Frankly, I barely registered it at the time, but the news excited Aggie for some reason, and she appeared more animated than I'd ever seen her.

Later that week, a surprising topic of mutual interest arose between us. It arrived in the form of another letter lying on the hall table addressed to her from the First State Bank of Galveston. Huh. This struck me as unusual. As far as I knew, my mother had never once in her whole life received correspondence from a bank. Finance and such matters were deemed men's territory. (I don't know why; there seemed to be no reason for it other than it had always been that way.)

There was no one around, so I picked up the envelope. I shook it gently and palpated it lightly. I heard no chink of coin, felt no rustle of bills. Being a helpful type, I carried it upstairs to our room, where Aggie sat at the desk, writing yet another letter. She covered it with her forearm to hide the contents from me.

"Look, Aggie, it's something for you from a bank in Galveston. What could—"

She turned in her seat and snatched it from my hands before the words had left my mouth. You'd have thought it contained a stay of execution from the governor. She held it with shaking hands for a moment, then took a paper knife and delicately eased it open, taking great care not to damage the contents in any way. What could warrant such treatment? She was too preoccupied to notice me leaning over her shoulder, but all I could see were several columns of numbers, similar to the documents that covered my father's desk at the gin.

She read it avidly, her finger tracing its way down the page. Arriving at the bottom figure, she muttered, "Oh, thank goodness."

"Good news, Aggie?"

Typically she'd rebuff a question of this sort, but now she sighed with relief and said, "My money is safe. Some of the bank records were washed away in the Flood, but they found mine. Thank the Lord, my money is safe."

This excited my curiosity. "You have money in the bank? Where'd you get it?"

"I saved it up from working at Poppa's store."

"How did you do that?"

"Office work. Poppa paid me to type-write letters and do some of the bookkeeping."

I mulled this over and said, "How much?"

"What?"

"How much did he pay you? How much do you have in the bank?"

She wrinkled her nose and said, "None of your business, Little Miss Busybody."

I thought hard to come up with some kind of sufficient incentive to make her tell me.

"Spill it," I said, "or I'll put Sir Isaac Newton in your bed while you're asleep." In truth, I wouldn't have done that to her or to Sir Isaac, a soft-bodied creature who might well have been injured in the brawl that would no doubt have ensued, but I thought the threat quite inspired as it came from my lips. Threat by newt. Really, it was one of my better ones.

She paled. "You wouldn't. Would you?"

"I might or I might not."

She narrowed her eyes. "I'll tell your mother."

I narrowed mine back at her and bluffed, "Go right ahead. See if I care."

So. We had ourselves a squinty-eyed standoff.

I said, "The family Salamandridae feels cold and slimy to the touch. It secretes a noxious protective film of—"

She caved, as I figured she would. Newts have many uses, after all.

"I guess it can't hurt anything," she said. "I've saved almost a hundred dollars."

"Wow! Gosh!" An astonishing sum for anyone, let alone an unmarried girl of seventeen. Suddenly the conversation was a whole lot more interesting. "That's amazing. How long did it take you?"

"About a year. Poppa paid me thirty cents per hour."

"What are you going to do with it?"

She hesitated. "I don't know yet."

I figured she was lying, but why? Still, that part didn't really interest me. What interested me were the many things you could buy with a hundred dollars. You could buy a decent horse, one that would transport you miles from home anytime you wanted. That was freedom of a sort. You could, if you were a typical girl, buy half a dozen gowns for a year of debutante balls, or a whole supply of fine linens for your trousseau. I suppose that was freedom of a sort. You could buy, if you were a different type of girl, a really good microscope and unlimited Scientific Notebooks. Definitely freedom of a sort. Or you could buy—it came to me in a flash—you could buy yourself something greater than all of these things. You could buy . . . an education. The thought was so audacious I could barely breathe.

Aggie said, "Are you all right? You look funny."

"Huh?"

"Are you going to swoon?"

"What?"

"You aren't old enough, but I've got some smelling salts here if you need them."

"I'm fine . . . I think."

My mind racing, I pestered her for details. She told me all I had to do was go to the bank with any little amount of money and ask to open a savings account. And yes, the bank would keep my money safe, where no thieving brothers could get their hands on it, and yes, the bank would give me back my money anytime I wanted it, and yes, they would even pay *me* money (she called it "interest") to look after my money.

The next day I marched down Main Street to the bank beyond the gin, cigar box in hand. I'd never been inside before, and for a moment, my courage failed me at the imposing brass doors. Nevertheless, I pushed my way in and stood blinking at the polished marble floor, the high ceiling with ornate moldings, the gleaming spittoons, the hushed atmosphere of prosperity and serious business doings. A far cry from the raucous clatter of the gin.

To one side stood a great steel vault, the door, at least a foot thick, standing partly open. To the other stood an oak and brass cage inside of which two mustachioed young men counted out cash for waiting customers. There was not a girl or woman in the place. To the rear, a portly fussy-looking man in a formal suit sat smoking a cigar at an expansive desk, deep in earnest conversation with a customer whose back was to me, whom I nonetheless recognized. Father. The portly man frowned at me and said something. Father got up and approached me with concern clouding his face.

"Calpurnia, what are you doing here? Is everything all right at home?"

"Everything is fine, Father." I held out my cigar box and said, "I have come to open an account." I heard my voice wobble, which I hated, but I plowed on. "I think they call it a savings account."

Father looked amused. "Why on earth do you need that?"

I thought quickly. "You're always telling us to save our money, so I thought this would be the best place to do it." Of course, his next logical question would be to inquire exactly what I was saving for. I hoped he wouldn't ask me. I didn't want to talk about it with him again. Yet.

To my relief, he merely said, "Hmm, yes. When I said it I was referring to the boys more than you, but it's an excellent idea, and you shall set a good example for them. Come, I'll introduce you to the president, and we'll get you started."

I curtsied and shook hands with the puffy bank president, Mr. Applebee, who struck me as pompous and having quite the air of being pleased with himself for no good reason that I could tell. I hoped I wouldn't have to do this every time I came in; it was like shaking hands with a big, dampish marshmallow. He had me fill out a paper with my name and address and such, and then led me to the brass cage, where I handed over my box. One of the tellers carefully counted my money twice and announced the total sum of $7.58. He wrote this figure in a small blue booklet and handed it to me, advising me to keep it safe and bring it with me each time I needed to make a "deposit" or a "withdrawal," and that "interest" would be added to my "balance" four times per year.

Father and I said our good-byes at the door. He headed for the gin, and I headed home, clutching the box that now held my new passbook. I stopped frequently to admire the handsome blue cover bearing the legend FIRST NATIONAL BANK OF FENTRESS in gold print, the notation of Opening Deposit of $7.58 written in a fine copperplate hand, and the many empty lines and blank columns waiting to be filled in with the record of my accumulating fortune. It was all very satisfying.

Relations between me and Aggie thawed a bit more. I was appreciative of her information about the bank and tried to show it in small ways. She in turn enjoyed talking with me about her "income and investments," although I didn't really understand everything she said. We compared notes about the progress of our savings. Plus, I guess that she felt a need to be nicer to me, now that I knew the secret of her savings. I had no way of knowing that she was hiding another secret, even more important, from us all.

AROUND THIS TIME, Travis began disappearing after dinner and not reappearing until bedtime. In fact, he was doing this almost every night, although I didn't pay much attention at first. With so many brothers tearing about the place, it was hard to keep track of them all. Then one morning, on our way to school, he looked as if he hadn't slept well, and I noticed scratches on his hands and bruises on his legs.

"Uh, Travis?"

"Hmm?"

I pointed to his wounds. "Anything you want to tell me?"

"Oh, that. I had a really bad night with Scruffy."

I stopped in my tracks. "Scruffy did that to you?"

"No, no, he'd never hurt me! It was the coyotes."

"The *coyotes*?"

"Well, not exactly the coyotes, but running through the bushes and stuff."

"Are you going to explain that to me or do I have to pull it out of you one word at a time?"

"Well, it's kind of a long story, Callie."

"Begin," I said impatiently. "I'm all ears."

"Okay. Do you remember when you told me that canines are happiest living with their own kind, in packs?"

I didn't remember, but I didn't say so.

"I started thinking that Scruffy needs the company of other dogs. So last week I took him to that empty lot behind the Baptist church where the town dogs like to meet, and I tried to introduce him. But for some reason they bared their teeth and chased him away. I guess they could tell he's not one of them, at least not a hundred percent. It's not fair, Callie—he didn't ask to be born half dog and half coyote, you know. It's not as if he could help it. And he couldn't help making his living on chickens."

I considered Scruffy's well-developed taste for poultry, and how it would probably doom him in the end.

Travis continued, "The next night I was visiting him at dusk when we heard the coyotes howling, way off in the distance. You know that high-pitched *yip-yip-yip* they make when they're gathering to hunt? Well, he pricked up his ears and got this wild look in his eye. That's when I realized he belonged with the coyotes! Why hadn't I thought of it before? They're such a scruffy lot, he'd fit right in, all sniffing and playing and hunting together. I even had a dream that same night that they made him the leader of their pack. So I started paying attention to where they gathered, and I found out that sometimes they meet on the far side of the river, just below the bridge. I sneaked out a couple of nights and took Scruffy over there, but we didn't see them."

I was impressed with Travis's resourcefulness, and how he had seemingly solved the Scruffy problem on his own.

"Last night was the third night we went to look for coyotes. We were walking along the river at dusk, and suddenly they were there, really loud and close by. When Scruffy heard them, he got that wild look in his eye again, and I knew that he belonged with them. I was awful sad, but I hugged him and told him, 'Good-bye, Scruffy. Your pack is waiting for you. They are your family now. This is your destiny.' He lit off in their direction."

Travis wiped his eyes, and I put my arm around him.

"I wanted to see the happy reunion so I chased after him in the moonlight and got scratched by all these prickle bushes. But it's a good thing I followed him, 'cos I could hear growling and yelping something fierce up ahead, and by the time I got there, three of them had him surrounded and were beating him up bad, just tearing into him. They were trying to *kill* him, Callie. They hated him. They wanted to *eat* him. But it's a good thing they're afraid of humans. I picked up a big stick and some big stones, and I chased them off just in time."

Travis wiped his eyes again. "Poor old Scruffy. He just wants to be part of a pack. But the dogs don't want him and the coyotes don't want him, and people only want to drown him or shoot him. Plus he's an orphan, kind of, and he lost all his brothers and sisters."

"Poor old Scruffy," I said, and meant it. I'd never known a creature to start out in life with Fate so cruelly stacking the odds against it. "Is he . . . is he gone?"

"He's back at his den," Travis said, perking up. "I guess I get to keep him."

I thought about this, and it struck me as fair enough. For although Fate had initially dealt Scruffy a rough hand, she was more than making it up to the coydog by giving him Travis.

"Nobody wants him but me," he said. "I guess that *I'm* his pack." He looked at me shyly. "You can be part of our pack too, if you want."

I could say nothing in the face of this except, "Okay. But he still has to be a secret, you know."

Lord, the secrets were piling up.

CHAPTER 21

SECRETS AND SHAME

The geology of Patagonia is interesting.... The most common shell is a massive gigantic oyster, sometimes even a foot in diameter.

AS I BRUSHED MY HAIR one hundred strokes at bedtime, I asked, "What is the sea like, Aggie? And the beach, what is that like? What about seashells? Is it true that you can just walk along and pick them up for free, or do you have to pay for them?"

"Pay? Don't be silly—who would you pay?"

"I don't know. That's why I'm asking."

"You pick up whatever you want, although why you'd bother, I don't know."

"For a shell collection, of course." One of my resolutions last New Year's Eve had been to set eyes on the ocean—any ocean—before I died, and since there was considerable doubt that this would ever happen, a shell collection would be a valuable thing to get my mitts on.

Aggie said, "I can't imagine why anyone would want a bunch of dirty old shells."

I found this conversation discouraging but persevered with,

"Have you ever seen a dolphin? I've read all about them. They're mammals, you know, warm-blooded. Not fish at all."

"How can they not be fish?" she said. "They live in the water. They have to be fish."

I stared at her in disbelief. For a girl who was privileged enough to live by the sea, she was dismally stupid about it.

I sighed and said, "Does the sun not sparkle on the dancing waves?"

She cast me a look. "Where'd you get *that* from?"

"Um, I read it somewhere."

"Right. Okay, well, I suppose you could say that's true when the weather's nice."

I said, "Tell me about the waves."

She looked perplexed. "The waves wash stuff up on the sand."

"What kind of stuff?"

"Oh, rotten fish, dead seagulls, driftwood, old seaweed, junk like that. And pee-yoo, it really does stink sometimes. Although once I found a glass fisherman's float, and once I found an empty bottle of rum that had floated all the way from Jamaica."

"Gosh! Was there a note in it?"

"No." She yawned.

"But did you keep it anyway? I'd love to have something like that."

"Whatever for? It's only a bunch of old junk."

The conversation was definitely not going as I'd hoped, but I pushed on. "Tell me about the tides."

"What's to tell? The tide comes in for a while and then it goes out again. Sometimes you can hear it."

"It has a sound? What does it sound like?"

"Well, when it's quiet, it makes a noise like this: *shoosh-shoosh*. Sometimes it's loud, when the waves crash on the rocks and make a big racket. It just depends."

"What does it depend on?"

She looked at me as if I were speaking Chinese. "How would *I* know?"

Her attitude struck me as very unsatisfying. How could she not know, how could she not find out, how could she not care? I wondered if something else had gone wrong with her in addition to her anemia and neurasthenia. Maybe she'd been injured in the Flood in some other way that didn't show. Maybe she'd been hit on the head and had all the curiosity knocked out of her. Question for the Notebook: What causes the waves? And the tides? Discuss further with Granddaddy.

The next day, a small package arrived for her and, casually loitering over the mail, I noted that the return address was one "L. Lumpkin, 2400 Church Street, Galveston." Who, or what, was an L. Lumpkin? I was about to carry it up to her when she dashed in from outside and fell on the parcel like a stooping falcon, clutching it to herself, face alight. Then she wheeled without a word and pelted up the stairs at full speed.

Goodness. How terribly rude. And how very interesting.

I found her in our room wrestling with the hairy twine

holding the package together. In exasperation, she screeched, "Scissors! Get me scissors!"

I ran downstairs to retrieve the pair in my knitting bag in the parlor, but by the time I got back, she had managed to pull the package apart. Inside was a box that she placed on the desk and opened reverently. Inside this box was a smaller box and a letter. Hands clasped to her bosom, she paused to savor the moment, whatever it was.

I made the mistake of murmuring, "What is it?"

She turned on me. "What does it take to get some privacy in this house? Get out!"

Offended, I said, "There's no need to yell. I can certainly tell when I'm not wanted." I left in a state of wounded pique, my feelings lacerated but my head held high. Here I'd been thinking we were friends of a sort.

I went downstairs and made the mistake of pacing the hallway, where Mother managed to snag me for piano practice.

As Aggie and I got ready for bed that night, she said, "Callie, where's the hairbrush?"

I plunked it down in front of her. A few minutes later, "Callie, have you seen the pumice stone?"

I plunked that down too, and was treated to the sound of her rasping her heels for five minutes.

"Callie, what have you done with the—"

"Nothing! Whatever it is! Find it yourself—I'm not your maid."

A frosty silence prevailed. I could tell she was bursting to tell me something but we studiously ignored each other until it was almost time to blow out the lamp. Finally she said, "All right. Can you keep a secret?"

Offended, I retorted, "Of course I can. I'm not a child, you know."

"Do you swear not to tell? Hold up your right hand and swear."

I did so, but even this seemed not to satisfy her and she said, "Wait, where's my Bible?"

"Really, Aggie."

She pulled her Bible from the wardrobe and made me place my right hand on it. Oh, serious business indeed. If you broke this kind of promise, didn't that mean you would go to H_ll? But what if you were tortured with hot pokers and flogged with the nine-tailed cat until you told? Would you be excused in that case? My knees trembled a little, as did my voice.

"I swear not to tell."

"And *never* to tell at any time, now and forevermore."

"*Never* to tell, now and forever. Amen."

Her whole face relaxed, and she smiled in a way I'd never seen before. Why, she wasn't bad-looking at all, a fact obscured by her habitual ill temper and all the worry and woe she carried about on her shoulders.

Mother had given her a carpetbag to replace the gunnysack she'd first arrived with, and she retrieved from it the small box I'd seen earlier. She bade me sit at the desk and handed it to me with great care.

I opened the box to find a cased photograph of a young man of twenty or so, trussed like a turkey in a tight suit and stiff collar, his hair plastered flat for the grand occasion of having his portrait made.

"There he is," she whispered, her expression going all soppy the way Harry's had when he'd wooed his first girlfriend.

I studied the pale moonish face, the skimpy mustache, the slightly buck teeth, the struggling beard.

"Isn't he marvelous," she breathed in a voice clotted with deep emotion.

Well . . . no. He looked rather like a smelt. To be charitable, some of this was probably due to having to hold his breath and freeze in place for the photograph, but some of it looked like an actual deficit in personality. I'd heard Granddaddy say there was no accounting for other people's taste, and here was living proof.

"Who is he, Aggie?"

"Why, that's Lafayette Lumpkin, of course. He's my beau. But nobody knows, and you mustn't tell." She squeezed my shoulder with an iron grip.

"Ow, that hurts. I *won't*. I *promised*. How'd you meet him?"

"He used to work as a bookkeeper in Poppa's store. But then he asked to walk me home, and Poppa fired him the very next day on some trumped-up charge. But he didn't do anything wrong. Poppa just wanted him out of the way."

"Why?"

"Poppa says his family comes from the wrong side of the tracks, and maybe they do, but I don't care a whit. Lafayette is a self-made man," she said proudly. "He learned accounting through a correspondence course, you see, and has made every effort to better himself, but it's not enough for Poppa, who's forgotten that he pulled his own self up by his bootstraps. He thinks I should marry a Sealy or a Moody or one of the other first families of Galveston. They're all rich as Croesus, but I spurn their advances."

She picked up the photo and hugged it to herself tenderly. Her gaze softened, and her voice went all dreamy. "My heart belongs to Lafayette."

Now, this was all very romantic, but exchanging secret letters with a man without her parents' approval was a dangerous game, one that could only end in trouble and tears. No wonder she swooped on the mail every day before anyone else could get a look at it.

"He's asked for my photograph—isn't that sweet? But I lost the only one I had in the Flood."

"There's a photographer in Lockhart, Hofacket's Portrait Parlor. Granddaddy and I went there and had our photograph made with the *Vicia tateii*."

She gave me an odd look. "You had your photograph made with that plant?"

"Of course. They say it's important to memorialize special occasions."

"They're referring to weddings and christenings and suchlike. Not plants."

"I'll have you know that finding a new species is a very

important occasion. Look," I said, opening the desk drawer and pulling out the portrait of Granddaddy, myself, and our discovery. "Look there," I said, pointing proudly.

"That's it?" she said with a touch of scorn, and tossed the photo aside as if it were nothing. Nothing. Most of the goodwill she'd been banking with me evaporated, and I sank into a snit. My photo of the vetch was every bit as important to me as Lafayette Lumpkin's was to her. And though I'll admit that the plant looked bedraggled and unprepossessing, suffering as it was that day from heat stress, still, it was a brand-new species and deserving of respect. There was just no interesting some people in the most important things.

"Wait a moment," she said, picking up the photograph and examining it keenly; I watched her absorb its significance as both a scientific and historic document. The light dawned within her. How gratifying. Up until this moment, she'd viewed me at best as a somewhat strange companion, at worst, an annoyance. Now she would take me seriously. Now we would have stimulating discussions on other subjects besides money. Now we could be explorers together. She tapped the embossed gold seal in the lower left corner that read *Hofacket's Fine Portraiture*.

"You said this place is in Lockhart?"

"It's kitty-corner to the courthouse. Why?"

"Why do you think?" she said, looking at me as if I were slow. "I can get my picture made for Lafayette. What does it cost, and when is the next trip to town?"

Gah. So much for exploring Nature and Science together.

"It costs a dollar, and I think Alberto's taking the wagon on Saturday."

"Good. I'll go then."

"I'm going too." I rapidly counted up the number making the trip, and realized that the addition of Aggie meant I would lose my spot on the spring seat up front, and I'd have to sit in the wagon bed. Still, a trip to the big city (population 2,306), with its many attractions, including electricity, was always worth it, with the library, the mercantile, the tearoom, and the bustling traffic. The library meant dealing with the elderly lady librarian, one Mrs. Whipple by name, a terrifying old bat who kept a close watch on the books, deciding whether children should be allowed them or not. She'd once humiliated me by refusing me a copy of Mr. Darwin's book *The Origin of Species*; fortunately, Granddaddy had remedied the situation by giving me his own copy, but still I trembled under Mrs. Whipple's sour gaze.

I asked Aggie, "How are you going to explain a portrait?"

"I'll say it's for Momma and Poppa, of course, to replace the one they lost in the Flood."

Gosh, here I was thinking I could be devious as all get-out when the situation demanded it, but Aggie had me beat all hollow. That girl could really think on her feet.

SATURDAY, MY FAVORITE DAY of the week, rolled around. I knocked on our own library door and heard the usual response of "Enter if you must."

"Granddaddy, we're going to Lockhart. Do you want me to return your library books?"

"That would be most kind. Also, let me give you this list of books I'd like to check out."

I took his list and ran for the wagon. Sitting up front were Alberto, Harry, and Aggie. Sul Ross and I sat on an old quilt in the back. I'd brought my copy of *The Voyage of the* Beagle, and kept him entertained by reading aloud from the exciting parts. He especially liked the parts about cannibalism, but I had to keep my voice low so that the adults in front did not overhear.

When we got to town, the others all piled into Sutherland's Emporium ("Everything Under One Roof") on the square, a massive department store all of three stories high and filled with enticements both practical and frivolous. I headed for the library.

The library was dim and smelled of paper, ink, leather, and dust. Ahh, the enchanting smell of books. Really, what could be better? Well, one thing that *could* be better would be the absence of Mrs. Whipple, the resident harpy.

I placed the books I was returning on the counter. Fortunately she was nowhere in sight, but I heard the swish of the threadbare black bombazine dress she wore in all weather, along with the faint creaking of her whalebone corset, and caught a whiff of mothballs, which meant she lurked nearby. Strange. Then she suddenly popped up from behind the counter like a jack-in-the-box, right in my face. I jumped about a mile and squeaked like a baby mouse, but even while jumping had to marvel at how her stout elderly form could be so springy and quick.

"Well," she said grimly, "if it isn't Calpurnia Virginia Tate, skulking about as usual."

How bitterly unfair! I knew how to skulk, and this was not skulking. Why did she have it in for me, this horrible custodian of the books? We were both book lovers, were we not? Logically, we should have been kindred spirits, and yet for some reason, we managed to perpetually enrage each other, seemingly without effort. Maybe it was time to make peace, bury the hatchet, extend the olive branch, make sincere apologies for our mutual wrongs.

Or maybe not quite yet.

Anger rose like bile in my throat. I bit it back and said in the most syrupy voice I could dredge up, "Good afternoon, Mrs. Whipple. I'm so sorry you thought I was 'skulking.' It's just that you startled me. Gosh, you're really agile for such a heavyset, uh . . ."

She flushed such an alarming beetroot color that I worried I'd gone too far and would be blamed for her death by apoplexy.

"I think," she said, "it's best that you leave. I'm too busy to deal with an impertinent chit such as you." She turned her back on me and headed for the Texas History section.

Evicted from the library! A new low! How on earth would I explain it to Mother? But speaking of chits, I remembered the note I carried from Granddaddy. In certain circles, the mere invocation of his name worked as a golden key to magically open doors that otherwise would have remained firmly closed to me; in other circles, composed mainly of the ignorant, the unwashed, and the unread, he was treated derisively as a loon, the "mad perfessor," espousing heretical ideas, likely unstable, possibly dangerous.

Mrs. Whipple knew Granddaddy to be a founding member of the National Geographic Society; she knew him to be in correspondence with the Smithsonian Museum, and whatever her own feelings about the theory of evolution, she had to grant that he was the most learned man from Austin to San Antonio, and likely beyond.

"Before I go, Mrs. Whipple, my grandfather wants me to check out these books." I extracted the note and smoothed it carefully on the counter. "They're for *him*, you see. For his research. His personal research."

She turned, and I could tell by the look on her face that she did see. Torn, tight-lipped, she nevertheless snatched up the list, ran her narrowed eyes over it, and then, without looking at me, wheeled into the stacks, barking, "Twenty minutes."

Good. There was time to browse the Emporium and maybe catch up with Aggie getting her portrait made. With a light heart and a light step, I headed for the square. We were lucky to have such a fine library when the majority of counties across Texas had none at all. Dr. Eugene Clark, a physician dying young, had bequeathed ten thousand dollars for its construction so that the young woman who had declined his proposal of marriage would have a proper library and lyceum in which to study literature and music. It had been built for love. And those of us in Caldwell County who could read were the beneficiaries.

I told myself, *Calpurnia, you're a lucky girl, even if you do have to deal with such a gorgon to check out books.* Actually, that was the tiniest bit unkind, was it not? Apparently it was more unkind than that, because by the time I'd made it to the square on this clear, fine day, a small black cloud of guilt had gathered on my internal horizon.

I wondered why Mrs. Whipple disliked me so much. I realized that if she'd had no particularly good reason before, she had a plenty big reason now, and I had handed it to her on a plate. I inspected my behavior, trying to shine at least a neutral light on it, but could not. At best I had been rude. At worst I had been cruel. I tried to put myself in her shoes (or rather, her creaking corset): a widow, elderly, eking out a scanty existence, having to put up with impertinent children like, well, me. She was the Keeper of the Books, and deserving of respect. No matter that she treated the books as if they were her own, reluctant to hand them over to careless strangers who might not accord them the respect they deserved, who might have grubby hands, who might commit the sin of underlining or writing in the margins, who might even commit the ultimate evil of losing one of the precious volumes! Unthinkable!

Ack, Calpurnia, you wicked girl. I'd have to make it up to her somehow. I would make a sincere apology to her to clear my conscience. Let her dislike me if she would; I would refuse to dislike her. She could not make me.

At Sutherland's I examined the scents and soaps and powders, far more plentiful and elegant than the selection at the Fentress General Store. A bar of fancy lavender soap in a decorative tin caught my eye, and I thought it a suitable gift for an old lady. I allowed myself the briefest of sighs before telling myself to buck up and then forking over a whole quarter. I didn't have enough left over for a root beer float, but never mind. Now that I had my own income, I figured there'd be plenty of floats in my future.

I wandered up to the mezzanine tearoom, where ladies sat in delicate gilt chairs among the potted palms and drank from bone china cups and ate teeny-tiny sandwiches with the crusts cut off (don't ask me why). I admired the pressed-tin ceiling, the slow turning of the two-bladed electric fans, the whooshing of the overhead pneumatic tubes carrying money and receipts back and forth across the store at a dizzying speed.

I went downstairs and found Harry buying cigars for Father. He said, "What have you got there, pet?"

"It's for Mrs. Whipple, the librarian. Do you think she'll like it?"

"Very suitable. But why are you buying her a gift?"

"I was mean to her." I explained the situation but did not tell him I had spent all my money, I swear. He commiserated and said, "Very commendable, pet. Come on, I'll buy you a float or a sundae, whichever you like."

"Gosh, really?" Life was looking up.

We sat side by side on swiveling stools at the fountain. Harry ordered a brand-new treat made from a split banana, an exotic imported fruit we'd never seen before. Of course, I had to order the root beer float. I admired the practiced ease with which the soda jerk assembled it, scooping the vanilla ice cream, adding the aromatic root beer, nicely calibrating just how high it would foam up in the tall tulip-shaped glass, almost but not quite overflowing, then topping it off with a dollop of glossy whipped cream and a shiny red cherry before sliding it to me on a frilly paper napkin with both a spoon *and* a straw.

I spooned up the whipped cream and pushed the ice cream to the bottom, discreetly slurping the fizzing slurry through my straw. Harry was kind enough to give me two bites of his banana split (there were definite advantages to being his pet), and it was such a marvelous treat that I resolved to have one of my own next time, even though they cost thirty cents!

Then I wandered through the various departments and admired the goods for sale. For some reason, they didn't carry books in stock. Maybe the store owner wasn't much of a reader, or maybe he figured the library was enough.

We went out to the street, where Harry and Alberto began to load up supplies. I wandered over to Hofacket's Portrait Parlor ("Fine Photographs for Fine Occasions") and was about to go in and look for Aggie when something in the window caught my eye. There, wedged between a photograph of a naked baby on a bearskin rug and an awkward countrified bride and groom in clothes rented for the occasion, was a familiar sight: Granddaddy and me and the Plant, on display for all the world—or at least all of Lockhart—to see. Goodness, we were locally famous. I wondered, could this be why Mrs. Whipple had it in for me? But no, she'd disliked me long before we'd discovered the Plant.

I went in, the tinkling bell overhead signaling my arrival.

"Take a seat!" hollered Mr. Hofacket. "I'm in the middle of a portrait here."

Then Aggie called, "Calpurnia, is that you? Come back here if that's you."

I pushed through the curtains into the studio where Aggie sat posed on an ornate wicker chair like a throne. In her lap she held a large spray of artificial roses and trailing greenery. She frowned at the flowers and said, "What d'you think? With the flowers or without?"

Mr. Hofacket looked up and said, "Why, hello, Miss Calpurnia. So nice to see you again." Mr. Hofacket had been much taken with our discovery and, if left to his own devices, would rattle on at length about the Plant's importance and the critical part he'd played in establishing the existence of a new species on the planet and how his close-up of *Vicia tateii* now resided at the Smithsonian, with his—Hofacket's—own embossed seal on the reverse, for anyone to see, forever and ever, and so forth and so on.

He inquired in respectful tones after Granddaddy's health and mine before I headed him off at the pass and asked him why he had our picture in the window.

"Well, missy, that's a good question. It's such a good question that half a dozen people come in here and ask it every single day, and then a lot of them stay to get their portraits done. It's what you might call a curiosity piece, a real conversation starter. Why, I remember one day—"

"With the flowers or without?" Aggie interrupted. "Sorry, Mr. Hofacket, but I don't have all day, you know."

"Right, right."

"So with or without?" Aggie stared at me with more than a flicker of impatience.

The flowers were fine approximations of the real thing, clearly made by someone who had studied the originals in Nature. "With, I think. They're very pretty. It's a shame that the colors won't show."

This sent Mr. Hofacket into gales of laughter at the thought of capturing color on a photographic plate. Aggie arranged the flowers while Mr. Hofacket loaded his magnesium flare and burrowed under his black cloth. "Hold real still," he commanded. "Three, two, one." The magnesium lit the room with a brilliant white light, leaving us momentarily stunned and blinded.

"Right," he said, "that should do 'er. You say you want two copies?"

"Yes, sir," said Aggie. "That's two dollars, right?"

"Right. Give me half an hour or so. They should be dry by then."

Aggie and I headed back to the Emporium but not before I pointed out the Plant in Hofacket's window. To my great satisfaction, she did look somewhat impressed, albeit grudgingly.

I left her fingering the fabrics and lace at the store and, screwing up my courage, headed back to the library to make my apology, present my gift, and perform whatever penance was expected of me.

I took a deep breath, steeled myself, and went in. To my simultaneous consternation and relief, Mrs. Whipple was nowhere to be seen. A small stack of books sat on the counter, tied with twine and bearing the briefest note: *Books requested by Captain Walter Tate, Fentress*. I tucked the books under my arm and carefully centered the pretty little tin of soap in the exact same spot. The brave part of me wanted to track her down in the stacks and follow through with my plan. The coward in me was highly relieved and thought, "Next time." This latter part seized the upper hand and whispered, "Hurry up, the wagon's waiting for you." Well, maybe it was and maybe it wasn't, but I chose to believe it and skedaddled out the door, congratulating myself on both my bravery and my cowardice.

And by the way, I know for a fact that Aggie made a trip to the post office first thing Monday morning on her way to school.

CHAPTER 22

THE VALUE OF LEARNING NEW SKILLS

A small frog, of the genus Hyla, sits on a blade of grass about an inch above the surface of the water, and sends forth a pleasing chirp: when several are together they sing in harmony on different notes. I had some difficulty in catching a specimen of this frog. The genus Hyla has its toes terminated by small suckers; and I found this animal could crawl up a pane of glass, when placed absolutely perpendicular.

GRANDDADDY'S LESSON PLAN next called for a frog, and we fortuitously came across a good-sized one at the inlet, not long dead, floating with its pale belly up. It was a *Rana sphenocephala*, the southern leopard frog, so named because of its distinctive dark spots. On inspection, the cause of death was not obvious.

"Will it do?" I asked Granddaddy. It looked only a little worse for wear.

"It will do," he said.

"I wonder what killed it?"

"Perhaps you shall find out when you do your autopsy," he replied.

We carried the frog back to the laboratory in my old fishing creel and pulled out the dissecting pan and tools. I was taking a real step up the evolutionary ladder, advancing to phylum Chordata, subphylum Vertebrata, meaning the frog had a backbone and spinal cord in common with humans, unlike the earthworm. And speaking of earthworms, where was Travis? He had agreed to watch this procedure. I fretted momentarily over whether I should retrieve him, then figured the time and trauma would not be worth it. It would be challenge enough to force him to study the results. And that boy wanted to be a veterinarian? How was that supposed to work?

Following Granddaddy's instructions, I turned the frog on its back and pinned each foot to the wax. I made an H-shaped incision the length of the belly through the smooth but tough skin and carefully pinned it back, then repeated the process through the substantial layer of muscle. There lay the innards: the surprisingly large liver, the tiny pancreas and wormlike intestines, the saclike lungs, the kidneys.

"Regard the heart," said Granddaddy, pointing it out with tweezers. "It comprises only three chambers, unlike the mammalian and avian hearts, which each have four. The frog heart mixes oxygen-rich and oxygen-poor blood before pumping it around the body; it is therefore not as efficient as the hearts of birds and humans, which pump only oxygen-rich blood, providing the organism with greater energy."

We concluded with the kidneys and cloaca and ovaries, showing the frog to be female, although no eggs were present. Perhaps a real herpetologist could have figured out the cause of death, but I found nothing obvious to explain it.

I took the tray to Travis in the barn, where he was sitting on a stool and entertaining the barn cats with a bit of string. He saw me coming and said, "Oh no. What is it this time?"

"Remember I told you we were moving up the evolutionary ladder? Well, we've made it to our first vertebrate. It's a leopard frog. You've seen them at the river."

I showed him the tray.

"Ooh." He moaned and put his head between his knees. But he didn't throw up and he didn't faint. I decided to call this progress of a sort.

We moved on to a stillborn baby rabbit, one of Bunny's progeny, and this time I insisted he watch. I tied the tiny pathetic creature on its back on a board and secured the paws with twine. Then I took a sharp pocketknife and made a careful incision down the chest and belly. I looked up in time to see Travis's eyes roll back in his head. I dropped the knife and caught him as he crumpled to the straw.

It turned out that my brother, who loved animals—or at least their exteriors—to distraction, could not, when faced with their interiors, maintain consciousness.

AFTER A LIFETIME of waiting, my type-writer ribbon finally arrived. I almost missed it, thinking the parcel on the hall table was one of the dime novels that arrived for Lamar twice per month.

I ran upstairs with my ribbon and found Aggie writing another of her interminable letters to The Lump (my private name for Lafayette). How she could wring such long missives out of such an uneventful life was beyond me.

"It's arrived, Aggie!" I panted.

She didn't even look up. "What's arrived?"

"My ribbon. We can start my lessons now."

"Oh, that." She stretched and yawned. "All right. Tomorrow."

"What about now?" I said, champing at the bit.

"I'm busy."

"You're only writing a letter."

"I'll have you know," she sniffed, "it's a very important letter. Maybe the most important letter of my life."

"Really? Then why don't you type-write it and I'll watch?"

"No, it's private. Go away."

"I *can't* go away. This is my room." At least it used to be.

"Well, it's my room too. Go away and draggle in mud puddles with your grandfather. That's what you two do, right?"

I didn't like her tone. I also couldn't deny it. Putting the best face on it, I said with stiff dignity, "We study all forms of Nature, all the way from pond water up to the stars."

She snorted. I thought furiously and said, "And besides, you're related to him *too*, you know. He's your . . . he's your"— and here I sketched a quick genealogical map in my mind—"your great-uncle."

I could tell by the startled look on her face she'd never thought of this. She came back with, "Only by marriage. Not by blood."

"Still counts," I said, "so you might be a bit nicer about him."

"Hmpf."

The next day she pulled the precious Underwood out of the wardrobe and set it on the desk. She removed her ribbon and threaded mine through various struts, saying, "Watch closely. I don't want to repeat myself." Then she rolled a clean sheet of paper into the machine and rapped out smartly: `The quick brown fox jumped over the lazy dog.`

Leaning over her shoulder, I said, "Why did the fox do that? Did the dog not mind it? I'd think any self-respecting dog would mind."

"No, silly, it's a typing exercise. It's one single sentence with all the letters of the alphabet in it."

I was too excited to take offense, and I also didn't want to contradict her by pointing out that there was no *s* in the sentence; you'd have to make either the dog or the fox plural. We switched places and I sat in the chair. She showed me how to place my hands at the "home position" and, with great excitement, I was off and running.

Except that I wasn't. Learning to type turned out to be tedious and dreary, not at all the magical experience I'd imagined. I'd been a bit worried that Aggie might not commit herself fully to the project, but I needn't have. She was true to her word and gave me terribly boring exercises (rather like piano scales) and checked on my progress daily, even grading my efforts like a real teacher.

We started with ASDF. Not even a real word. The keys kept sticking together, and I spent more time unsticking them than actually typing. Really, the only fun part was the small satisfying *ding!* at the end of a line, the bell warning you that you were reaching the edge of your paper. Then it was time to whack the return lever as hard as you could, sending the carriage crashing back to the beginning of a fresh line.

"Keep the fingers arched as if you're playing the piano," she reminded me about a million times. "Don't let your fingers collapse." I complained about these exercises bitterly but only under my breath. After all, the whole endeavor was my idea and involved considerable cash outlay, so I could hardly gripe about it to her or anyone else.

Aggie grumbled that my constant practice was getting on her nerves, a reasonable complaint, so I moved a chair and small table into the trunk room. I spent a half hour in there every day, pecking and clacking, ASDF, ASDF, ASDF. Then I moved on to FDSA. This was progress? Finally we moved on to real words, improvement of a sort but not as exciting as it sounds. I typed cat and mat and sat until I thought I would scream. It was worse than the *McGuffey Reader*. Then I moved on to sad and lad and mad until I thought I would scream. The trouble was that my left little finger, by far the weakest, had to hit the a, a letter that, if you examined any sentence at random, lurked everywhere; you couldn't get through a single line without it. This meant all of my a's were quite a bit fainter than the other letters, giving the lines a mottled look and marring their precise symmetry. Still I persevered. And I improved.

So engrossed was I that I did not notice my brothers crowding the trunk room doorway, staring at me. I looked up, startled.

"*What?*" I said.

"Uh, nothing. We just wondered about the noise."

"Well, if it bothers you, shut the door."

At the start I sounded like this:

Clack . . .

Clack . . .

Clack . . .

Not too much later, I sounded like this:

Clack . . . *clack* . . . *clack* . . .

And not too much after that, I sounded like this:

Clackity clackity DING! CRASH!

After weeks of this, I went to Granddaddy in the library and said, "Do you have a letter you need to send? I'm practicing on the type-writing machine."

"Ah," he said, "another giant stride forward into the new century. Here is a rough copy of a letter I was about to write in pen. See how you go with it."

I rushed back to my "office," took out a piece of pristine white paper, and rolled it onto the platen. For a moment, I paused with my fingers above the keys so that I would remember my first real typing job, then began.

Dear Professor Higgins,

Enclosed please find a few seeds of the _Vicia_
tatei, which you have reqested. I thank you
kindly for the _Vicia higgensei_ seeds received
by post earlier this week. They arrived in good
condition. I look forward to germinating your
specimans, and entering into a fruitful
exchange of ideas regarding the conparative
anatomy and physology of the two.

I remain, sir, faithfully yours,

Walter Tate

Fortunately I read it over to make sure there were no mistakes and discovered four of them! Ack, what a mess! My first formal commission, and I had botched it. I carefully typed it over, checked it twice, then ran to the library.

Granddaddy read it with me leaning over his shoulder. He signed it with his ink pen, blotted his signature, and beamed.

"Marvelous! Why, it wasn't all that long ago we communicated by pressing a sharp stick into a wet slab of clay. Truly the machine age is upon us. Well done. Here," he said, reaching into his waistcoat pocket, "a little something for your trouble."

I backed away. "Oh no, Granddaddy, I couldn't." The thought of taking a dime from this man who had given me so much shocked me. He'd given me my life, really. He'd opened my eyes to the empire of books and ideas and knowledge. He'd opened my eyes to Nature; he'd opened my eyes to Science. From others I would take a dime, but not from him.

"I couldn't possibly," I protested. "But I'll take the letter to the post office right now, if you'd like."

"I'd like that very much," he said, pulling a stamp and an envelope from his desk. "And when the days lengthen, we will germinate these seeds together and see what we come up with."

I ran to the post office. And then I ran to Dr. Pritzker's office, eager to share my new skill with him. He was out on a farm call, so I spent a happy hour on one of the hard chairs reading about the treatment of spasmodic versus flatulent colic in the equine.

CHAPTER 23

MY FIRST SURGERY

In conclusion, it appears to me that nothing can be more improving to a young naturalist, than a journey in distant countries.... But I have too deeply enjoyed the voyage, not to recommend any naturalist, although he must not expect to be so fortunate in his companions as I have been, to take all chances, and to start, on travels by land if possible, if otherwise, on a long voyage.

DR. PRITZKER was at first rather skeptical about typed labels, but after I ran up a batch to show him, he changed his mind.

"That looks very professional, Calpurnia. You're hired. I'll pay you a penny apiece."

Now, this may not sound like a lot of money, but Dr. Pritzker, being the only vet for miles around, was in much demand and prescribed at least a dozen drenches and salves and powders every day, all requiring a label. I calculated on the spot that I could make at least fifty cents per week!

"Yessir!" I said, and stuck out my hand. We shook on our deal, which for some reason amused him.

I got better and better on the type-writer, and made fewer

and fewer mistakes, and made more and more money. But now I had to face the problem of the machine being at home, when I really needed it at Dr. Pritzker's office. I had worked out a system in which I would run to his office the moment school let out, run home and type up the labels he needed, and then run them back. All this running back and forth was proving tiresome. But what to do? Buying a machine was out of the question as they were prohibitively expensive. But maybe I could . . . rent one.

I waited until Aggie had received another letter from The Lump and was in a good mood. I found her propped up on the bed, darning a sock.

"Say, Aggie, I was wondering . . ."

"Wondering what?"

"It's about your machine."

She looked up sharply. "You haven't damaged it, have you? I'll wring your neck if you have."

"No—ha-ha—nothing like that." With Aggie, the term "good mood" was a relative one.

"And you are still using your own ribbon, right? Don't you dare use mine."

"I'm *not,*" I said, offended that she thought I'd reneged on our deal.

"Then what?"

"Well, I'm typing labels for Dr. Pritzker . . . and I thought . . . since you're not using it . . . I wondered if I could take it to his office and use it there."

She laughed. "Not a chance."

"You know I'd take good care of it. No one else would touch it."

"Forget it." She returned her attention to the darning egg.

I played my next card, the one I knew would get her attention. "I'll pay you."

She looked up. "What do you mean?"

"I'll rent it from you. So I can take it to his office."

"How much?"

"I'll give you ten percent of what I make from typing."

She said, "I'll do it for fifty percent but you better not put a scratch on it."

"No. That's too much."

We haggled away and eventually settled on twenty percent, with my having to give her an accounting and her rental money every week. Why she would bother to dicker over such trifling sums when she was making good money of her own, I didn't stop to wonder. I guess I figured that when you'd lost everything in the world, it only made sense that your days would revolve around money. I carefully loaded the Underwood into its case and dragged it to the office in J.B.'s wagon. Dr. Pritzker made a space for it on the corner of his desk.

The next time I typed a letter for Granddaddy, I got his permission to show it to Dr. Pritzker before mailing it.

Well, Dr. Pritzker was mighty impressed with that and asked me to type out his letters and bills for him as well as labels. My afternoons were filled with such dispatches as "Enclosed please find the bill for services rendered re: gelding Snowflake" or, if someone had not paid on time, "Your bill for treatment re: heifer Buttercup is now overdue. Please remit."

The truth is that the typing got sort of monotonous after a while, but making money of my own and occasionally getting to watch Dr. Pritzker when an animal was brought in was more than exciting enough to make up for it.

And then poor Samuel got an infection in his foot from being trod upon by a recalcitrant bull and was ordered by Dr. Walker to stay in bed with the limb strictly elevated above heart level for a full week. I immediately volunteered to go with Dr. Pritzker on his farm calls.

He looked dubious and said, "What about Travis? You don't think he'd like to go instead?"

"Uh, he's in bed too. With, uh, the croup. Otherwise, I'm sure he'd be more than happy to help." I couldn't bring myself to spill the beans that my brother fainted at the *thought* of blood, much less the sight of it.

So I raced to the office after school to help the doctor load up his supplies. And although the blacksmith had adapted the harness and reins for Dr. Pritzker so that he could drive with one hand, he still required help hitching his buckskin, Penny, to the buggy. You might think that a veterinarian would have the most attractive horse in town, but not so. With her narrow chest and sickle hocks, Penny's conformation was not the best, but she was otherwise healthy and calm, and he'd got her for a good price.

"Appearances aren't everything," he said, and I, in sympathy with Penny, chimed in with, "Of course not."

The first few days I rode with him in the buggy, we got some odd looks mixed in with the smiles and waves, but I sat up straight and did my best imitation of a real veterinarian's assistant. When we got to the farms, I fetched a bucket of water and handed him his soap and towel while he consulted with the farmer regarding the animals' complaints. Frequently the farmer would make such unhelpful statements as "he's not himself" or "she's off her feed," comments so useless that I wondered how Dr. Pritzker could ever make a diagnosis from such vague information. Nevertheless, with close questioning and a careful physical examination, he would elicit the facts he required while I handed him his instruments and took notes for the "patient's" file.

The high point came when we called at the Dawsons' ranch and found a cow lying on her chest in a stall. Tied to her tail was a note scrawled in pencil: *Belly all swole. Plees fix.*

Mr. Dawson and his sons were out branding and there was no one to help. Except me.

The poor cow looked miserable, drooling and moaning with each breath, her left side grossly distended. We did our usual routine with bucket and soap and water, and I opened the cloth roll of instruments while he performed an exam.

By now I had trained him into teaching me what he was doing. He said, "See here on the left, there's an impaction of the rumen, or first stomach. I shall have to anesthetize her to clear the blockage. We'll have to wait until the Dawsons get back."

Stoutly I declared, "I can do it. It's one ounce of alcohol plus two ounces of chloroform plus three ounces of ether. Shake well before using."

He looked at me doubtfully. "You've been a big help to me, Callie, but really—"

"You have to watch the respirations carefully," I said, doing my best to sound confident and knowledgeable. "Too little, and the cow will thrash. Too much, and the cow will die. Right?"

"That's right. But you could get hurt. And what on earth would your parents say?"

Well, I had a pretty good idea what they'd say but I wasn't going into it right then, and before he could think of any other protests, I was removing the corks from the pungent chemicals. I mixed them together in a clean bottle and shook it well.

I took out the anesthesia cone and said, "Ready, Doctor," in my best professional voice.

He looked tense and muttered something under his breath that sounded a lot like, "God, don't let me regret this."

I tied the cow's halter rope short and pushed the blotting-paper cone over her muzzle. She was too ill to protest. I began to dribble the chemical mixture onto the cone. As she inhaled it, her eyelids drooped even further, and she finally dropped her head to the straw. I flicked her eyelid as I'd seen Dr. Pritzker do, and she did not blink. Now the trick was to keep dripping the mixture at a steady rate to keep her under while he worked. But not so far under that she wouldn't wake up.

"Very good," he said, looking a bit more relaxed.

He picked up the trocar, a thin tube with a sharp pointed end, saying, "We'll try this first. Maybe this will clear her."

Whoever believes the practice of surgery to be a delicate matter would have been shocked by what happened next. He plunged the instrument with great force straight through the cow's side into her distended stomach, releasing a great whoosh of gas into the stall, followed by a jet of semiliquid grass. The liquid drained for a few seconds and then dribbled to a stop.

"Damn," Dr. Pritzker said, and I was ridiculously proud of the fact that he forgot the need to apologize for saying such a bad word in my presence. I was no longer a mere girl—I was his working assistant. "The trocar's clogged. We'll have to open her up. Bistoury."

I handed him the long curved knife. He made a small incision in the skin behind the last rib and then pushed down hard on the knife, enlarging the incision to six inches, then made a stitch between the skin and the lower part of the stomach. He stuck his whole hand inside the cow's stomach and started pulling out huge handfuls of muck. You could see the distention slowly subside the more he extracted.

"What has this old girl been up to?" he said. "I've never seen one quite this bad before." When he pronounced himself satisfied, he sewed up the stomach and then the skin.

"All right," he said, "time to bring her up."

I stopped dribbling the anesthetic but kept the cone in place in case she started to thrash. She slowly regained consciousness and, at the end of it all, hauled herself to her feet and looked around with a renewed interest in life. Saved!

I reeked of chemicals and had a smudge of manure on my pinafore but was otherwise unscathed.

Dr. Pritzker said, "Well done, Calpurnia. You have a real talent for this." Then he looked a little furtive and said, "But, uh, we don't need to tell your mother or father about today, do we?"

"No, sir!"

"Oh, good. That's good."

This time we both washed up in the bucket and shared the soap and towel. I couldn't stop grinning for the rest of the day.

CHAPTER 24

DOGS, LUCKY AND NOT

These wolves are well known, from Byron's account of
their tameness and curiosity, which the sailors, who ran
into the water to avoid them, mistook for fierceness....
They have been observed to enter a tent, and actually pull
some meat from beneath the head of a sleeping seaman.

UPON HEARING THAT ANOTHER dog disaster soon followed in
our lives, you would naturally assume that it involved the coydog at the dam, but not so. It involved Father's prize bird dog,
Ajax, along with Homer, one of the Outside Dogs. Apparently
they had chanced upon a rattlesnake den in the scrub. I always
figured that was why deadly creatures like rattlesnakes possessed rattles—to prevent this exact kind of ruination—but the
dogs imprudently decided to investigate, probably egging each
other on, and barely made it home before collapsing on the front
porch. Fang marks in stark evidence on their muzzles and fore-
paws told the sad story. Father was at the gin when it happened.
Sul Ross ran to fetch him and then ran to find Dr. Pritzker. By
the time they arrived, both dogs' faces were terribly swollen,

almost beyond recognition. Ajax gasped for breath, a horrible rasping noise; Homer whimpered in pain.

Dr. Pritzker bent low over first Ajax and then Homer. I could tell from his expression that there was nothing to be done. "I'm sorry, Alfred," he said to my father. "I'm afraid I can't help them."

Father looked more upset than I had ever seen him. The dogs, especially Ajax, had been his faithful companions for years, keeping him patient company in the cold autumn hours before dawn, huddled together for warmth in the blind, waiting for the call of the geese overhead. They had built a powerful bond between them, Ajax and Father.

Samuel fetched Dr. Pritzker's old revolver from the buggy and loaded it with two cartridges.

My father found his voice and said, "I . . . I suppose I should do it."

"No, Alfred," Dr. Pritzker said. "I hope you will allow me to do it. You take these children and go inside."

Father hadn't noticed that Sul Ross and I had been joined on the lawn by Harry and Lamar.

Father said to us, "Go inside, all of you." He nodded at Dr. Pritzker and followed us into the house, where he went straight to the sideboard and poured himself a glass of whiskey. The first shot rang out, and I flinched. Father gulped the drink down in one long swallow. I had never before seen him drink spirits in the middle of the day. The second shot rang out. He left the room without a word. We heard him trudge up the stairs, one slow, heavy step at a time.

I stood at the window and watched Samuel wrap each of the limp burdens in a gunnysack and carry it to the buggy. I was beyond grateful that Travis wasn't there. I hoped he was down at the river with his coydog.

When he returned home that evening, I don't remember who told him the news. I only know it wasn't me.

Father remained subdued for days. And then Dr. Pritzker came for dinner one night and casually—very casually—let drop that Ollie Croucher's retriever Priscilla had whelped six fine pups, all healthy, not a runt in the bunch, and they would be weaned and ready to go in a few days. The doctor said, "I'm thinking of taking one myself."

J.B. piped up with, "Ooh, puppies. Can we get one?"

Mother said, "I don't see why not." She smiled encouragingly at J.B. and then at Father and then at Travis, saying, "I'd bet you'd like that too, wouldn't you? We could go and look at them on Saturday. Wouldn't that be fun?"

J.B. agreed that it *would* be fun; Father smiled wanly and said that he thought it a good idea; Travis only tucked into his dinner, oddly silent. I tried to catch his eye, but he would not look at me. His not looking at me spoke volumes.

Just as I expected, he motioned me out to the front porch after dinner. He whispered frantically, "I need your help, Callie, I need your help to bring Scruffy home. It's the perfect time for a new dog, even Mother said so."

"I know, but she was referring to a purebred hunting dog."

"Scruffy can hunt. He's been hunting chickens all his life."

"You mustn't tell a soul about that—it's part of the problem."

"Will you help us? Will you stick up for him?" My little brother was so filled with anxiety I thought he might burst. "You could tell them he's not a crazy wild animal. You could tell them he'd make a good pet for us."

"Okay, I'll do what I can for you and for Scruffy. But, Travis, haven't you noticed? It's not like I have a whole lot of say in what goes on around here."

He visibly relaxed. "Thanks, Callie. We'll go see him tomorrow. We'll make a plan together."

We went back inside to get ready for bed. Travis might have slept well that night but he had managed to transfer some of his anxiety to me. I lay in the dark, scheming about how to convince our parents to adopt Scruffy.

The next day found me following Travis along a deer trail, or perhaps a coydog trail, through the thick undergrowth downstream from the gin. Scruffy came out of the bushes, glad to see us. He had filled out nicely, and his coat was glossy. Travis had even put a collar on him.

"See?" said Travis proudly. "Doesn't he look good?"

"Well, he does look a whole lot better," I admitted.

"He is kind of a working dog, you know. He caught a rat the other day. Will you take a look at these sore spots on his flank? I've been washing them with soap and water, but they still won't heal over." Travis grasped his collar. "Good boy, Scruffy. You'll be all right."

I looked at one of the open wounds and gently separated the edges with my fingers. Scruffy whined a little but that was all. The wound itself was not wide but looked chronic. I wished I had one of Dr. Pritzker's probes with me to check on its depth. I patted Scruffy, and he licked my hand again, bearing me no grudge for causing him discomfort. A good dog.

Travis said, "It doesn't look very big, so why doesn't it heal?"

"It's not very big at the surface but I think it's deep. There's something down in there that's stopping it from healing, probably a shotgun pellet."

He frowned. "Can you fix it?"

"It's an actual operation. First you have to dig out the foreign body that's in there, then you have to scrape out the tract or cauterize it with a hot iron so the flesh heals properly."

"But can you do it?" he said anxiously.

"I could give the anesthetic, but Dr. Pritzker would have to do the surgery," I said.

"So will you ask him? I bet if you ask him, he'll do it. Tell him I can pay him out of my allowance. Mother will like Scruffy a lot better if he doesn't have any sores."

"All right, I'll talk to him about it." I looked at Scruffy critically. "And after he's healed, I think we should give him a bath with some of the fancy soap that Mother brings out when we have guests. That would improve him some too."

"That's a great idea," said Travis, grinning at me in admiration.

"And I think we should trim some of that fur around his ruff. Maybe trim his tail so it's not so bushy. I can do it with the scissors. That will neaten him up some."

"Okay, great!" Travis beamed his very best smile at me, the truly irresistible one, the one that caused friends and strangers alike to cave in to his entreaties, including the ones that inevitably led to trouble.

"Then we could make a bow out of one of my hair ribbons," I said, "to make him look cuter." It was going to take a whole lot more than that, I thought, but I kept this to myself.

"See?" Travis said, ruffling Scruffy's fur. "He's going to make a really good pet."

Travis crouched down and put his arms around Scruffy, leaning his head against the warm fur. They looked so happy together, the boy and his dog who, while not the best-looking dog in the world, made a really good pet. I hoped that Mother and Father could look past the pedigree and the appearance to see what I saw, that Travis had finally found the *right* pet.

"When are you going to talk to Dr. Pritzker? It needs to be soon. We don't have a whole lot of time. We're supposed to look at the puppies on Saturday. If we end up getting one, there might not be a place for Scruffy."

"All right. I'll ask him tomorrow afternoon."

But before tomorrow afternoon came, unlucky fate struck, and it struck in the unlikely form of Viola.

We were finishing breakfast when we heard a muffled boom from the back of the property.

"What was that?" said Mother.

"Sounds like the twenty gauge," said Father. The shotgun was kept on a hook on the back porch for varmint control.

A minute later, Viola came into the dining room. "Shot a coyote, Mr. Tate, in the weeds between the corncrib and the henhouse. Maybe sick, from the way it was limping."

Travis and I stared at each other, horrified disbelief dawning between us. He leaped up, knocking over his chair, and sprinted from the room. I jumped up in hot pursuit, ignoring the confused cries and general hubbub in the dining room. I pelted out the back door at top speed behind him, yelling, "Maybe it's not him! Maybe it's really a coyote!"

We reached the corncrib and followed a bloody trail through the tall weeds. All I could think was, *It's too much blood, there's too much blood*. And there on the ground lay the "coyote." Only, of course, it was not a coyote. But it was alive. Panting and whimpering, but alive.

"No!" Travis cried in anguish, staggering at the sight of blood on Scruffy's hindquarters.

Oh, Travis, not now, I prayed. *Don't go all wobbly on me now.* "Don't look at the blood. Get the wheelbarrow and hurry."

He turned away and ran to the garden shed. I ran to the barn and grabbed a saddle blanket.

By the time we met back at Scruffy, Father and Harry and Lamar had arrived and were shouting confused questions and orders at us: "That doesn't look like a coyote." "Why does it have a collar?" "Don't touch it—it's probably rabid." "Where's the shotgun? I'll put it out of its misery."

"No, you can't," I cried. "It's Travis's dog." I put the blanket over Scruffy to keep him warm and to hide the blood.

"Travis doesn't have a dog," Father said.

"Yes, I do," Travis said through his tears. Now that he didn't have to look at the blood, fortitude returned to his frame.

"Yes, he does," I said. "Help me lift him into the wheelbarrow. We have to take him to Dr. Pritzker."

"That thing?" said Lamar. "It's only a mongrel. Father, shall I get the shotgun?"

"His name is Scruffy," Travis cried.

They stared at us in confusion. Scruffy whined from under his blanket.

Father grumbled something about a man not knowing what was going on under his own roof, and disobedient sons, and too many animals, and no more pets. He looked deeply troubled, but I could not tell if it was due to Travis's sobbing or Scruffy's yelping. Surely the mangled dog reminded him of Ajax, and just as surely, it reminded him of Travis's long string of terrible pets.

Lamar said, "That thing's not worth saving. Heck, it's barely worth shooting." He and Father turned and headed back to the house. Were they heading for the gun? Or for help? I thought I knew the answer but there was no time to dwell on it.

"Help me," I said to Travis and Harry, but Harry only held up his hands and backed away.

No help there. I reached slowly for Scruffy's collar because you never knew what a dog in pain—even the best-behaved dog in the world—would do. But he did not snap, only yelped as Travis and I lifted him into the wheelbarrow. A bloody hind leg slipped out. Travis reeled and squeezed his eyes shut, and I quickly adjusted the blanket to hide it.

"Good boy," I said, whether to Travis or Scruffy I wasn't sure. "You can look now. Hurry, before Father gets back." We each took a handle and pushed off toward the drive. Harry, who hadn't said a word, watched us go. He wasn't going to help but he wasn't going to hinder us, either. Perhaps that was the best we could hope for under the circumstances, but still, the part of me that had always been his pet knew I would not forget this moment.

It was tough going in the gravel drive, the front wheel foundering in a slow-motion nightmare. Travis checked his blubbing and saved his breath for the hard work at hand. When we made the street, he fell and we almost dumped the wheelbarrow over. He got up with skinned hands and knees without a word of pain, grabbed his handle, and we were off again, breaking into a clumsy trot and pushing our burden for all we were worth. No noise issued from under the blanket. I pushed grimly and could only think, *What if Dr. Pritzker's not there, what if he's out on a call, what if he's not there?*

We rounded the corner with our makeshift ambulance right as the doctor was unlocking his door. Relief flooded my heart as never before. He looked at us in surprise as we raced up.

"We need your help," I wheezed. "Our dog's been shot. It was a mistake. Viola thought it was a coyote."

"It's not a coyote, it's our Scruffy," Travis gasped.

"Bring him in, bring him in," Dr. Pritzker said, holding the door for us. But the wheelbarrow was too wide to fit through, so Travis and I had to lift him from the barrow. The blanket fell off as we carried him to the table. Blood dripped on the floor. But Travis did it. He did what needed to be done. We managed to arrange Scruffy on the table, and then he said, "I think . . . I think I'll just sit down for a little bit." He plopped down in a chair and dropped his head between his knees.

Dr. Pritzker gave him a funny look and said to me, "Is he all right?"

"He's, uh . . . yeah. I'll explain later. Can you save this dog?"

Dr. Pritzker frowned at the patient, who was panting at a frightening rate.

"What was he shot with?" he said.

"Twenty gauge," I said, "birdshot."

"Good," he said, "better than buckshot."

Travis surfaced long enough to mumble, "You can save him, right?"

Feeling oddly calm, I said, "I'll get the anesthetic." Now that we were there, now that I knew help to be at hand, and now that I had a part to play in providing that help, most of my fear subsided.

"Muzzle first," Dr. Pritzker said. I helped him buckle on a leather muzzle. Scruffy made no protest.

"He's never bitten anyone," Travis said, head still down.

"Doesn't matter. All injured dogs get a muzzle. One of my rules of practice. Ready with the chloroform?"

I slipped the cone over the muzzle and applied the anesthetic. Scruffy's eyelids sagged, and his breathing slowed. Dr. Pritzker slowly explored the matted, bloody fur on his hindquarter and grunted.

"What's wrong?" said Travis, quickly looking up and just as quickly averting his gaze.

"Nothing wrong with the hip. But part of the lower leg is shattered. He'll probably never walk on it again."

"But you can save him, right?" Travis said.

Dr. Pritzker frowned. "I may have to amputate at the stifle—that's the knee—but that's no kind of life for him. He's not a purebred so he's not worth anything. Besides, who wants a three-legged dog?"

"I do," said Travis. "I want him."

"Me too," I said in unity with my brother. I unrolled the instrument pack, readied the sutures, and waited for Dr. Pritzker.

He looked at the two of us. After a moment he sighed, "All right."

He probed and sewed and debrided, and extracted chips of bone before saying, "Well, I'll be. The popliteal artery is intact. Talk about good luck. Maybe I can save the leg, but I make no guarantees, understood?"

"Yessir," Travis mumbled.

Dr. Pritzker had just finished sewing up the fascia when Father and Harry came through the door.

"Ah, Alfred," Dr. Pritzker said, "I'm just closing up here. I'll be done shortly. Step carefully, there's blood everywhere."

Travis moaned.

"Oh," added Dr. Pritzker, "and you might take your boy outside. He's looking a little green around the gills."

Father harrumphed, but he and Harry each took an arm and led Travis to the bench outside.

I could hear Travis taking deep breaths. Father gave him a moment and then said, "Young man, what's the meaning of all this? Out with it."

Travis explained the story of Scruffy, haltingly at first, then picking up steam. About how he was part terrier and part coyote, and how the dogs didn't want him, and the coyotes almost killed him, and how Mr. Holloway tried to drown him, and how Mr. Gates and now Viola had shot him, and that he, Travis, was his only friend in the world and would not let him down now.

Father said, "It's half coyote? No, no, we can't have a creature like that about the place. It's just not safe. Look, my boy, I've decided to take one of Priscilla's new pups and turn it into a hunting dog. They're seven weeks old and ready to wean. You can pick out one for yourself and raise it as your very own dog. You can even have the pick of the litter."

Travis grew louder and more vociferous. "I don't need a

puppy. I already have a dog, and his name is Scruffy. He's the only one I want."

He continued to argue his case. I regretted that I wasn't out there to help him, but I was too busy handing the doctor bandages. Poor old Scruffy, lying there in a pool of blood. He didn't look much like a dog, or a coyote, or a coydog. He didn't look like much of anything except a bloody mess. But he was still breathing.

We applied a dressing to the leg and then I remembered his other old wounds.

"Dr. Pritzker, there's an old fistula here. Would you take a look at it? Since he's under? I'll pay."

"Calpurnia Virginia Tate," he sighed, "you don't have to pay me."

I handed him a probe, and he dug around for a minute before triumphantly extracting a deformed slug of metal half the size of my little fingernail. Then another. And another.

"Look at that," he said. "He's been shot before, and more than once. He's a tough little scrapper, and a lucky dog to boot. Maybe you should call him Lucky instead."

"No," I said, "he has a name. His name is Scruffy."

FATHER REMAINED UNHAPPY about the situation for some time. Travis was allowed to keep his pet, but it had to live at the gin, and he was under strict instructions not to bring it home. Travis washed him and brushed him and taught him how to fetch and shake a paw.

After the wounds healed, we took turns walking him and exercising him a little more each day. The muscles around his good hip grew strong in compensation, and he developed a comic hitching gait that served him well. He got to the point where he could run like blazes, at least over the short distance.

Then came the day when he caught a rat at the gin and fortuitously delivered it to the loading dock, where Father happened to be smoking a cigar. Scruffy laid the dead rat at his feet and looked up expectantly at Father, who looked at it in surprise. He puffed his cigar and appeared thoughtful, probably thinking about how the rats plagued his business. Then he bent down and patted the reddish-brownish head, saying, "Good dog."

And just like that, Scruffy transformed himself from an outcast coydog to an extremely valuable working dog. Father himself brought him home that night, where he settled in on the front porch so quickly you'd have thought he always lived there. And from the porch, he and Travis initiated their stealthy joint campaign to turn him from an Outside Dog into an Inside Dog and eventually even an On The Bed Dog, previously unheard of in our house.

So Scruffy became part of the Tate family pack. Travis had finally found the right pet.

That was the happy ending to the story of Scruffy, one of the most exciting things to happen in our house that year. We couldn't know that yet more excitement lay ahead.

CHAPTER 25

A PUFFER FISH OF ONE'S OWN

[I]f your view is limited to a small space, many objects possess beauty.

ONE EVENING OVER DINNER, Mother smiled and said, "Tomorrow is Aggie's eighteenth birthday. Tomorrow, she becomes a real adult."

Did Aggie blush a little? I think she did.

"I suppose," Mother went on, "we shall have to get used to calling you Agatha, since you'll be a proper young lady."

"Oh no, Aunt Margaret, I've been called Aggie my whole life, and I'm used to it."

"It's a shame your parents can't be here, but we'll all do what we can to make up for their absence."

Later, when I kissed Mother good night, she whispered, "I want you to buy a nice birthday present for Aggie."

"Uh," I said, contemplating my bank balance and wondering how much I'd be expected to spend. I hated the thought of spending my hard-earned cash on fripperies; I'd even stopped buying myself any candy at all. Talk about sacrifice!

"Here's a dollar. Buy her something nice, mind."

"Sure!" That cheered me up no end. The next day, I went to the general store and bought some lilac sachets and a tin of scented talc, appropriate gifts for a brand-new grown-up lady.

For her birthday dinner, Viola made Aggie's favorite, beef Wellington, and a dessert of angel food cake. Father opened a bottle of champagne with a resounding pop and poured her a half glass.

"Oh, it tickles!" She giggled after taking her first sip. I don't think I'd ever heard her giggle before. She looked flushed and—dare I say it?—almost beautiful in the chandelier's flickering candlelight. She opened her gifts and exclaimed over them kindly. She read aloud a letter from her loving parents, which included a substantial check, and the news that they hoped to send for her in another month or so. We gathered around the piano and sang to her, then I floundered my way through a new tune called "The Blue Danube" by Mr. Johann Strauss. Was it my imagination, or did Mother's teeth click every time I hit a sour note?

When I was through, Mother said, "That was lovely, Callie, and I'm sure it will be even nicer once you actually learn the piece. Aggie, dear, perhaps you'd care to play us something?"

Aggie took my place at the keyboard and launched into a perfect rendition of the same tune. Not only was her playing note-perfect, she was what they call lyrical, and we all swayed along to the music. Fortunately, my own sense of self-worth was not invested in musical performance, so I did not begrudge her praise. We applauded her enthusiastically.

Really, it was the nicest time in the house since news of the Flood.

I wondered how it was that one magically changed from child to adult at the stroke of midnight. I wondered if Aggie suddenly felt different at the striking of the clock. I wondered if she felt like Cinderella, only in reverse.

I PROBABLY WOULDN'T have woken up at all if a mosquito hadn't insisted on biting me on the eyelid. Half awake, I heard a faint rustling. Probably the snake again. I rolled over on my pallet and was about to drift off when I realized that Aggie was moving stealthily across the room. I could see her in the faint moonlight, feeling her way to the wardrobe.

"Aggie," I whispered, "are you okay?"

She froze.

"I can see you, you know," I whispered.

"You have to be quiet," she whispered back, and I was surprised to hear an undertone of pleading in her voice.

"What are you doing? You can light a candle if you like."

"No candles!" she muttered hoarsely. "Be quiet and go back to sleep."

"Not until you tell me what's going on."

She opened the wardrobe and, to my surprise, took out her carpetbag. She placed it on the bed and then fumbled her way back to the wardrobe and began pulling out her clothes.

"Okay," I said, "now you really have to tell me. Or I'll wake Mother and Father."

"No, you mustn't," she begged.

"Then you better tell me."

Although I couldn't see her expression, her long pause told me she was wrestling with what to say next. Finally she said, "I'm going to meet Lafayette Lumpkin. We're running away to Beaumont. We're going to get married."

"Oh, Aggie!" The boldness of her scheme took my breath away. Nice girls from nice homes did not do such things. "You'll get in so much trouble."

"Hush! Keep your voice down. We'll be all right if we can get married before anyone catches us. I'm eighteen. I can marry."

"But what about your parents? You'll break their hearts. What about *my* parents? They'll be furious." What she was doing was audacious beyond belief and would heap shame upon our family.

"There's a letter on the dresser that explains everything."

"What about your money?"

She patted her bag and said, "I took it all out of the bank today. With my savings, we can set him up in business. He says there's lots of oil in Beaumont, and a man who gets his foot in the door early can make a lot of money. We're going to be rich."

I thought this pretty unlikely but said nothing. I watched her stuff her clothes into her bag and tiptoe to the door. She turned with her hand on the knob and said, "He's waiting for me on the road to Lockhart. Please don't say anything until breakfast. I'll send you a present if you don't. *Please*, Callie."

I realized I held her future in the palm of my hand. One

outcry from me, one word of alarm, and all her plans would fall apart.

I considered: On the one hand, no sisterly love had bloomed between us. On the other, we had grown to tolerate each other's ways. And she had taught me some valuable lessons.

I protested, "I'll get in such trouble."

"No, you won't. Just pretend you didn't hear me. You can tell them you slept through the whole thing."

I weighed the chances of such an argument holding water and said, "They'll kill me."

"Please, Callie. You swore on the Bible."

"That was about the photograph. Not such a thing as this."

"*Please,* Callie. You can have my Underwood."

I sighed, knowing that I would probably regret my decision forever. "All right. I won't tell until breakfast."

"You promise?"

"I promise, Aggie."

"You know, you're not such a bad kid after all."

"You don't have to leave your Underwood. I won't tell anyway."

"It's too heavy to carry. I'll have to get another one. You keep it. It's yours. Good-bye."

"Bye, Aggie, and good luck."

But these words struck me as insufficient to the moment. Now that she was leaving, I wanted her to stay, or at least offer some reassurance that we were not parting ways forever.

"Will you write to me?" I whispered.

But she gave no reply. She merely stepped through the door, closing it behind her with the faintest click, and just like that, she was gone. How easily she slipped loose of us, of our house, our family, of me.

If you think I lay awake staring at the ceiling all night, scratching my eyelid and trembling in awe of her actions and fear of the consequences, you would be right. You think there wasn't H_ll to pay in the morning? Oh yes indeedy.

I entered the dining room feeling queasy, straining to look nonchalant. Mother, sipping coffee out of her favorite Wedgwood cup, looked up and said, "Is Aggie coming down to breakfast? Is she not well?"

"I don't know," I said, fighting to control the quiver in my voice. "She's not there."

Mother frowned. "What do you mean, 'not there'?"

"I found this on my dresser," I said, handing over the letter. Then I took my place at the table and pretended to my usual appetite, a difficult piece of acting if ever there was one. I forked up my eggs with a shaking hand.

Coffee slopped over the side of Mother's cup and stained the white damask tablecloth. "Alfred!" she cried. "She's gone!"

A hue and cry went up. Father and Harry and Alberto each took a horse and galloped off to San Marcos, to Lockhart, to Luling. Telegrams were sent to the sheriffs of adjoining counties. And I was threatened with various gruesome punishments to spill the story but stuck hard and fast to my claim of waking to find her gone.

A thundercloud of fear mixed with fury hung over the house for days. The only good thing (besides the Underwood, of course) was that I got my bed back. For a few days, it felt much too soft, and I actually missed my lumpy cotton pallet on the floor. But that soon passed.

Uncle Gus and Aunt Sophronia were apoplectic and blamed my parents for everything, despite Aggie writing them and begging their forgiveness and absolving my parents of any blame. We later found out that Aggie and Lafayette had made it to Austin, married there, and then boarded the train to Beaumont, where they rented a cottage and set Lafayette up in business as a landman with Aggie's carefully hoarded money. Then came the news that they were expecting their first child and were happy as clams at high tide.

And speaking of clams, Aggie never did write to me, but a few months later, a wooden crate arrived with my name on it. It contained no note but was packed with a fine collection of strange and wonderful seashells nestled carefully in the excelsior. I spent many happy hours cataloguing them with Granddaddy, learning about the angel wing, the sailor's ear, the cat's paw, the lightning whelk. There was even a dried *Diodon*, a puffer fish of my very own. I tied a long slender blue ribbon around its midriff and thumbtacked it to the ceiling, where it swam in currents of air, swaying gently in the breeze from the open window. I loved my puffer fish. I also loved my magnificent horse conch. Not only was it almost a foot long, but when you held it to your ear, you could hear the distant *shoosh-shoosh* of the waves.

So I did not go to the beach. But the beach came to me.

In the end, I let my newt go, except that he wasn't really "mine"—he was just on loan from Mother Nature, and I had learned all I could from him. He deserved to go back to his drainage ditch and live out the rest of his newt life in peace.

And as for that old snake? Well, he comes and goes. He's around here somewhere, but we don't mind each other. Granddaddy reminds me that he will one day grow too big to make it through the gap in the corner, and then we'll have to make other arrangements. But that's all right with me.

ACKNOWLEDGMENTS

First of all, a warning to young readers: Do *not* pick up or touch any wild animal, especially one that looks hurt or is out during the day when it is usually out only at night. This *especially* applies to bats. Such an animal is likely to be diseased.

My endless thanks to my husband, Rob Duncan, and to my writing group, the Fabs of Austin: Billy Cotter, Pansy Flick, Nancy Gore, Gaylon Greer, Kim Kronzer, Delaine Mueller, and Diane Owens Prettyman. Thanks also to Trevor Nance, Lee Ann Urban, Nancy Mason, Ana Deboo, and Julia Sooy.

I consulted various experts for help with this book, but any errors, omissions, distortions, or general screwups contained herein are strictly my fault and no one else's. Thanks to Special Agent Byron San Marco of the Austin Bureau of Alcohol, Tobacco, Firearms and Explosives; Byron Stone, MD; and veterinarians Doug Thal, DVM, and Andy Cameron, DVM, both of Santa Fe, New Mexico.

Thanks to Diana Weihs, MD, and James Tai, MD; Lynne Roberts and Laurie Sandman; Robin Allen (Master Knitter); and George Pazdral, MD, JD.

A big *woof* of gratitude goes to the real-life Scruffy for providing inspiration for much of this book. She is our very own coydog, supposedly half Chow and half coyote. We found her running wild and living off handouts near the river in Fentress, starving, scrawny, and—let's face it—not the world's most attractive creature. But we adopted her into our pack, and now she is a beloved member and very cute in our eyes. Thanks, Scruffy!

The Galveston hurricane of 1900 remains, to this day, the largest natural disaster in US history. As many as ten thousand lives were lost. For those readers interested in further information about the storm and its tragic aftermath, go to *Isaac's Storm* by Erik Larson. (Another warning: This book is not for young readers.)

The following also aided me in the writing of this tale: *The Voyage of the* Beagle by Charles Darwin, 1839; *A Special Kind of Doctor: A History of Veterinary Medicine in Texas* by Henry C. Dethloff and Donald H. Dyal; William B. E. Miller and Lloyd V. Tellor's *The Diseases of Livestock and Their Most Efficient Remedies*, published in 1884, which I stumbled across in a used-book store; and *The Handbook of Texas Online*, at tshaonline.org/handbook/online.

For more information on children abducted and raised by the Comanche, see *The Captured* by Scott Zesch and *Comanches: The Destruction of a People* by T. R. Fehrenbach. Many of the abductees who were eventually returned to their white parents had a difficult time fitting back into society. Some even returned to their adoptive Comanche families. And, yes, some people do claim that it is possible to predict the weather with a jar of bear grease. (See the MountainMonthly.com entry on G. Gordon Wimsatt.) I have not seen this in action—although I would dearly love to—and cannot vouch for its veracity.

Finally, the biggest thanks of all go to my wonderful agent, Marcy Posner, and my equally wonderful publisher, Laura Godwin.

For information regarding upcoming appearances, please go to jacquelinekelly.com.

The writing of this book was fueled by Haribo gummi bears.

DON'T MISS THE
BEGINNING OF CALPURNIA'S STORY.

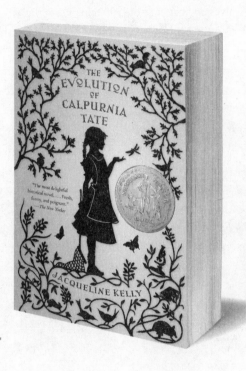

Read Calpurnia Tate, Girl Vet,
the chapter-book companion series to
Newbery Honor Award–winning novel
The Evolution of Calpurnia Tate, and
The Curious World of Calpurnia Tate.

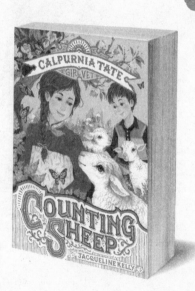